THE SECRET AT NUMBER 6

Kaylie Kay

For permission requests write to the publisher at

https://kayliekaywrites.com/contact

Dedication

To all the new crew, and those who dream of being crew, this one is for you xxx

"Once you have tasted flight, you will forever walk the earth with your eyes turned skyward, for there you have been, and there you will always long to return."

~ Leonardo da Vinci

Contents

Prologue

Bea, one year earlier.

Bea couldn't read them; her parents were definitely worried, nervous, in cahoots about something... she'd never seen them like this before. They were sitting in the conservatory, her in the chair, them huddled together on the sofa opposite. Small talk had long since been exhausted.

'Did someone die?' she asked. Gran, Aunty Dot, an elderly relative?

'No,' her mum managed a small smile. 'No one died.'

'Well can you please just spit it out as you're both making me nervous.' They had called her down from her bedroom with 'something they wanted to talk to her about,' but seemed to be struggling now with *actually* talking about it.

Her mum and dad looked at each other, and she could tell that whatever the news was, neither of them wanted to be the one to share it.

'You know I love you, don't you?' her dad eventually started. She nodded slowly; there really was no doubt about that, he told her every day, and twice a day at least since she had moved back in following the breakup with Will. 'To the moon and back?'

His reference to their favourite bedtime book made her smile; her favourite, and earliest childhood memories were those when he put her to bed, and they shared a story. She nodded again, urging him on.

'And that you were my first child?'

Well, as the eldest of the three daughters she had always presumed so....

Her mum shifted forward in her seat now, stepping in to help him.

'What your father is trying to say is that he is your father in every sense of the word, except for biologically.' She said it so quickly that Bea had to replay it before she understood it.

'Huh?' She thought she understood, but she needed her to say it again, just to make sure.

'Your biological father was someone else, but I met your dad when you were just a baby and so he has always just been your dad,' she explained quickly. Was her voice shaking?

'It doesn't change anything...' Bea's dad shook his head, his eyes locked on to hers, sad and pleading.

The house fell deathly silent as the 'news' settled. Bea was lost for words, but so, it seemed, were they.

'Why?' she started slowly with the first question that popped into her head, feeling her heart racing in her chest. 'Why are you telling me this now?' she asked, 'I'm nearly thirty years old.' She pointed out the obvious, that they had kept this a secret from her for almost three decades. Had she really needed to know? If she had, then surely she should have known a long time ago?

Her mum gave a small shrug and looked down. 'We should have told you many years ago.'

'Uh-huh,' Bea said, feeling a wave of... was it anger? Upset? She didn't like it, whatever it was, it made her feel uncomfortable inside.

'It was my fault,' her dad spoke up. He glanced sideways at her mum, who nodded, giving him permission to carry on. 'I didn't want you to not think of me as your dad. To me you were always my daughter, but I was worried, I still am, that you would think of me as something else, and not *your dad* if you knew. When your sisters came along it made it even harder, I didn't want you to feel different to them, less loved. Ever.' He looked straight at her and Chloe felt the anger subside for a second as he continued. 'Then, after Barry...' He hung his head now, his face in his palms.

The anger came back like a wrecking ball into her stomach as Bea realised why he had *needed* to tell her... She rolled her eyes and threw up her hands. 'Really, Dad? Was that *ever* really likely to happen?' What were the chances that she would ever need one of his kidneys like Barry's son had?!! She fumed inside. Bea knew he was crying, but she couldn't comfort him. What right did he have to be upset? *He'd* known all along, it was *she* who had been lied to. Or was she angry because he had told her at all, had she really needed to know?! Either way, only *she* had the right to be upset right now! She glared at her mum now.

'So, who was ...' she paused, looking for the right word, 'my *biological* father?' She heard the sarcasm in her voice, knew that she was being unkind, but couldn't stop herself.

'He was a pilot. His name was Anthony McGhee, and I was very much in love with him. He was older than me, married, and after I told him I was pregnant I never saw him again. He just disappeared.'

'Wow.' Bea leaned back now, winded by the brief, and blunt, summary of how she came into this world. Neither of her parents could look at her. She pushed herself up from the chair. 'I think I need to get some fresh air.'

Chapter One

Maddie: I feel like it's just hit me. Can't believe it's our first day on Monday! I'm panicking I missed something!

Jo: Me too gurrrl! I wrote myself a checklist if this helps:

{screenshot}

Maddie: You're amazing!!! Looks like I've done it all... just one of my references to come back, and my (hopefully clear) criminal record check haha!

Jo: You're welcome. Meanwhile I've no idea what to wear, what to bring, where to go...

Megan: Smart casual they said. I'm doing jeans and shirt. Jo this checklist is gold!

Paul: Short dress and heels for me then!

Jen: Can't wait to see that lol

Paul: You think I'm joking?! Anyone else staying in the Premier Inn apart from me and Jo?

Megan: Me!

Jade: Nope, I've got a room in Horley, worked out cheaper

Chloe: Just off to look at a room in Crawley

Jo: A bit last minute gurl!

Chloe: Yep...always... eek!

The small white car bearing the estate agency's blue and gold logo told her that she was in the right place, and Chloe pulled her mum's four-year-old Ford Focus up in front of it. She glanced in her rear-view mirror and checked herself before getting out, in sync with the smartly dressed man who was here to show her around.

'Chloe Bashford?'

'Yes, that's me.' She accepted his outstretched hand and shook it lightly. She wondered if it was him that she had spoken to on the phone yesterday, the one who had assured her that he had the 'perfect property,' and not to panic. 'Pleased to meet you.'

'And you, I'm Mike,' he smiled widely, his tanned skin creasing around his eyes. 'Did you find your way here alright?'

'Yes, thank you.' She had set off from her home in North London at the crack of dawn, anticipating the Friday morning traffic to be exactly how it had been, awful, but it had still been preferable to a packed underground and then a train out here to Crawley.

'So, Number 6 Addison Road...' He rubbed his hands together and looked up at the building next to them. Chloe forced a smile despite the sinking feeling in her tummy; if it had been him on the phone, he had lied. It was far from perfect. 'You need a room for five weeks of cabin crew training, I understand?' Chloe nodded. 'And have you seen any other properties?' he asked, still smiling. Chloe shook her head, kicking herself for leaving everything to the last minute as she always did, wishing that she had other options up her sleeve right now. Of course, everyone else in her training group had secured their digs weeks ago when their start date had been confirmed, when they'd found each other on Facebook and set up the WhatsApp Group probably, but she'd even been late to that party. It was only when Jo had tracked her down on Facebook and invited her to join them that she'd even realised there was a list of all the people on her course amongst the million emails and forms she had been sent.

He laughed. 'Don't look so worried.' Apparently, she hadn't hidden her feelings very well. 'It is a bit old-fashioned, but the rooms are spacious and clean and the rent is cheap compared to a lot around here, and one of the girls you'll be sharing with came through me just a couple of months ago. She's a flyer too, so you'll have lots in common and some help with those exams.'

Chloe managed a smile now. *Flyer*. She was going to be a *flyer*, cabin crew, flight attendant... all she had to do was get through this next five weeks and she would have wings with which she could fly. Did it matter if she was staying in a house that looked like *this*, that made her feel like *this* before she had even stepped inside? Had she really expected to find a modern, luxury house-share for a bargain price at the last minute, if ever?

'Are there any other tenants?' Chloe asked; it was a big house for two people.

'Just one, another lady.'

'Does she fly too?' she asked hopefully.

Mike shook his head. 'I don't think so,' he said. 'She was already here when I first showed someone around, but I believe she works in aviation too.'

Chloe smiled; she hoped that she did. Taking a deep breath, she looked along the cracked tarmac driveway up to the old, red-brick building. It might have been grand once, a huge bay window to the right of the front door, two wide windows above, detached by a good few metres from the house next door. It wasn't so much the house though, although it could maybe do with the wooden door and window frames being replaced, but it was the garage that was next to it, separated by a narrow path that led to the back garden, which was setting the tone for her. Creeping ivy wrapped around from its side, picking at the small patches of olive paint which clung to its almost bare metal front. The huge tree that loomed over from where it grew somewhere behind, seemed to scratch its roof with its gnarled, leafless fingers. The garage alone gave the whole property an air of foreboding and neglect. She shivered, feeling the bitter wind as it rushed past them.

'Shall we?'

It is just five weeks, and you need somewhere today. Suck it up, Chloe told herself. 'Don't judge a book by its cover,' her mum would have said, or perhaps today she would tell her not to judge a house by its garage? Chloe zipped up her jacket sharply and followed the agent up the uneven path.

The black and white tiled floor in the long hallway was a welcome surprise, old enough that it had become fashionable once again. Dark red carpet with worn down pile covered the stairs, the same carpet as was in the long living room that he had just led her into.

'So, this is the lounge-cum-dining room, shared by all the tenants. As you can see it's a lovely big space...'

Chloe wasn't listening to him, she was taking it all in, deciding whether she loved the old-fashioned look or hated it. A floral, overstuffed three-piece suite sat at the end of the room with the bay window that looked out onto the road, gathered around a Persian rug that clashed wildly with it. On the opposite wall the dark mahogany sideboard with its thin curved legs matched the nest of tables and television unit... only the flat screen TV gave any clue that they were in the 2020s and not the 1980s.

At the other end of the room a dining table in the same wood sat empty in front of a dresser, *its* shelves empty too. She could almost imagine how it would have looked before, when whoever had chosen this furniture had lived here; family pictures and ornaments no doubt adorning the shelves, pictures hung on the Regency-striped walls.

'...the landlord has said that tenants are welcome to leave their personal things in here.' Chloe nodded as she tuned back into what he was saying. Okay, it was old fashioned, but it wasn't awful, she could soon make it nice with a few bits and pieces. Maybe she could make use of the table to do a jigsaw? Watch TV with her housemates?

He was leading her out now, down the hall and into the kitchen. The winter sun had broken through the clouds and was beaming through the window, making the yellow walls glow. Sage-green wooden cupboards lined the walls high up and low down. A metal sink sat under the window, looking out onto an overgrown garden, and a door to the left led to a small utility room with a washing machine and back door through it. Against the wall to her right was a small round table with three chairs. It was homely and 'cute', for want of a better word, and she imagined herself eating breakfast at the table with the other girls, talking about flying... a smile must have slipped out as Mike was standing there smiling back at her now.

'I'm so sorry, I was miles away,' she apologised, suddenly aware that he had been talking to her.

'I could see, somewhere nice I hope,' he grinned. 'So, I was saying that is all downstairs, shall we see what could be your room?'

Chloe nodded.

At the top of the stairs Chloe counted five closed doors around the wide landing. Mike opened the first two to reveal a small toilet and a separate bathroom with washbasin. A collection of girls' toiletries was scattered haphazardly across the windowsill, and bottles were bunched together on the corner of the olive-green bath. A small electric shower hung over one end and a shower curtain with a blue seaside scene was pulled halfway along.

'This would be your room.'

Chloe turned away from the bathroom to see Mike was holding open a door at the other end of the landing now. She stepped past him and looked around. The room was huge, much bigger than hers at home, with pink flowers climbing up the paper on the walls and the same heavy curtains as downstairs. A single bed lay under the window, a new duvet and pillows still in their packaging on the bare mattress. She felt quite sure that before it had become a shared house, this would once have been the master bedroom, with a bed big enough for two.

A white, kidney-shaped dressing table with glass top and vanity mirror sat next to the bed on the left-hand wall, and opposite stood a white, modern wardrobe with sliding doors. The same red carpet ran through from the rest of the house into here. From the window she could see down to the street below. 'You would need to bring your own bed covers but everything else you need is here, I think.'

Chloe pictured the room with her own things in it, her sheepskin rug on the floor, makeup on the dressing table, her own bedding. It would be absolutely *fine*. 'I'll take it,' she said, turning to Mike with a smile.

Getting into her car, Chloe looked back up at the house one last time. The sun was shining now and that feeling in her stomach had almost gone. In two days' time she would be back here with her things, making friends with her flying housemate and whoever else lived here, ready to start her training on Monday morning. *Everything always turns out okay in the end* was her motto, and today was proving to be no exception.

Chapter Two

Liv: Sorry I've been super quiet in this chat, been really busy, but looking forward to meeting you all tomorrow!

Megan: You too babe. Tomorrow! How did that happen??!!!

Jo: Me and Paul are on our way down now whoop whoop!! Anyone up for drinks in the Premier inn bar later?!

Megan: I won't be in til later tonight. Have fun and I'll see you in the morning :)

Darren: I'll join you for a couple. Let me know when you get there. Are we all heading over in the morning together?

Jo: Sounds like a plan. Premier inn Crew lol! SatNav saying three hours but Paul's driving like a loon so could be quicker!

Jen: Does anyone else feel sick? I'm so nervous

Megan: Oh babe, we're all in this together. It's my second airline so I'm good, but I remember that feeling well. We'll look after you. Is it 8am guys?

Jo: Yes, 8am to get your ID at security and then cafeteria at 9

Megan: Great. Whoever gets there first save us all a BIG table!

Chloe tried her best to look confident as she walked along the corridor. She could hear the noise of chatter coming from the cafeteria at the end and stopped briefly to check herself in a glass picture frame, smoothing down her freshly highlighted hair that she had pulled back into a ponytail. She looked smart in her blazer, which she had paired with black jeans and a bodysuit, new white trainers on her feet. She slipped the lanyard that the security man had just given her around her neck and looked at the picture on her shiny new ID badge, wishing that she had smiled for it, before taking a deep breath and walking towards the noise of her new life.

In the large open hall with its high industrial ceilings, small round tables filled the middle of the space, and long rectangular ones lined the edges. A deli-style counter ran along one side, behind which two ladies shuffled quickly up and down serving the dozen or so people who were queueing there. Chloe scanned the room, trying to recognise anyone from the photos on the group chat. Someone waved from one of the long tables on the far side, and she checked over her shoulder that there was no one else behind her before she waved back and walked quickly over.

'Chloe, cutting it fine, girl.'

Chloe recognised Jo by her raven black hair and flawless caramel skin. 'Not how I'd planned it,' she laughed, sliding into the end of the bench on the far side and looking at her watch. She'd made it with just five minutes to spare. 'Buses aren't my thing.' It was true, she'd always been more of a train girl, but the underground didn't run this far out so she was going to have to work them out whether she liked it or not.

'Nice to meet you,' said a pretty blonde girl with pink cheeks and wavy hair, the one who had waved at her, holding her hand out across the table. 'Megan.'

Chloe shook it lightly, smiling back at her and then around the table at the other faces which until now had just been names and two-dimensional photos. Most of them seemed to be in their early twenties, like her, some were older. A selection of notebooks and folders were scattered amongst them, notes from their hours and hours of eLearning, like the ones in her own bag. 'Nice to meet you all,' she said, raising her right palm to them. 'I'm Chloe and I'm nervous.'

This made some of the others giggle.

'You're not alone, pet,' said the one she recognised as Paul, shaking his head slowly. He didn't sound how Chloe had imagined he would, his voice really deep yet vulnerable somehow, and he had the same accent as Jo, broad Manchester. 'Chuck in a bit of a hangover there too.'

'Oh dear,' Chloe laughed, instantly fond of him.

She wondered if she should take out her folder too, but there seemed little point; what could she gain from five minutes when her brain felt so foggy? Even last night when she had tried to refresh herself it had seemed impossible to remember anything.

'Are we all here?' Megan asked. 'Where is Liv?'

'She said she was driving up from Brighton each day.' Chloe recognised the person speaking as Darren, the ex-policeman, at the far end of the table. He looked different from his photos, but as the only one with a bald head in the group it had to be him. 'I'll put a message on the group.' Chloe's phone pinged, reminding her to switch it to silent, as the message hit the group chat.

A loud handclap was followed by a call of 'Group 352?' making them all stop talking and turn to look up at the two people who had just appeared behind them. A man and a woman, both dressed in navy polo shirts with the airline's logo, and black trousers, grinned down at them.

'That's us,' confirmed Megan as some of the others nodded.

'Well, welcome to your cabin crew training,' he said, opening his arms wide. 'I'm Ben, and this is Vanessa.' Vanessa smiled at them and gave them a small wave. 'If you'd all like to follow us then we will get this show on the road!'

****

Chloe walked along the street with the two bags of shopping she had picked up at the grocery store by the bus stop. She was exhausted; the day had been long and she had hardly slept in her new room last night, but despite the tiredness her head was buzzing. Every once in a while a small laugh would slip out as she remembered something funny, but mostly she couldn't stop smiling to herself at the way a group of strangers felt as familiar as family already.

So far Megan was her favourite. She had a gentle calmness about her, probably helped by the fact that she had flown before, and Chloe somehow felt more relaxed about everything when she was sitting at her side. Next came Paul, the dependable joker with a heart of gold who had shown so much genuine concern when Liv had been inconsolable about being late on her first day. To be honest, Chloe couldn't help but feel that Vanessa could have been a little nicer about it. Had she really needed to make her feel quite so bad? Had she needed to go on and on about how she couldn't afford to be late for a flight, running over the company lateness policy at that very time, in front of everyone... that could have been saved for later, surely? Just her opinion.

That aside, she had loved getting to know everyone, and learning all about what her new life was going to be like. Had her bags not been so heavy she might just have skipped down the street!

Turning the corner of Addison Road, Chloe stopped for a second and put them down, shaking out her hands to bring the blood flow back to her fingers. A cyclist zipped past her on the pavement, almost riding over her shopping.

'Careful!' she called after him, picking the bags back up out of harm's way. It was a longer walk than she had expected, but Mum had needed her car, and she certainly couldn't afford to buy one in the near future. The cyclist gave her an idea. Perhaps she could borrow her brother's bike, bring it back with her next weekend?

She was sure Zac wouldn't mind as long as she kept it safe, he would probably even lower the seat for her...

One more street to go. She ignored the muscles that were screaming in her forearms, pushing forwards... if only Number 6 wasn't at the far end of it.

Reaching the house, Chloe walked up the path and glanced left at the garage. It didn't look as forbidding in the sunshine as it had on Friday, although it still gave her a small shiver. At the door she put her key into the lock and pushed it open. She stood for a moment, took out her earphones and listened, listened to the same silence inside as she had been left with after Mum dropped her off last night, the same silence she had woken up to this morning. She put the earphones back in, grateful for the music, and hoped that at least one of the other girls would be home this evening, because as much as she was feeling positive, excited about her day, that uneasy feeling in her stomach was trying desperately to get back in, and she wasn't sure if she could keep it at bay if she had to spend another night here alone.

The door clicked shut behind her as she carried her bags through to the kitchen, where she unpacked them on the table. She turned and cast her eyes over the closed cupboard doors, trying to decide where would be okay to store it, finally opening one at the top. Inside a few jars of pesto, a bag of granola and some pasta sat haphazardly on the top shelf next to an enormous tub of protein shake. Underneath were two wine glasses, an oversized mug with red hearts on, some glass tumblers and a mismatched collection of plates, bowls and cutlery. Chloe wondered what the rules were… did they have a cupboard each or just put things anywhere? She closed the door and opened the next one, answering her own question immediately. Tins and jars stood in uniform rows, labels all facing forward, small tubs neatly stacked next to jars of herbs and spices. On the shelf below was a pile of matching plates and bowls, and cutlery laid in perfect alignment on top of some paper towel. She closed the door. The third cupboard was empty, and she piled in her shopping, not thinking about where to put things, bread next to pasta, chocolate cereal next to crisps… a jar of peanut butter and her favourite coffee. She was neither healthy nor organised like either of them, but maybe she would be the in-between person that would bridge the gap between them, she wondered.

The fridge was a similar scenario, two shelves telling two different stories. One neat and organised with things you could cook with, one full of fruit, some limp looking salad unopened in its bag and two bottles of white wine. Chloe was already veering towards the one who tried to be healthy but liked to have fun, thinking that the other one most likely had a touch of OCD. She closed the fridge door and looked around for a kettle. A pot noodle would do for tonight, she wanted to have a look through the things they had covered today and make sure she knew it all before they got onto the 'nitty gritty' tomorrow, as Ben had called it.

The front door opening took her by surprise, and she turned quickly to see a girl in the same uniform she would soon be wearing dragging a small case through into the hall. The girl let out a loud sigh as she kicked off her heels, dropping her handbag down next to the case with a thud and pushing the door shut behind her with her foot. She kept her head down as she walked in her stockinged feet towards Chloe, looking at the phone in her hand. Chloe fixed a smile on her face to greet her…

'Oh my God!' The girl clutched her chest as she almost walked into Chloe, the shocked look on her face soon turning into a smile, and then a laugh. 'I'm so sorry, I presumed there was nobody in. You must be the new housemate,' she said, holding out her hand.

'Er, yes, yes, I'm Chloe,' she said, shaking her hand.

'Lovely to meet you, Chloe, I'm Bea, and I've just had a bloody long day,' she said, letting go of her hand and opening the fridge. 'Fancy joining me for a glass of wine?'

Chapter Three

Paul: How are you Liv?

Liv: Ok, thanks so much for your support earlier everyone, I'm not normally that sensitive

Jo: Girl don't apologise, I'd have been a mess if it was me!

Liv: I'm going to leave super early tomorrow, Nick will have to get the girls to school... he's not going to like that much!

Jen: What does he think about you flying?

Liv: He's okay, knows it's always been my dream, but we shall see. Hopefully I can go part time pretty quickly!

Megan: I'm sure it will work out :) Guuys, I can't find the course they told us to do in my online learning. What's it called again?

Jo: {screenshot}

Megan: Ah, cheers babs

Maddie: Had the best day today, thanks so much everyone, love you all {hearts}

Paul: Love you too sweetcheeks

Jen: Paul you're sooooo cheesy

Megan: Howling

'So, tell me about yourself,' Bea said as she poured them both a glass of Pinot Grigio, filling them almost to the top.

'Er…' Chloe felt her face flush, as if she were at an interview again. 'Well, I'm from North London, still live at home…'

'Flown before?' Bea interrupted, handing her a glass and sitting down at the table.

'No, only on holiday.'

'Excited?' Bea grinned. Chloe pulled out a chair and sat opposite.

'Very,' she grinned back.

'Nervous about the exams?'

'Er…' Chloe stalled. She hadn't really thought too much about them yet. She had done well at school, but this was all so new and unknown that she hadn't a clue what to expect. 'Maybe a little.'

'Aw, you'll be fine.' Bea took a sip of her wine. 'Hopefully your trainers will give you a wink when it's something you need to know. Who have you got?'

'Er, Ben and…' she couldn't for the life of her remember the girl's name. 'Have you been somewhere nice?' she asked, turning the questioning back on her housemate of whom she knew nothing yet.

'Yes!' Bea's face lit up. 'Three nights in Cancun. It was wild! We went into the jungle, had a night at Coco Bongo's… have you heard of it?' Chloe shook her head; she was feeling a little dizzy with the amount of energy Bea had and the speed at which she talked, as she proceeded to tell her every detail of her trip. She was topping up their wine glasses now, even though Chloe was less than halfway through hers. 'Oh my word, you are going to love it!' she carried on, not losing any steam. 'Flights are busy, mind, but they are nice passengers, just happy to be going on holiday.' Chloe nodded, taking a sip and twirling the glass in her fingers; she could feel it starting to warm her body now, the stress of the last few days seeping away as she imagined herself on a white sand beach with palm trees... 'Chloe?'

Chloe shook her head and focused back on Bea, who was smiling at her and waiting for an answer to her question, the one she hadn't heard.

'I'm so sorry, I was just picturing myself on the beach in Cancun,' she said dreamily. 'What was the question again?'

'You'll be on that beach before you know it,' Bea smiled. 'I just asked if you had a fella?'

Chloe shook her head and looked down for a second as she allowed herself to think about him. It had been six months since Lucas had ended things, six months since the day she thought her life was over if she didn't have him by her side. They had been childhood sweethearts, together since they were fourteen years old. 'We need to see other people,' he had said, and she hated him for saying *we,* because she didn't need to at all, she would have been quite content to go through the next stage of life with him, and the next. She had an inkling that it was Isla Green with the big boobs and fake tan who had tempted him, made him want to try other girls, sow his oats wider. Men were weak, her mum had said as she consoled her, many of them weren't programmed to settle for one person, especially so young, she said. It wasn't because she wasn't as pretty as Isla, or because her boobs were too small, or her lack of womanly curves, some men preferred their women that way... but for now she should go and be free, free as a bird, and see what adventures she could have without the constraints of a relationship.

The next day her mum had called her over to her laptop. 'How about doing this?' she asked, drawing Chloe's attention to the advert for cabin crew at Osprey. It spoke of adventures, seeing the world, meeting new people. The crew in the picture seemed to be smiling right at her, calling her to come and join them. Suddenly the grief she had felt was replaced with excitement, a feeling of destiny, an opportunity she never would have looked at if Lucas hadn't set her free... free to fly. It still hurt a little, if she were honest, but she was okay with a little.

She sucked in a deep breath as she looked back up, and smiled as wide as she could at Bea. 'I've been free and single for the last six months,' she said.

'Good girl!' Bea said approvingly as she got up to take a second bottle of wine from the fridge. Chloe watched her, so glamorous, glossy chocolate hair twisted up, makeup immaculate, tall and elegant, and so *positive*. She wanted to be like Bea. 'Best way to be when you're so young, nobody holding you back.'

Chloe wondered if Lucas would have held her back, if he'd have wanted her to stay at home...

'No more for me, thanks,' Chloe said, putting her hand over her almost empty glass. She could feel that she had nearly reached her limit, and she still hadn't eaten.

'You're right,' Bea said. 'I've got a date tonight, wouldn't do to be drunk when he arrives,' she laughed.

'Boyfriend?' Chloe asked, confused by her contradiction.

'*Noooo*,' Bea giggled. 'Just a date. Have you met Kathryn yet?'

'Who?'

'The other girl that lives here.'

Chloe shook her head and drank the last of her wine. 'What's she like?

'Odd,' Bea said, suddenly serious. She leaned forward, her elbows on the table, fingers steepled. 'Not like us.' She pointed to Chloe and back to herself. 'One small glass while I tell you about her?'

'Oh, go on then.' Chloe gave in, pushing her glass forward. What harm would one more do?

Chloe felt almost drunk as she poured the boiling water into the noodles an hour later. She could hear the shower running upstairs and marvelled at how her housemate was still able to consider going out after all that wine. She was intrigued to meet Kathryn, who apparently worked long shifts in Crew Scheduling. Quiet, reserved, weird, were three of the words Bea had used to describe her, although Chloe wondered if it was maybe her refusal to drink wine with her, ever, that was the main sticking point. She was happy to stay open-minded though, perhaps she liked doing jigsaws, or getting stuck into a great book?

She turned the tap to cold as she waited the three minutes for her dinner to 'cook,' filling up a glass with water and drinking it straight down, followed immediately by another... Bea was definitely going to be a bad influence during her time here, she could tell, but she loved her already and couldn't wait for them to share more wine, to hear more of her tales about how her own life was going to be...

Chapter Four

Maddie: It was nice to meet you all today, let the fun begin tomorrow!!

Jen: Nice to see you all too. Don't know about anyone else but I'm zonked!

Megan: Same, but need a drink and food. Anyone in Crawley?

Paul: Me and Jo are in the Punchbowl, come and join us! Not having many though after last night!

Jo: Yeah right haha!

Megan: Great, see you in ten.

Jen: Tea and an early night for me... is this an acceptable time to go to bed?!

Paul: Absolutely not, get your arse to the pub you lightweight

Jen: This girl needs her beauty sleep. Have fun guys but I'm out!

Chloe: Having a drink with my new housemate or would have joined you... have fun and see you in the morning everyone.

Maddie: See you all in the morning. I'll save us all a table if I'm the first one in again :)

'*Soooo*, now things are going to get more serious.' Ben stood in front of the screen at the front of the room and smiled at the class. Chloe was sure there was an evil glint in his eye as he said it. 'Group 352, welcome to the world of S. E. P.' He performed a flourish as the letters came up in giant capitals. 'Safety,' he pointed to them one at a time, 'Equipment and Procedures.' He looked around at the group, who were sitting behind tables in a U shape around the edge of room. Everyone was silent, and Chloe was regretting that last glass of wine. She glanced sideways at Jen, who looked terrified. Next to her Liv seemed to be struggling to keep her eyes open, tell-tale bags under her eyes. Chloe felt sorry for her, trying to juggle being a mum and doing all of *this,* without a very supportive husband going by the few comments she had thrown out to no one in particular when she had arrived all flustered and only just on time this morning.

'Don't be so scared,' he laughed. 'Me and Gemma are here to make sure you all graduate as full safety-trained cabin crew at the end of this course.' Gemma, dark hair in a bun, red lipstick, smiled up from behind the laptop in the corner. Chloe was relieved that Vanessa from yesterday had been replaced, if only for Liv's sake. 'And as long as you put the work in I am sure that you are all more than capable of passing these exams. Be in no doubt though, you will *all* need to put the work in....'

He paused and looked around at them again, making sure they all understood what he meant. Chloe's stomach sank. She wondered if her brain was even capable of retaining information any more after so many years off from any kind of studying... what if she failed? The eLearning had been okay, but she'd had the workbook to refer to. Now it was getting much more serious. She felt her face flush at the thought of it. *Don't be ridiculous,* she told herself, *it can't be that hard...* Her skin prickled as it tried to expel the alcohol. Why had she had that last glass of wine???

A picture of an aircraft came up on the screen, under the title "Flight Controls," and as Ben clicked something in his hand, obscure names like elevator, *spoilers* and *ailerons*, not to mention *flaps* – both *leading edge* and *trailing edge...* flashed up with arrows pointing to various parts of the wings and tail.

'*Soooo,*' Ben clapped his hands together. 'Who remembers this from their pre-course work?'

Chloe's heart was beating so hard she thought it would burst out of her chest and she felt an overwhelming urge to run, to get up and run the hell away. Her head thumped and her mind was as blank as a plain sheet of paper; all those hours of studying she had done were for nothing... she didn't remember a thing. Not. One. Single. Thing.

****

At lunchtime the chatter around the table was almost euphoric. They had all survived the morning, even managed to understand what Ben and Gemma were teaching them at times. It seemed that Chloe had remembered some things after all, they had just been hidden behind her wall of panic. Now she felt quite confident, and the hangover had worn off too... things were really turning around, and it was only one o'clock.

'Great photo, Jo.' Megan turned her phone around. Chloe leaned in to see the Instagram post, raising her eyebrows at the 237 likes that had already accumulated. In the picture, Jo had taken down her hair and kicked one leg out behind her as she kissed the nose of the oversized model aircraft that stood in the lobby. It actually hadn't occurred to Chloe to take any photos yet, but then she didn't really post, just liked to see what others were doing on the socials.

'Thanks,' Jo grinned. 'I'll be setting up my Only Fans in no time. Wait until I get that uniform.'

Megan laughed out loud. 'You'll make a fortune.'

'Oh I know I will,' Jo winked.

'Well I want a cut for taking that photo, mind,' said Paul.

'What's your Insta name?' Maddie asked. 'Are you on TikTok?' With that the conversation around the table swiftly turned from SEP to social media as they swapped details. Now they would be able to see what their classmates got up to once they got their wings, be able to follow each other's journeys.

'Chlo, what's your Insta?' Megan asked.

'Oh, I don't have much on mine, it's a bit mixed up,' she said, showing her page. So far there was a few sunsets that had caught her eye, some of Sam, the family spaniel, a picture from a family wedding with her mum, dad and brother and a couple of a night out with friends. There was no theme, no co-ordination.

'I'm sure that will change once you're flying,' Megan said, taking her phone from her and typing her own name, MeggyMoo, into the search bar. She tapped

FOLLOW on her behalf. 'Mine's a bit mixed up too,' she said with a grin.

A small laugh slipped out of Chloe's mouth as she scrolled down through the pictures of cows and calves; Megan looking so pretty in rubber boots amongst the straw and mud. Megan's feed was 50% cows, 50% glamorous dresses or pictures of her in her previous airline's uniform. She looked up at Megan and raised her eyebrows as she waited for an explanation.

'I live on a farm,' she laughed.

'Brilliant. Absolutely brilliant.' Chloe was in awe; herself a city girl who had always longed to have open fields to run through as a child, she returned to scrolling through the pictures of Megan's remarkable life.

'Everyone ready to go back and touch some portable equipment?'

Chloe reluctantly looked up to see Ben standing at the end of their table.

'Ooh yes,' Paul said playfully.

'Enough of that from you.' Ben shook his head, his lips pulled into a thin line that was trying not to smile. 'Follow me, guys,' he said to the rest of them, 'and phones away once we get in the room, please.'

'Damn,' Chloe heard Jo complain behind her as they walked down the corridor. 'I was hoping to get a photo in the lifejacket, my followers love a bit of rubber.'

Chapter Five

Rasia: Guys I'm heading to the crew room in the hotel to eat my pot noodle! Need to decompress before I start studying again!

Jo: Good idea, see you down there, feel dead

Darren: I can't, I need to study, anyone else worried about the exam or just me?!

Maddie: Me too, I'm terrified. Do you think we need to know how often the Beacon transmits a signal, and the exact distance a flare can be seen from? Whyyy do we need to know all of this??!

Megan: Be along in a minute... will bring cheese and crackers! Just an hour though...

Jo: Beaut! Same, no leading us astray Paul, gotta study!

Paul: What you trying to say?!

Liv: Wish I was staying with you guys

Jade: Me too, could literally cry... this house is awful and the family talk so loudly I can't hear myself think

Paul: Come and join us here, more the merrier

Jade: I wish, had to pay up front :(

Jo: You're welcome to come and share my room if you need to babe, got two beds xxx

Jade: That's so kind of you, thank you xxx

'Whereabouts is your room again?' Megan asked as they left the training building together that evening.

'Just the other side of Crawley,' Chloe answered. 'You're so lucky staying just there.' She wished so much that she had booked in at the hotel, but the prices had gone right up by the time she had got around to checking and it was way beyond her budget.

They both looked along to the purple-trimmed hotel a short way up the road on the other side. The wide street seemed never-ending, stretching into the distance, flanked by warehouses and offices of various shades of grey to match the sky.

'Right,' Chloe said as she checked the time on her phone, noticing that the WhatsApp group already had thirty messages and they had only just left the building. 'I'd better not miss this bus. I think I'm going to bring a bike back with me at the weekend, get some exercise in.'

'Madness,' Megan laughed and raised her eyebrows up at the dark grey cloud coming in their direction. 'See you tomorrow, babe.'

'See you tomorrow,' Chloe said and turned in the opposite direction towards her bus stop. She walked quickly, as the clouds had just blocked out the sun and she felt a drop of water touch her hand.

The rain came down thick and fast, bouncing off the pavements and running down her face. To her relief the bus arrived quickly, and Chloe thanked the driver for saving her from a soaking. She sat down in the window and watched the swollen droplets race down the glass; people outside sheltered under trees along the road or ran, holding bags over their heads in futile attempts to stay dry. It was over as quickly as it started though, and by the time she reached Addison Road the shower had passed and a beautiful rainbow stretched right across the road. Her mum always said that a rainbow was someone's way of saying goodbye when they had just died, but Chloe preferred not to think of people dying, and just liked to think that it was a beautiful act of nature with a smidgen of science behind it.

She walked up the hill and turned into the driveway, surprised to see a blue BMW parked there. She walked past it, glancing in at the leather seats and fancy dash, and quickly decided that it didn't belong to Kathryn. Letting herself in she stopped as always and listened at the open door. A giggle from upstairs told her that Bea was home, and a second laugh, a man's voice, meant that she had a visitor, and probably one with a BMW.

The evening sun drew her down to the kitchen and she stood for a moment looking out of the window. An urge to feel the warmth of it on her face pulled her to the back door and she turned the handle, which wobbled in her hand. The wooden door had swollen over the years, and she yanked it twice before it opened properly.

Outside, dandelions grew a foot tall along the side of the garage, and weeds poked through cracks in the pavement just as they did at the front of the house. The grass out here was long, but not so long that it hadn't been cut in recent months. Bushes lined the sizeable garden, and trees hung overhead. She caught a glimpse of old fence panels behind, leaning into the bushes that now bore their weight. It was probably a nice garden once, when it was cared for. She looked back at the house. A bench sat under the kitchen window, iron arms with wooden slats in between. She walked back to it, brushing the few drops of rain off with her hand and lowered herself down slowly, just in case it broke, relieved that it just creaked a little. Safe, she exhaled and leaned back, feeling the warmth of the sun on her face. She closed her eyes, and ignored her phone that vibrated in her pocket as a message came through... she would enjoy this for a moment first.

A rustling sound startled Chloe, and she lifted her head up to see what it was. It was coming from behind the garage, but before she could get up to investigate, a woman appeared holding a bunch of weeds in one hand.

'Oh, hello,' she said, rubbing her forehead with the back of her free hand. She was tall, with wild, auburn shoulder-length hair and freckles to match. Maybe in her late thirties or early forties, but it was hard to tell. Her clothes were just as Chloe had imagined they would be, like her mum, skinny jeans and a thick, knitted cardigan, with flat boots on her feet. She didn't smile, but she hadn't expected her to. 'Just doing some gardening,' she said, holding up the weeds. 'You must be the new tenant,' she said as a matter of fact.

'I'm Chloe, pleased to meet you.' Chloe stood up. 'Do you need a hand?'

'Er, no, thanks.' She shook her head. 'That's enough for one day. Nice to meet you,' she said and turned towards the house... and then she was gone, dropping the weeds by the back door as she passed through it.

'Bye,' Chloe said, too late for her to hear. She stood for a moment and re-ran their short conversation; had she made a bad first impression? Should she have engaged her more in conversation? Chloe regarded the small pile of weeds that she had dropped. Maybe it would make a good impression if she added to it, helped her with the gardening? She walked over to where Kathryn had come out from and peered down the back of the garage, quickly changing her mind. It was a jungle behind there, thick with brambles and weeds that would take weeks to clear by hand, by which time she would be moving out... and who knew how many spiders and insects were hiding away down there, the small window with its yellowed glass and crumbling frame covered in a thick layer of cobweb. She shivered and stepped back; she would find another way to get on Kathryn's good side, she was sure, but spiders were a no-go.

Chapter Six

Jen: Guys, can anyone help me with what seatbelts are in each demo kit... it's so confusing

Megan: {screenshot}

Here's a summary I made up to try and remember them.

Jen: You're amazing, thanks so much. I'm struggling to get all this info into my head

Liv: Me too, and my little angels are refusing to go to bed:(

Megan: Handover to your husband babe

Liv: Don't even get me started...

Jo: I feel like he emphasised age and weights for kiddie life jackets a lot... reckon that will be in the exam

Chloe: I agree

Rasia: Night one revising and my head might burst

Jo: #STRESSED

Megan: If anyone wants to meet early tomorrow I'm happy to help

Jen: Yes please!! I revise so much better when I can talk through things! Too tired now, nothing is going in

Paul: I'll take any help on offer, what time?

Megan: 7:30 in the cafeteria? Should be quiet then? Or the classroom if you prefer?

Jo: Cafeteria, then we can get a coffee

Liv: Sod it, he can sort the kids out, I'll be there, I can't get anything done here. Did I tell you I used to be a teacher;)

Paul: NO! You kept that one quiet, start calling you Miss!

Liv: Just primary, but I have a few tricks for remembering things that might help someone.

Maddie: perfect, thanks so much, I'm gonna get an early night then.

Darren: Cheers Megs, and Liv, I'll be there.

Chloe had decided on the living room for her revision, as the noises coming from Bea's room were in no way conducive to learning. She sat at the dining table, laptop open, scrolling through page after page of portable equipment. On a notepad she scribbled durations and instructions, pre-flight checks and locations… her brain hurt. Added to that was the WhatsApp group that had beeped constantly all evening…

Chloe muted the group; she was getting nothing done while she was constantly reading their messages and the collective anxiety of the worriers was doing nothing to aid her own. She took a deep breath and covered one side of the notepad with a piece of paper.

'Portable Oxygen, turn anti-clockwise to start, lasts two hours fifteen on low flow…' she recited, moving down through the endless list.

It was dark outside when she heard the two sets of footsteps come down the stairs, and the front door open, and close moments later. A small knock at the semi-open living-room door followed by 'Hey,' made her finally look up from the paperwork. 'How's it going?'

Chloe groaned and held up the page she was on in the manual. Bea leaned in to see it.

'Ah, Portable Equipment,' she laughed. 'The joy! Is it going in?'

'Actually, yes, I think it might be,' Chloe said. In fact she was quite sure she had almost nailed it. She was fortunate to have a very analytical mind and could remember small details easily. In another life she would have loved to have been a detective, examining forensic evidence and solving the most difficult crimes, but she didn't want to be a policewoman first and deal with the worst of humanity, so that had ruled *that* career out for her.

'It's a lot to take in at once, I found it *so* hard,' Bea said with a sympathetic smile that suggested she wasn't buying her confidence. 'Do you want a cuppa?'

'That would be lovely,' Chloe smiled back. 'White and one please.'

'Coming up.'

Chloe tested herself on the last few lines and sat back, pleased with herself. This was a perfect time for a break. She picked up her phone; 126 messages on the group since she had looked last, but she had no desire to read them yet. Bea returned with two steaming mugs and a packet of biscuits.

'You are truly amazing,' Chloe said as she put the cup and biscuits down next to her.

'Ha, I've been where you are not so long ago, I remember the pain.' She hovered in the door, sipping her own tea. 'How was today?'

'Good,' Chloe said as she wrested a biscuit from the packet. 'Long, but good.'

'It's so much to take in, hey?' she said again.

Chloe nodded. 'I had no idea how much crew needed to know.'

'Uh-huh. Do you need any help?'

'I think I'm okay, but thank you,' Chloe said gratefully, handing the packet back.

Bea put her hand up. 'Not for me, you keep them. If your trainers are nice they will help you out in the exams, just put your hand up and they'll reword the question for you.'

'Thank you, you're an angel.'

'You're welcome,' Bea smiled. 'Right, I'm going to let you get on, I need a shower, JFK early in the morning.'

'Oh, Bea,' Chloe said, suddenly remembering something as she was pulling the door shut behind her. It opened again and Bea's head poked around it.

'Yeah?'

'I met Kathryn earlier, in the garden,' Chloe whispered. She hadn't heard her in the house all evening but presumed that she was in her room.

'Oh, how was that?' Bea whispered back.

'She was gardening, seemed nice enough,' she shrugged.

'Gardening?' Bea frowned.

'Well, pulling weeds out behind the garage.'

Bea pulled a confused face, before mouthing 'Weirdo,' and making Chloe laugh. 'Night, love,' she said at normal volume.

'Night, Bea, and thanks again.' Chloe held up her mug.

'Welcome,' Bea called as she walked away.

'Right,' Chloe turned the page of her notebook. 'Back at it, girl.'

****

In bed that night Chloe quickly scrolled through the now 187 messages. Her mind whirred with the information she had spent all evening absorbing, but in comparison to some of them in the group she had to admit that she felt quietly confident. Only tomorrow would tell if she was justified in that. She heard the far door across the landing open, the one to Kathryn's room, and light footsteps going down the stairs. It was a shame that she wasn't as open as Bea, but Chloe was determined to make a friend of her one way or another, she was sure that there must be *something* they had in common.

Chapter Seven

Liv: Is anyone here yet?

Megan: I'm here, long table at the back of the room where we had lunch yesterday. I've decided that it's 'Our' table :)

Darren: Just leaving the hotel if anyone is walking across?

Jo: Wait for me

Liv: Just parking up, won't be a sec.

Paul: I'm outside, just having a cig

Jo: Tut tut

Liv: I might take up smoking at this rate lol

Maddie: Me too

Chloe chose sleep; she was an owl, not a lark. The cafeteria was heaving by the time she arrived at 0850, the air thick with conversations and excited chatter. She spotted the group immediately on 'their' table as Megan had so cutely put it, weaving her way across the room to where they sat.

'Morning,' she said brightly.

Maddie looked up at her from her manual, a pained expression on her face. 'How come you're so cheerful?'

Chloe shrugged, pulling over a chair and sitting down next to Megan. A faint smell of stale cigarettes wafted up her nose and she knew without looking that Paul was to her left. The table was quiet, most people's heads down as they used their last few minutes.

'Morning, Chlo,' Megan said, looking easily the most relaxed on the table. 'Good sleep?'

'Yes, thanks.' She had slept like a baby in fact, the past few days catching up with her and putting her almost into a coma. She felt great for it this morning though, her mind the clearest it had been for days despite its workload.

'Right, who's ready for their test?'

Ben stood over them. Chloe noticed that he had a habit of just *appearing* with no warning, always with his hands together and a big cheesy smile on his face.

'Can't wait,' someone said dryly.

'You'll all be fine,' he said with the confidence of someone who had seen this exact same worried group of newbies week after week. 'Let's get it over with.'

They all followed him in silence along one of the many corridors that made up the maze of a building and into a room where computers lined the walls. Chloe sat at the one nearest the door and put her bag under the table.

'Everything away, people.' Chloe hadn't even noticed that Gemma was already in the room until she spoke. 'Turn your computers on and when it asks, put in your company email and payroll number. Would anyone like a blank piece of paper?'

Chloe wasn't sure what she needed one for but put her hand up nonetheless as Gemma walked past her. Her earlier calm waned, and she could feel her heart rate and temperature slowly rising. She took deep breaths, dropping her shoulders to ease the oncoming anxiety as she had done in her college exams. She followed Gemma's instructions until the exam start page stared back at her from the screen.

'Okay.' Gemma looked around the room slowly. 'Put your hand up if you're stuck, we can reword a question, but we can't help you with the answer. When you're ready, press start.'

Chloe turned back around and clicked her button, her heart giving one big *thud* as she did so.

Where is the elevator located on the aircraft?

Blank, her mind was completely blank. She had concentrated so much on the Portable Equipment she'd forgotten everything else. She stared at the screen for a moment before giving herself a shake. *C'mon, Chloe, you know this stuff.* She flagged it to come back to later, when her brain was back working.

The next few questions were the same and she felt the panic burn in her chest. She looked around and saw both of the instructors leaning over her classmates... what could she ask though? She understood the questions, she just didn't know the answers.

What are the pre-flight checks of a smokehood?

Aha! She smiled, finally one that she knew; she ticked the answer confidently.

What age can you use a ...

How long does a ...

Click, click, click, Chloe sailed through one after another. She could hear muffled whispers as hands went up around the room, and sighs from Darren who was sitting next to her. At the last question, with twenty minutes still to go, she went back to the beginning.

Now she remembered, 'the elevator is on the horizontal stabiliser,' she could see the picture in her mind.

Click, click, click...

She hovered her mouse over the submit button. Just one question was still flagged, but her need to get out of the room far outweighed her need to score 100% when she only needed 88%. She had already seen one of the girls leave the room and she wanted to be out there too.

Congratulations you've passed!

Score: 100%

Chloe pushed her seat back triumphantly and pulled her bag out from under the desk. She caught Ben's eye as she stood up and returned his thumbs up to signal her pass.

Outside the room the air felt so much clearer, so much easier to breathe. She followed the signs back to the cafeteria and looked for her classmate, who was sitting on the far side.

'Oh my word,' Jen said when she saw Chloe walking over to her. 'How did you find it?'

'A struggle at first, but then I got some easy ones at the end. You?'

'Yeah, same. There was definitely some tricky ones in there though, I think they are worded to catch you out.'

One by one people joined them.

'Did you get that question about...?'

'How long does a fire extinguisher last?'

Paul walked over to them now, his face white. 'Are you okay, Paul?' someone asked.

'Yeah, just scraped through,' he said, falling into a seat and leaning back, his eyes raised to the ceiling.

'Are we all out now?'

'Jo's still in there.'

Chloe looked at her watch; surely the thirty minutes was up now. 'Do you think she's okay?' she asked.

Paul shrugged. 'She had Gemma with her, but they wouldn't help me much so I doubt they would her. Do you think I've got time for a cigarette?' he asked to no one in particular.

'Nope,' Jen said and tipped her head in the direction of Ben, who stood across the hall beckoning them towards him.

They followed him in silence back to the room and took their same seats. Jo sat with her back to them across the room, she didn't turn around.

'So, we just need you all to close down your computers,' Gemma said, waiting until all of the screens were black.

'Well done, everyone. We will be moving on to decompression and turbulence now, so once your computers are off, if you take everything with you and meet us back in the same classroom we were in yesterday in twenty minutes.'

'I have no idea where that is,' Chloe said to Megan as they left the room. Her sense of direction had never been great, always one to follow the crowd and not take much notice of the route.

'I have a rough idea, but hopefully someone else will know,' Megan replied.

Chloe looked over her shoulder and saw Paul put his arm around Jo. Her energy from the last two days seemed to have left her completely, her infectious smile nowhere to be seen. Chloe wanted to give her a hug but didn't know if she should.

'Coffee?' she asked Megan.

'Yes, I just need a quick wee though, can you grab me a latte and I'll meet you there in five?'

'No problem.' She walked back to the cafeteria alone and joined the queue, wondering where the rest of the group had gone, thinking about Jo. Her stomach growled, reminding her that she had skipped breakfast, and she scanned the counter for inspiration.

'A toasted muffin, please,' the woman in front of her said to the server.

'Good idea, that sounds perfect,' Chloe thought out loud. The woman turned part way around and Chloe recognised her instantly.

'Kathryn,' she exclaimed, 'I didn't realise that was you.' Her hair was tied up today, and she wore a smart white shirt with tailored black trousers and low heels. *Very officey*, Chloe thought.

Kathryn smiled, but it didn't quite reach her eyes. 'Oh, hi,' she said, pushing her dark-rimmed glasses back up the bridge of her nose. 'Nice to see you. How are you getting on?' she asked politely.

'Great,' Chloe answered, wondering if she really meant it when she said it was nice to see her. 'So, you work in here then?' she asked quickly, undeterred.

'Yes, on the second floor.'

'Oh wow,' Chloe said, surprised by how much went on within the four walls of this building. She had presumed that it was just for training, other parts of the airline going on elsewhere. 'It must be so interesting, trying to coordinate all those flights and crew,' she said, picturing a room full of big screens and whiteboards, people wandering around with microphoned headsets on.

'Er, yes, yes I suppose it is,' Kathryn said as she tapped her phone on the card reader and took her muffin from the server. 'Well, must get back. Good luck with the training,' she said, and she was gone. Chloe watched her stride purposefully across the hall and through the door to the stairwell. For the second time Chloe was left in her wake feeling like her conversation was unfinished.

'Madam?'

'Oh sorry,' Chloe said to the server, who was waiting patiently for her to place her order. 'Two lattes and a toasted muffin, please.'

'Who was that?' Megan asked, suddenly at her side. Chloe had no idea how long she had been standing there next to her.

'Oh, my house mate, she works in crew scheduling.'

'Wow,' Megan said, taking their lattes from the counter. 'Now that's someone useful to know.'

Chloe considered this for a moment; it hadn't crossed her mind before. 'I suppose it is,' she said, *or it would be if only she would talk to me.*

Chapter Eight

Jo: Guys I'm freaking out, I've got to learn everything for tomorrow's test and go over all of today's for my resit. I lit can't cope.

Megan: Right, get yourself together and meet me in the crew room in half hour, we'll do it together.

Paul: I'll be down too.

Jo: Noo, it's okay, thanks though... think I'll be better off studying on my own

Paul: Was it something I said?

Jo: Ha, no offence babs, just need to concentrate and not good at that when I'm with others, as you know!

Paul: fair enough. You can do it girl... I can't lose you, who else can make me laugh the whole way down from Manny!

Jo: It's a rare skill I have!

Chloe: Oh Jo, my number is on here if you want to call me at any time for help

Jade: We're all here for you girl.

Megan: And I'll be in the crew room all evening if you change your mind, I need to get out of this room

Darren: Wait, where is this crew room you speak of?

Megan: Keep up Darren, where've you been luv?! 2nd floor, turn left out of the lift. There's a kettle and microwave in there and a few sofas

Darren: Well well, who knew! Definitely be down a bit later, this room feels like a prison cell. Good luck with everything Jo.

Jo: Thanks everyone. Gonna turn my phone off for a bit, see you all in the morning.

Paul: Meet you outside the front 8:30?

Jo: I have to be in at 8 for the resit so I'll see you in the classroom after. :(

Paul: I'll be downstairs at 7:30 and walk you over.

Jo: xxx

There was a different car in the driveway that night when Chloe returned home, an old estate with so much mud sprayed up its sides it was difficult to tell that it had once been black. Looking in through the window she could see pieces of paper, old receipts and wrappers, scattered across the passenger seat and floor, a layer of dust across the plastic surfaces. She couldn't imagine Bea being a passenger in a car so dirty, not that it could have been one of her beaux as she was away, wasn't she? She opened the front door and listened to the silence that filled the house. Walking through to the kitchen she listened between steps, still silence.

'Hello?' she called, just loudly enough that someone upstairs might hear. Nothing.

Chloe shrugged; it was a mystery that would have to wait, she hadn't eaten since lunchtime and her stomach was crying out for some dinner. She opened up the fridge and took out the tortellini and tomato sauce that had been in her head the whole of the journey home, popping a piece of the ricotta-filled pasta into her mouth, uncooked, as she tipped the rest into a saucepan.

The back door opening, the shake of the door handle followed by a hard push, startled her as she drained the pasta minutes later, but what startled her more was the person who came into the kitchen. A man of probably late fifties, head shiny on top and grey hair cropped short around the back and sides. He was short, shorter than her even, maybe five foot five, dressed in casual beige trousers and a small-checked shirt under a navy V-neck sweater. He looked down as he wiped his feet on the worn coir mat. Chloe coughed to let him know that she was there.

'Oh, hello,' he said, looking as surprised to see her as she was him.

'Hi,' Chloe said back, wondering if she should be worried that a strange man had just walked into the house, albeit a small one. 'Can I help you?'

He stopped, holding the door handle still, as if he might just walk straight back out. 'Oh, sorry,' he said, before letting out a very unmanly, nervous giggle. She held in a laugh, his threat level immediately reduced to nothing. 'I'm the landlord, Andrew, and you are?' He stretched out a small hand.

'Oh.' Chloe put the empty pan down on the draining board, wiping her wet hands on her hips before shaking it. His grip was much tighter than she was expecting, painful almost. 'I'm Chloe,' she said, trying not to wince. 'I just moved in on Monday. Lovely house,' she said, pulling her hand back as soon as he released it. He nodded but said nothing as he studied her, a smile on his face now. 'Did you used to live here?' she asked, trying to fill the silence.

'Yes,' he said. 'Mother was here until last year.'

Chloe nodded; that fitted in perfectly with her assumptions about the décor, but she stopped short of asking if she was dead.

'Is everything okay for you?' he asked eventually.

'Yes, thank you,' she replied. She glanced sideways at her pasta, steam rising from the sink.

'Well, I must be off, let you have your dinner,' he said. 'I just wanted to check on the place on my way past.' Chloe nodded. 'Nice to meet you,' he said as he made to go out of the back door.

Suddenly Chloe had a thought. 'Just one thing, Andrew,' she called out, making him stop and turn around. 'I was just wondering,' she asked, trying to form her words in the most amiable way. He looked at her, eyebrows raised in anticipation. 'If I were to bring my bike here,' she started, 'would I be able to keep it in the garage?'

He didn't answer for a moment, just rubbed one side of his face with his palm and looked upwards. 'Well, I would love to say yes,' he said slowly, 'but the garage is so full of Mum's things that there isn't a spare inch in there. How about,' he brought his hand down to his chin and tapped his lips with his forefinger thoughtfully. 'How about you just bring it right on into the hallway? Plenty of room there for it, and if anyone complains you just tell them I said it was okay,' he said. He seemed pleased with himself for coming up with a solution. 'Right, really must dash, nice to meet you,' he said again, and was gone.

'You too,' Chloe called after him. She looked back down the hallway and shrugged. Sure, there was room but there was no way her mother would have let her park a bike in the hallway at home, it wasn't the nicest of ornaments, and she could imagine it getting in the way when Bea tried to get in with her bags. She'd clear it with them both first, and if there was any pushback, she would give up on the whole idea.

Her phone pinged and she picked it up as she sat down at the table with her dinner. The WhatsApp group was off already, everyone panicked about tomorrow's exam after reality had well and truly set in this morning. She switched it to silent; her own worry was enough of a burden, without getting drawn into everyone else's. An evening of study was ahead of her, although she felt so tired all of a sudden that she doubted she would get much past nine o'clock with it.

****

She must have nodded off, as it was dark outside when she lifted her head up from her pillow, but the sleep had been light, and the front door closing had been loud enough to wake her. She rubbed her eyes and picked up her iPad, rereading the page where she had left off, hoping that the decompression and fire drills were going in more effectively than it felt they were.

She picked up her phone and scanned through the last few messages. Jo hadn't been back on the group and Chloe wondered how she was doing. She couldn't imagine how stressed she must be; failing an exam was one thing, but failing your first one was not a good footing to start on. At all.

Chloe picked up her pen and shook herself off; napping wasn't going to help her with her own exam, but then nor was fidgeting like she was because she was suddenly desperate for the loo.

Opening her bedroom door she was surprised to see Kathryn on the landing, mostly because she was on her knees doing something with a screwdriver to the door of her bedroom, which was next to hers at the front of the house. She didn't stop what she was doing either, just gave her a quick side glance. 'Hi,' she said.

'Oh, hi,' Chloe said, stopping and studying. 'Do you need a hand?'

'I'm good thanks,' she replied, twisting the screwdriver into the edge of what Chloe could now see was a shiny new door handle.

'Was it broken?' she asked, curiosity getting the better of her.

'No, but I lost the key somewhere.'

'Ah,' Chloe said, mulling it over. She looked at her own door handle. There was a hole where a key should go, but she definitely hadn't seen one anywhere in her room. It hadn't crossed her mind either, but now that she thought about it, she guessed it made sense to lock your door in a shared house.

'I saw the landlord today,' she said casually as she passed her.

'Oh, really?' Kathryn didn't stop what she was doing and she didn't turn around.

'Yes, he came to the house.'

'Uh-huh.'

'He was just checking everything was okay, I think.' Chloe stopped outside of the toilet door at the top of the stairs. 'Have you met him?' she asked.

'Yes,' Kathryn replied bluntly. She sounded completely disinterested.

Chloe wasn't giving in that easily, surely their mutual landlord deserved a conversation? 'He was nice enough, very short though and a funny laugh, don't you think? Apparently he used to live here with his mum, but I think she died a year ago and all her things are still in the gar...'

Kathryn had finally turned around towards her now. She was still kneeling on the floor, but just with one knee, as if she were about to get up, and she was tapping her chin with the screwdriver. The intense way that she was staring at her made Chloe feel uneasy and she stopped talking mid-sentence. 'Go on,' Kathryn said with a nod after a moment's silence. 'What else did he say?'

'Er.' Chloe shifted her weight from one foot to the other as she tried to recall what else they had talked about in their brief encounter. 'Oh yes,' she pointed her finger up in the air, 'I asked him if I could keep my bike in the garage, but he said it was full and that I should keep it in the hallway. Would you mind that? Please say if you do.'

Kathryn said nothing, was just nodding still.

'Do you mind?' Chloe asked again.

'No, not at all,' she said suddenly, and then she smiled. Chloe beamed back at her. Kathryn had *smiled*, a *real* smile, at *her*...the ice had finally been broken!

Her joy was short-lived.

Kathryn turned abruptly back around. 'Excuse me, I had better get this done or I'll never get my tea.'

'Oh, of course, don't let me stop you,' Chloe said. 'I need to get on too,' she added, aware that she might have come across a bit too keen. 'Just a quick loo break before I get back to the books...' she rambled as she shut the door between them, sighing once she was safe inside. Why was it so hard to make friends with her, and why did she care so much?

When she emerged, Kathryn was gone. She washed her hands quickly in the sink next door, noticing how Bea's things were scattered everywhere that she looked. Her own toiletries stayed close at hand under the sink in their Victoria's Secret bag, but there was nothing of Kathryn's in here that she could tell, no doubt they were locked away behind that door of hers... On her way back to her room, Chloe couldn't help herself trying Bea's door handle and was inexplicably pleased to find that, like hers, it wasn't locked.

Later that night, as she tried to get to sleep, Chloe pondered the door situation. Did the fact that she and Bea didn't worry about locking their doors mean simply that they had nothing to hide? She knew that she didn't, and nor did she have anything worth stealing, and she could only presume that Bea felt the same… BUT, if that was the case, did that mean, in turn, that Kathryn *did* have something to hide or something worth stealing? If so, what was it…?

Go to sleep, Chloe, you are getting carried away, everything doesn't always have to have a reason…!

Chapter Nine

Chloe: Good luck Jo, you'll smash it

Megan: Yep, good luck lovely, hope you get some easy questions

Paul: Go on my girl, you can do it!

Maddie: thinking of you Jo, good luck darling

Jade: Good luck Jo xxx

Rasia: Good luck xxx

Liv: Good luck Jo, make sure you take your time and ask them for help if you need it xxx

Megan: Yes, get them to reword the heck out of it!

Jo: Thanks everyone... just going in... see yous on the other side...

The air smelt of burned toast this morning in the cafeteria. Chloe saw her group straight away, sitting along their table on the far side. No one was talking when she reached them, and no one apart from Megan even looked up, they were all just hunched over their manuals and notebooks in their own little worlds. The looming exam coupled with wondering how Jo was getting on was a total buzz-kill. Megan took her bag off the seat next to her that she had saved for Chloe and she sat down.

'Any word?' Chloe asked quietly. Megan just shook her head.

'It's five to nine, should we go down do you think?' Darren asked.

'Reckon so,' Paul replied. He picked up his phone from the table and looked at the screen. 'No news is good news, right?'

No one answered.

In silence they followed Darren back down to the computer room; down to the one room that they were all beginning to dislike. Inside Jo was sitting in the same seat as yesterday. Like yesterday, she didn't turn around.

****

As she made her way home that evening there was no break in the clouds, no sun shining through them or rainbows to lift the mood. Chloe shut the front door behind her and went straight up the stairs, dropping onto her bed with a loud sigh. She wished Bea was home, because right now she could do with a large glass of wine and someone to talk to who would understand what she was feeling, understand the insecurity that had descended on the whole group as they watched Jo face being sent home. She wondered if anything like this had happened on her course. She closed her eyes and allowed herself to drift off for a moment to somewhere warm and sunny, until the shrill beep of her phone disturbed her.

Any special requests for tea tomorrow?

It was a swift and simple text, but it worked magic. Going home to see her family was exactly what she needed.

Fish and chips and Netflix? she texted back.

New Season of Crime Scene?

Perfect!!!

Great, can't wait to hear about your week xxx

Chloe jumped up, shaking off her mood. Right now she had passed both exams with 100%, and she needed to do whatever was necessary to make sure she carried on that way. She felt terrible for Jo, she really did, but she had at least passed the new exam today and hopefully she would get through the verbal resit tomorrow… in the meantime *she* had studying to do. She also needed to pack a bag so that she could go straight home from training, where she would get herself into her comfies and under a blanket on the sofa, ready to binge-watch crime dramas with her mum; a perfect Friday night would be her reward for this week.

She pushed her hands into the small of her back and stretched backwards, staring mindlessly out onto the street. A lone figure caught her attention as it approached the house in the darkness, and she watched as Kathryn turned onto the driveway. She took a step forward, expecting to see her cross onto the path and into the house, but she didn't. Chloe moved up close to the window and looked down on the front garden, but Kathryn was nowhere to be seen. She watched for a couple more minutes but there was no sign or sound of her coming into the house.

Intrigued, Chloe opened her door and tiptoed down the stairs. She opened the front door as quietly as she could, looking outside, along to the garage. The sound of the back door opening surprised her, and she quickly pushed it shut just as Kathryn appeared from the kitchen.

'Oh, hi,' Kathryn said casually.

'Hi,' Chloe said. 'Er, I thought I heard someone at the door,' she said, her hand still on the handle.

'Oh, right. I forgot my key, good job that back door is never locked,' Kathryn said. She didn't even look at Chloe as she made her way past her and up the stairs.

'Uh-huh,' agreed Chloe, who until that moment hadn't realised that it wasn't. She heard her unlock her bedroom, open and close it and lock it again from the inside, strange behaviour from someone so blasé about the house being so open? Also, it had been a few minutes between her reaching the house and coming in the back door… what had she been doing in that time?

Chloe found herself mulling it over as she went to the kitchen to get her dinner. Was it her or was Kathryn's behaviour strange? Was it the idea of watching some good old crime documentaries tomorrow night that was making her even question it, or had Bea been right all along? She opened the back door and stuck her head out into the cold night air. There was no light in the garden, even the moon was absent behind the invisible clouds. What had she been doing in those few minutes? she wondered. Why was her behaviour so very odd? What was in that room?

Chapter Ten

{Jo has left the group}

Megan: Well that's the saddest thing

Maddie: I keep crying, I think it's all got to me. How could they just throw her out like that?

Jade: Yeah, I can't believe they wouldn't help her out more

Megan: My last airline were exact the same, three chances and you were out.

Rasia: SO unfair

Liv: Actually broke my heart seeing them lead her out like that, the poor girl :(((((

Darren: What did Gemma mean when she said she'd be back?

Megan: I must have missed that?

Darren: She said something along the lines of 'like Captain Maggie' or something to Ben, sounded like an inside joke. Just wondered what they meant by it?

Megan: Absolutely no idea, defo an inside joke by the sounds of things? Are we still going for drinks? I seriously need a bottle of wine right now.

Paul: I'm just gonna grab a shower… half hour downstairs?

Darren: Yeah you need one fella ;) See you in half hour.

Paul: watch yerself Dazza!

Megan: Ahhh Paul, thought you were taking Jo home. Glad you're joining us!

Paul: I would have but she wanted to take the train. Needs a bit of time on her own I reckon.

Rasia :(xxx

Chloe: Enjoy everyone, send Jo our love Paul, tell her 'everything will always turn out alright in the end' xxx

Megan: Aww I like that Chloe. Can't believe you've blown us out though...

Chloe: It's my motto, sad I know but lol! Sorry, already promised my mum. Will come next time!

Megan: You'd better....

It was good to be home.

Chloe put the last of the plates in the dishwasher and shut the door. 'Mum...'

'Yes?' Her mum turned around from the sink, where she was washing the roasting tins. Her dad had already disappeared off to get ready for work. He was a concierge in one of the top London hotels and Chloe loved hearing his tales of the bizarre demands made by the rich guests in the small hours, from drugs to prostitutes and everything in between.

'Did you ever wish you'd played the field?'

Her mum stopped what she was doing and laughed. Chloe's parents had been childhood sweethearts, just like her and Lucas, only neither of *them* had felt the need to see what they were missing. 'Well, I can't speak for your dad, but I guess it crossed my mind once or twice over the years.'

'Mum!' Chloe was shocked to hear the admission.

'What?' Her mum giggled. 'I didn't *do* anything, just wondered what life might have been like with someone else. You know, a rich Italian, a sexy singer in a band...' A dreamy expression came over her face.

'Mother!' Chloe snapped her out of her thoughts. 'You practically cheated right then!' she laughed. Her mum shrugged, the smile still on her face as she went back to scrubbing her pan.

'You asked,' she said.

'Wish I hadn't.' Chloe shivered at the thought of her mum with the rich Italian and the sexy singer... She had wanted to know though. Her mum was still extremely attractive, only forty-six, and still stayed slim and fit thanks to her love of running and yoga. She'd had her brother at just nineteen, Chloe a few years later, and had then decided that their family was complete. She and Zac had enjoyed a lovely childhood, growing up in a standard British semi with normal parents who rarely argued, and put them first for everything. Chloe would have been happy to have what they had, too, but now that particular future had been written off for her, she wondered what her new one would be? Should she play the field like Bea, or maybe throw herself into a sensible job and climb the career ladder once she had tried flying for a couple of years? Was there another Mr Right out there for her, or was she destined for a string of Mr Right-Nows?

'See you girls in the morning.' Her dad came in and kissed them both goodbye, taking a treat from the jar on the side and giving it to Sam, who had just come in and sat expectantly at his feet.

'Bye, love,' her mum said. Chloe shot her a look over her dad's shoulder as she hugged him; she had practically just cheated on him. Her mum just smirked.

'Right,' she said as the door shut behind him, and tipped her head at the clock. '*Crime Scene*.'

'Shit,' said Chloe, flicking on the kettle to make the hot chocolates. They only had five minutes to get in position.

'I'll get the biscuits,' her mum said, hastily opening the larder cupboard.

'Tonight we look at the case of a missing man from Kent, whose body went undiscovered for fifteen years…' started the presenter. Chloe tucked her legs up underneath her and sank back into the deep cushioned sofa next to her mum. Sam jumped up and made himself comfortable between them. *'… and you won't believe where they found him.'*

****

Chloe wished she felt excited to be back, but she wasn't, and she hesitated before getting out of the car. There were no lights on at the front of the house except from the hall, and it looked cold and unloved. Her mum was already out and was wresting Zac's bike out of the boot for her.

'Here, I'll get that,' she said, turning the handlebars around and slipping it out easily. She had been blessed with her dad's common sense thankfully, and not her mum's lack of it.

Propping it up against the car, she hugged her mum.

'Are you okay?' her mum asked, standing back and looking at her knowingly.

'Yeah,' Chloe sighed. She was okay.

'It's only four more weeks.' Her mum put her hand on her shoulder.

'I know. It's just this house.' Chloe looked over her shoulder. 'It just doesn't feel...' She didn't know how to finish her sentence.

'Like home?'

'Yeah, I suppose,' she said. She had never expected a shared house to feel like a home though, she had known that it would be very different to what she was used to, but it was something more, *there* was something more, but she couldn't quite put her finger on it. Maybe it was more about the people in it? Perhaps that was it, she wondered, but that didn't seem to explain it either. Perhaps she would never be able to find the words to finish her sentence.

'Will you come in for a cuppa?' she asked, knowing that just having her mum in it would warm the old place up.

'I can't, love, I've got to pick your brother up from the station.' Her mum wrapped her arms around her now.

'Oh yeah,' she said into her shoulder. She had forgotten that Zac was arriving back from his girlfriend's tonight, she hadn't seen him all weekend, just spoken to him on the phone when she asked him about the bike.

'Go on,' her mum said with her best encouraging voice. 'Get inside in the warm.'

'Okay. Love you, Mum,' she said and kissed her on the cheek.

Chloe wheeled the bike up the path with one hand, her rucksack in the other, and rug rolled up under her arm. At the front door she turned to watch her mum drive away, brushing off the feeling of being abandoned, knowing that it was childish and pathetic.

The sound of the door suddenly opening behind her made her jump, and she spun around to see Bea stood there with a huge smile on her face. 'Well look who's home!' she cried. In an instant Chloe felt better, if not a bit silly for letting her negativity get the better of her; it really wasn't that bad here when Bea was home. 'What the hell is that?'

'A bike,' Chloe laughed as she wheeled it by her. Bea curled her top lip as she leaned it against the wall and dropped her bag and rug on the floor next to it.

'Well, I can see that.' Bea looked at it, her forehead creased. 'But for who, and why?' she asked slowly.

'For me to get to training, and the shops. I hate the bus,' Chloe explained. 'Do you mind if I leave it here? The landlord said it was okay?' she called down the hall. Bea had already disappeared into the kitchen and didn't answer.

'Wine,' she said, holding up an empty glass to Chloe as she walked in. Chloe saw the half empty bottle on the table.

'Go on then,' she smiled. 'Just the one...'

Chapter Eleven

Rasia: Just drove past Heathrow on my way back down and saw an Osprey Plane taking off... Wonder where it's going?

Darren: Reckon that's the New York. Will be us soon up there kids!

Paul: Spotter

Darren: you got me!

Maddie: SO regretting leaving this Dangerous Goods until Sunday eve. I'm just staring at the book and nothing is going in.

Megan: I'm watching Sully, does that count as revision?

Maddie: Lol, absolutely!! Honestly though, I think I'm having a breakdown. Please tell me the exam is easy?

Megan: Deep breaths, you'll be fine, just take lots of notes on the videos. Let us know when you're done so we know you're ok xx

Chloe: Little bit excited for this aircraft visit tomorrow! Good luck Maddie xxx

Megan: Welcome back Chlo!

Chloe: Sorry I've been quiet, couldn't keep up with all the messages haha

Jade: Me neither, glad I'm not the only one! Looks like you all had a good weekend though. Let's get week two done!!

Chloe felt as if she was going on holiday as they walked through the airport. She loved everything about being here, even if she wasn't *actually* going anywhere! The group followed Ben as he led them through security, where a lady checked their IDs against names on a list. Chloe held her breath as she went through the metal detector, and let it out again once the danger of being sent to the body scanner had passed. She watched as Megan stood, legs apart and hands above her head as the machine captured her image. She wondered how much it could *actually* see.

They had four instructors with them today, something to do with ratios for escorting they said, and for needing to split into small groups once they got on the aircraft. They were all so excited, every face wearing a grin as they emerged into the departure hall and waited for the others at the edge of the sea of holidaymakers who filled every seat, shop and restaurant.

Megan clutched Chloe's arm. 'That'll be us soon, babe,' she said as a crew member from their airline walked past them, talking on her phone while pulling her trolley bag behind her. They watched her walk into the coffee shop and up to the counter, the boy behind greeting her with a much bigger smile than he had the person before. Chloe wondered if she realised how people were looking at her, how they watched her out of the corner of their eyes and over the tops of their newspapers. She wondered if she herself was going to feel a little embarrassed the first time she did this trip to work, or would she love it? It was amazing what uniforms could do, they turned mere mortals into superheroes, after all.

'Right, that's us,' Ben said, taking his position at the front again.

Chloe had no idea where they were heading, didn't have a boarding pass to say what gate they were going from, and no one had seen fit to share that information with them. They followed him alongside the travellator, where people stood still and let the belt move them along the long corridors. Past empty gates, and others where people queued up outside. Tel Aviv, New York, San Diego... Chloe would happily have got on any of them right now.

Finally, Ben led them into Gate 37 and through the empty room with its empty rows of seats. On the far side a security guard opened the door for them.

The jetway echoed as they walked down it and finally emerged at the door of the aircraft. Megan hadn't let go of her arm yet, and Chloe felt her squeeze it. She turned and grinned at her.

On board Gemma called out names and split them into lettered groups. Chloe found herself with Paul and two of the others now, as Megan was plucked away and taken off in another direction.

'So, group C, my group,' Dan called them. 'Your aircraft visit is going to start in the middle, where we are going to begin your familiarization with every crew member's favourite place...' They stood in silence and waited for him to enlighten them. 'The crew rest area, of course!' he said, and beckoned them with his hand to follow him.

The plane had a musty smell, despite the fact that it had been cleaned and looked spotless. Chloe had never seen one empty before, never boarded first. Neither had she been on such a big one; family holidays had entailed short flights to Europe on budget airlines. Here, every seat had a TV screen in the back of the seat in front. Each seat also had a pillow and a blanket; she was quite sure she had never had such comforts given to her by an airline before, only by her mum who would pack everything they needed and more for the journey. And headphones too, she noticed now, sticking out of the seat pocket, sealed in little plastic bags... Chloe wasn't looking where she was going and walked straight into Paul, who had stopped in front of her.

'Oops, sorry,' she apologized. He gave her a smile and moved sideways so that she could see past him.

'So, up here in this cleverly hidden little stowage,' Dan was saying as he reached up above the jump seat at the door, 'is the magic key,' he said, holding a small silver key up in the air. He walked over to where a doorway stood right in the middle of the aisle and slipped it in the lock, pulling it open. 'Follow me, people,' he called from behind the door, which now blocked the aisle and their view.

The person in front pulled the door back and squeezed past it. When it was Chloe's turn she was surprised to see that behind it was a flight of stairs going down into the belly of the aircraft. They had looked at equipment in crew rest, and she had seen diagrams, and yet it hadn't occurred to her that it was down in the depths of the cargo hold. She followed Paul down and stood on the bottom step. The ceiling was low down here, and small submarine-style bunks lined the walls, each with a curtain half pulled along it.

At the other end Dan stood, bent over slightly, waiting patiently for their chatter to die down. 'It's not luxury, but I promise you will grow to love it,' he said. Behind him Chloe could see that the end bunk was bigger than the others, in height at least. The others seemed to have little more than two feet above them, and she wondered if she would feel claustrophobic.

'I'll take the big one,' said Paul.

'Only if your manager doesn't want it, fella,' Dan said. 'A lot of them choose to be in this bunk as it's next to the phone in case you need them in an emergency.'

'I bet they do,' Paul muttered. It made sense to Chloe though, and she was okay with hierarchy.

'Do you get in your pyjamas and everything?' someone asked.

'If you want,' Dan answered. 'Some do, if it's a long break. I prefer to sleep in my pants myself, there isn't much room for getting changed. Oh, and don't be surprised if people just strip off in front of you, no one cares down here. Get that skirt off and get yourself into bed, no time to waste.'

Chloe processed this as Dan proceeded to point out the smoke detectors and the safety equipment. *So,* she counted the bunks, *six people come down into this tiny room, whip their uniforms off, climb into bed and go to sleep*. What a bizarre concept that was, what a strange world she was going to be part of.

'Any questions?' he asked when he had finished. No one answered. 'Let's go back up, then,' he said, and nodded at Chloe. 'Lead the way.'

Out in the cabin Dan pushed the door almost closed. 'One last thing,' he said. 'The door doesn't self-lock. So, unless we want passengers thinking it's a toilet and wandering down in the middle of the night while you're asleep in your undies, slide the latch across on the inside when you go down.' He opened the door again and quickly showed them the latch. 'Then, when you come back up, make sure you lock it from outside.' He used the key to lock it. He reached up again, before walking past them to lead them down to the back galley. Chloe looked up at where he had been, but she couldn't see where he had pulled the key from, or put it back, for the life of her.

****

The ride home had been invigorating once she had found the cycle lanes and managed to navigate her way through the back streets. She wasn't a fan of cycling on the main roads, quite sure that she would be one of those people that the lorry driver just 'didn't see,' as he drove over her if she was brave enough to take the shortest route each day. It was quicker than the bus though, and she felt less sluggish as she reached the house than she normally did after a day in training.

A small Amazon parcel sat on the doorstep, and she smiled when she saw her name on it. Her new puzzle had arrived, a thousand-piece picture of New York City at sunset that would set her up for a perfect evening. She opened the door and pushed the bike inside, wriggling her backpack off her shoulders.

'Hey,' she called to Kathryn, who she could see in the kitchen.

'Oh, hi,' she called back. Chloe could smell something delicious cooking and followed her nose down to where Kathryn was now stirring a pot on the hob.

'Wow, that smells amazing,' she said, leaning over and breathing in the steam, aromas of ginger and coconut hitting the back of her nose.

'Oh, thanks.' Kathryn gave her a small smile. 'It's just a vegan curry.'

'Oh, you're vegan?' Chloe asked and Kathryn nodded. 'Me too, well, veggie, I struggle with cutting out dairy altogether.' She felt proud of herself as she said it, having managed four whole weeks without meat so far.

'Same, I cheat sometimes.' Kathryn smiled again and Chloe thought how pretty she looked when she did so. 'Want some?' she asked.

Chloe felt a burst of happiness. 'I'd love to try a little, but only if you've got enough?'

Later that evening Chloe smiled to herself as she sat and picked out the edges of the puzzle at the table in the living room. She had finally broken through with Kathryn, and somehow by jumping that hurdle the house felt different. Sure, she was *quirky*, but that was okay, at least she felt as if Kathryn *liked* her now, that she wouldn't feel awkward just saying hello anymore. She heard the front door open and Bea curse as she walked into the bike, the sound of it rattling in protest. She jumped up and put her head out into the hallway.

'Are you okay?'

Bea was bent down, rubbing her toes. She looked up at her, forehead furrowed with pain and annoyance.

'I'm so sorry, the landlord said to put it there, it wasn't my idea, I promise.'

'It's okay, I've got nine other toes,' Bea said with a tight smile.

'I'll move it, it's not raining, it can go in the garden.' Chloe walked over quickly and took the handlebars, leading it outside like a naughty child, leaning it up against the back wall. 'Sorry,' she said when she came back in.

'Don't worry, thanks for moving it though,' Bea said as she limped across the kitchen.

'That's fine, I'll take it back at the weekend.'

'Uh-huh.'

Chloe's heart sank when she didn't disagree with her. 'I did ask if I could put it in the garage but he said it was full,' she said.

'Who did?' Bea asked, sitting down at the table and lifting up her injured foot. Chloe wondered if she had listened to her at all, knowing that she had mentioned the landlord at least twice now.

'The landlord,' she said.

'You mean the agent?'

'No, the landlord, he came here the other day.'

'Oh.' Bea seemed surprised. 'Sorry, what did you say about the garage again?'

'He said it was full of his mum's stuff. I'm sure I could squeeze the bike in there though.' Chloe wondered if he would notice. 'Is there a key around for it anywhere?'

'Nope,' Bea said with absolute certainty.

'Are you sure? He might have just hidden it,' she said, remembering the key from crew rest.

'Well if he has then he has hidden it well, I've looked,' Bea said, getting up. 'I'm going for a shower, I'm being picked up in an hour.'

'Bea,' Chloe said as she turned away.

'Yes?'

'I really am sorry about your toe.'

Bea finally smiled, and Chloe felt herself relax a little. Just as she was making friends with Kathryn, she had managed to piss off Bea, and she really didn't want to do that. Living in a shared house was more of a challenge than she had anticipated.

'No worries, I'll live,' Bea said as she limped away.

Alone in the kitchen Chloe stared out of the window contemplating the missing key. It really was possible that there was one around here somewhere, she had seen enough crime programmes where spare keys had been compromised, hidden on tiny shelves and in obscure places, just like the one for crew rest earlier. Perhaps Bea just hadn't looked in the right places...

Chapter Twelve

Darren: Morning guys, everyone ready for the pool party?!

Megan: If only it was… and if only it wasn't 6am! I look half dead without my make up too!

Paul: No change there then Megs. Got my Mankini ready ;)

Megan: Oi!

Maddie: God help us!

Rasia: I'm really nervous guys. I can't swim very well.

Megan: Oh babe, we'll all help you out. Anyone else wearing comfy clothes for after? Leggings and hoody?

Paul: I was a lifeguard during college, no one will be drowning today!

Rasia: I'm more worried I won't pass than I am about drowning but thanks Paul lol

Chloe: I'm not great either Ras, we'll swim slowly together! Yes to comfy clothes Megs. I'm sure it will be okay for today?

Rasia: Floating on my back is my favourite stroke haha! I just had some lessons so can just about do the length, but not sure how it will go with clothes on.

Paul: Just wear something light, you'll be grand

Rasia: I wish I had your confidence. Give me ten exams back-to-back over this.

Maddie: Bloody ridiculous that we have to do it anyway, I think. Surely if your plane crashes in water you ain't gonna survive?!

Jen: My thoughts exactly :/

Paul: One word: Sully

Chloe's wet clothes made her bag heavy on her shoulder as they waited for the bus to take them back to the training centre.

''Thank you so much, Chloe.'

Chloe smiled at Rasia. 'I didn't do anything, you got through it yourself, babe.' Well, maybe she had swum a little bit slower to stay with her, discreetly passed her the lifejacket that she had already blown up while the trainers weren't watching, pushed her up onto the raft... It seemed she was better at swimming than she remembered, and she was grateful to have been able to have helped someone.

'I don't think so,' Rasia smiled. 'Honestly, I couldn't have done it without you. Or you,' she said as Paul appeared. 'Thanks for pulling me out of the water first.'

'No problem at all,' Paul said.

'Right David Hasselhoff, aren't you?' Chloe teased. Paul frowned. '*Baywatch*?' He shook his head now. 'Don't worry,' Chloe laughed, obviously not everyone had been subjected to reruns of eighties and nineties programmes like her.

'I'm starving,' Paul said, rubbing his tummy.

'We'll have a breakfast break when we get back,' Ben said as the bus pulled up.

Back in the cafeteria Chloe sat down and pulled her lunchbox out of her bag. It was getting expensive buying food every day, and the training wage was only just going to cover her rent. What little savings she had from her supermarket job were diminishing quickly, and so, like most of the others now, she had packed some snacks to keep her going.

'Grapes?' she offered Megan.

'No thanks, babe, bit healthy for me,' she said with a grin, putting her bag down on the seat next to her. 'Bacon sandwich all the way, do you want anything?'

'No thanks,' Chloe said. She had a banana for after, and a sandwich for lunch. She looked over to the queue, wondering if she should at least treat herself to a coffee, she wasn't *that* poor. A movement caught her eye and she squinted to see who was waving, surprised and pleased to see that it was Kathryn, and she was waving at *her*. She waved back but stopped herself from getting carried away and going over, she didn't want to scare her off when they were making such positive steps. She felt that Kathryn was just a little reserved and didn't let her guard down easily, but inside was a lovely person that not many people got to see. She felt flattered that she was showing that side of herself to her.

'Anyone fancy meeting for a drink tonight?' Paul asked from the end of the table.

'Maybe a couple,' someone said. 'Not a crazy one though.'

'No, just a couple,' Paul agreed. 'This is all getting a bit heavy for me now, I just need something to take the edge off.'

'Uh-huh,' someone else agreed.

'Actually, maybe straight from training?' Chloe said, the idea growing on her. 'We are finishing early today, right?' The early start was sold to them by the promise of an early finish. She could get an Uber back, as she hadn't brought the bike in today since it didn't have any lights and it had been practically the middle of the night when she left the house.

One by one everyone agreed. They needed to enjoy their time here, it wasn't meant to be all stress and no fun, was it? Maybe a couple of drinks and bonding would give them the reset they all needed.

'What did I miss?' Megan asked as she sat down, the smell of bacon *almost* tempting Chloe to give up on being a vegetarian.

'Drinks straight after training,' Paul said.

'Fab idea,' Megan said with a smile.

'Just a couple,' Chloe said, reiterating it for her own benefit. A couple wouldn't hurt, but more than that and they would only have themselves to blame if they lost another of their group to the next morning's exam.

'Yes, Mum,' Megan grinned.

****

It was six o'clock when Chloe sensibly put herself in a taxi. The others were still there, she had tried her best to guide them but had admitted defeat when Paul announced 'just one more,' and left them to it. They were all grown adults after all, though she couldn't help feeling that Paul was a little dependent on alcohol; not that it was her place to worry about him, but he reminded her a lot of her brother, and her family had been through years of trying to keep him on the right path. Thankfully his current girlfriend seemed to be a calming influence on him, or maybe he had just grown up. Either way he was heading in the right direction now, getting up for work on time every morning and starting to think of his future, leaving behind those friends who still weren't quite there yet. At twenty-six it was about time.

She was still thinking about him when the taxi pulled up at the house. It was dark already and it was starting to rain. She turned on the torch on her phone and approached the garage, feeling her skin prickle as goosebumps broke out on it. However she felt about the place, she needed to get inside it so that Zac's bike wasn't left out in the rain.

She knelt down and shone the light on the horizontal handle, which sat just above the floor in the middle of the metal door. Her grandparents had had a garage like this, and she could remember her grandfather pulling it up, the door sliding inwards, into the roof.

She yanked it up, knowing that it wouldn't be so easy, but trying nevertheless. A keyhole in the middle of the handle teased her, something so small yet so powerful that it kept everything inside hidden away from the world. She pulled a hairgrip from her hair, which she had thrown up in a messy bun after swimming, and poked it into the hole like she had seen in old films, but without really knowing what she was doing and to no end.

'Dammit,' she cursed, giving the handle a final shake and standing up. She shone the torchlight around the edges of the door and ran her fingers along them. Nothing except flaking paint and dirt. Along the floor she kicked loose stones with her foot, moving around to the side and shining the light up and down the wall, moving the weeds aside, first with her foot and then with her hand. Nothing. She walked along the narrow path between the garage and the house, reaching the garden and stopping at the rotten wooden door at the end of the wall that would have been used once to get inside. She hadn't noticed it before, it was almost hidden by some kind of climber plant that seemed long dead, but its tentacles still clung to the wood. Beneath the handle was another keyhole with no key. Around the back she faced her fears and squeezed herself down to the window, trying to ignore the cobwebs as she looked behind them. The torchlight shone through the dirty glass and she could make out the rough shapes of whatever was inside. Boxes perhaps, piled high, old furniture maybe.

Defeated, Chloe brushed her hands together to remove the worst of the dirt and made her way to the back door of the house, which was predictably open. Inside Bea was in the kitchen, in her uniform, making herself a coffee.

'Oh, hi,' she said.

'You made me jump,' Bea said, 'did you forget your key?'

'Actually, no. I was looking for the key to that damn garage,' she explained, 'so that I can put my bike in it.'

'Well, good luck with that, I've searched high and…' She stopped short of finishing the phrase, distracted by something on her phone as she picked it up from the side and put it in her bag. 'Anyway, I'm off for the next week so don't worry about bringing it inside. I don't mind really, just not very good with pain,' she smiled.

'Ooh, a week?' Chloe was instantly distracted by the talk of her trip. 'Where are you going?'

'Singapore and then on to Sydney.' Bea fastened the lid onto her travel mug.

'*Niiice.* I can't wait to see Australia,' Chloe cooed. She had always wanted to go Down Under, and it was almost within her reach.

'It's a long one though,' Bea said, walking into the hall. 'Three night-flights. Worth it once you get there I guess, both great cities apparently. It's my first time to both.'

'Exciting, sounds great to me!' Chloe said. Anywhere sounded great to her.

'Right, I'd best be off, see you next week,' Bea said, just as Chloe was about to ask her why she wanted to get in the garage. She picked her handbag up from the floor and slotted the mug into it.

'Have a great time,' she said, deciding it wasn't important and could wait. She watched as Bea wheeled a larger than normal case out of the front door and into a waiting taxi. The rain was coming down now, and Chloe opened the back door again, bringing the bike back inside. As she closed the door she instinctively wanted to lock it, but remembered that there was no key in the lock here either. *What is it with this house and its lack of keys? Surely it is basic security to be able to lock a back door at night?*

With the bike parked back in the hall she came back to the kitchen. She needed some food to soak up the three beers she'd had before getting down to the business of studying. As her pasta boiled she stood and stared at the key-less back door. Surely, the agent would have made sure at some point that there was one here? She looked up and around, then stared at the empty keyhole and imagined the key in it... perhaps it had been taken out and put somewhere, perhaps it had fallen... She looked down, and as her eyes reached the floor she noticed that the small step had a lip which jutted out slightly, a gap between it and the floor. She leaned over and slotted her fingers underneath, feeling something move amidst the dirt and dust when her finger touched it.

She went quickly into the kitchen and got a knife, sliding it underneath and pushing the object out. Onto the floor slid a single silver key.

'Yes!' said Chloe, jumping up and punching the air triumphantly with the key in her fist, before putting it into the lock and turning it. She felt an overwhelming satisfaction in the sound of it locking, and wondered how long ago it had fallen out and been mindlessly kicked under the step? How long, if at all, anyone had spent looking for it.

As she stood back her victory subsided when she realised that she had only solved half of the mystery. There was still the matter of the other key, the one to the garage, and she had an overwhelming feeling that it was nearby; it would make sense after all to keep the spare garage key close to the back door, wouldn't it? She looked up for inspiration and her eyes fell on the shelf to the side, the one above a row of coat hooks. It was empty from what she could see, but she stood on her tiptoes and ran her hand along it anyway. When she was unable to quite reach the wall at the back she got one of the chairs from the kitchen and stood on it, this time making sure her fingers covered every inch as she ran them along...

A small clang made her heart jump as the key hit the floor.

Chapter Thirteen

Maddie: I can't take it anymore, I'm sooooo tired

Jen: Babe I'm literally pulling out my fake eyelashes with this revision.

Paul: Anyone want to meet early again. Too tired to do this tonight after the early start.

Chloe: Glad to see you all got back at a decent hour :)

Megan: Don't worry Mum, we were all well behaved. Agree though, too tired to study!

Jade: What was it we need to know again?

Maddie: Pilots Like Wet Feet

Darren: ?!

Maddie: Protection Location Water Food :)

Darren: Ahhh! Do love a good acronym!

Maddie: Honest though, I feel like my brain is at its limit and I might be due to fail something.

Paul: I hear ya sista. Fried.

Liv: We aren't losing anyone else. 7:30 in the cafeteria tomorrow?

Paul: Becoming a habit this!

Liv: Haha, reminds me of the old Breakfast Club before school lol

Maddie: Love you Liv, Love you all. Feeling a bit emosh tonight!

Liv: Get some sleep, nothing will go in while you're tired.

Paul: Yes Miss!

The pavements were wet from the night's rain as Chloe cycled to training the next morning. Lost in thought she veered at the last minute around a huge puddle, narrowly saving herself from a soaking. She had confirmed that the key fit in the lock of the front garage door, but in the dark she couldn't find a light inside. Even without one though, she could see that the landlord hadn't been lying, it was full to the brim in there, boxes piled up right to the door. At some point in the next week, before Bea came back, she was going to have to look at it in the daylight and see if she could make some room, but daylight was limited on these short winter days. Maybe she would have to stay Friday night, she thought, sort it out on Saturday morning before going home? For now the bike was staying inside, and so far Kathryn had managed to avoid hurting herself on it, or at least she hadn't heard any dramatic cries when she had come in late last night.

Arriving at the training centre she locked the bike up in the racks and went inside. She laughed when she saw the first arrivals of their group on their table having their tutorial. Liv was holding everyone's attention with her notepad held up, tapping at things with a pen.

She walked over and sat down quietly with them, trying not to disturb the lesson.

Next to her, Paul was rubbing his face. He was concentrating hard on what Liv was saying but he looked as if he was about to cry. She reached over and touched his hand to get his attention. 'Sit next to me,' she said quietly. 'I'll help you if I can.' She was quite confident this morning and hated to see him so worried.

'Thank you,' he said with a grateful smile. Chloe hoped she wouldn't regret it, that he knew how to ask for help without the instructors seeing or hearing. She needn't have worried though, apart from a single tap on her knee, to which she read the question on his screen without turning her head and mouthed the letter B to him, he didn't really need her. Sometimes, she thought as they both finished at the same time, people just needed to get past the panic to realise they actually knew their stuff.

'That was actually alright,' he said as they walked back to the cafeteria together. She had resisted her urge to be among the first few out and hung back in case he had needed her.

'Yep, see, you know it up there.' She pointed to her own head, looking up at him. He was a little older than her, with a strong jaw and nose, but the softest blue eyes. He looked much like her brother, and she felt protective of him.

'I always hated exams,' he said.

'Didn't we all,' Chloe agreed. 'I never heard anyone say they enjoyed one yet.' Paul nodded, a smile on his face.

'Anyway, one more down and only two more days until the weekend.'

'We all need to celebrate if we make it through this week without losing anyone else,' Paul said.

'Actually,' Chloe said, realizing that that would fit in perfectly with her plan to stay Friday night, 'that's the best idea you've had yet… let's do it!'

'No going home at six?' He raised his eyebrows as he looked at her.

'Promise,' she said with a wink, linking her arm through his.

Chapter Fourteen

Bea

The last of the passengers filed past her at her door.

'Goodbye,' she said, trying to hold her smile even though she could literally feel the crow's feet forming around her eyes with every second that passed.

'Thanks so much for your help,' said the man whose AirPod she had just found. What was it, she wondered, with passengers losing AirPods? It seemed she couldn't go a single flight without finding herself on her knees searching for one. So far, she had about a 70% success rate, meaning that the plane must be hiding a whole bunch of the things in its nooks and crannies.

It had been a long flight overnight to Singapore, but with a four-hour break in crew rest she felt surprisingly okay. Then with the time difference turning her mid-morning into early evening, it seemed perfectly acceptable that she should be quite ready for a glass of wine, or five.

'Clear down the back?' the Flight Manager called over the PA. Bea looked back at her zone before sticking her thumb out in the aisle to confirm that there was no one left.

'Let's get off then,' came the reply.

No one needed to tell her twice; excitement built up inside her as she anticipated the night ahead, her expectations high for this city after the stories she had been told. She quickly changed her shoes, ditching the mumsy flats and loving the coldness of her high heels as she slipped her tired feet into them. Four months flying and she felt as if she had never done anything else, but then it was in her blood, she had been born to do it, hadn't she?

In her five-star hotel room she opened the water bottle into which she had decanted gin and tonic from the plane. She poured herself a glass and stood in thought for a moment at her floor-to-ceiling window. Outside, the city spread as far as the eye could see, skyscrapers lit up by a million lights, neon signs and colourful displays illuminated the night sky, and far below her traffic coursed through the busy streets. She wondered if her dad had ever come here, and if he had, what did the city look like to him, back then? Would he have stood so far up? Did he see any of what she could see now? They were the same thoughts she had everywhere she went, and maybe one day she would find the answers.

****

'Ah there you are. Here,' Andre said in his smooth Dutch accent above the noise of the bar, putting another daiquiri into her hand. She was standing outside watching what was going on as she waited for Stephen, the purser from economy, to finish his cigarette.

'Oh, thanks,' Bea said, quite certain that it was her turn to buy the drinks, but every time she was nearly finished with one, another was in her hand before she had a chance to get to the bar. Perhaps it was the benefit of being the only girl out, she wondered, as aside from the three pilots only two other crew had turned up, both of them boys. She didn't think she would ever understand crew who stayed in their rooms all trip. Yes, some people needed to save their allowances or were tired, but how could anyone miss out on *this*? Up and down the marina bars were buzzing with people having the time of their lives. It was warm outside, the cold of home a distant memory as summer lingered on here and drew people out. So far, she had met people from all over the world, some who lived here, others just passing through like they were, but all of them enjoying the party.

'Sorry, buddy, can I get you a beer?' he asked Stephen, realising that she wasn't alone.

'I'm good, just going in, but cheers.' Stephen put out his cigarette under his foot and headed in. Andre stood between her and the door, blocking her way.

'So, how are you enjoying your first time in Singapore?' he asked. He was tall, and she had to step back to look at him without craning her neck. Handsome too, she noticed, thick curly hair that was long on top, and a stubbled chin that made him look like a bit of a rogue compared to other pilots.

'*Lovvvving* it,' Bea said, taking a sip of her drink and wincing slightly at the taste of tequila.

'Yes,' he said, looking around with a smile on his face, 'it's quite a special place. Everyone's favorite trip.'

Bea nodded, she could understand why. 'I'm lucky to get one so soon.'

'Four months, you said?'

She nodded, having told them at the hotel bar earlier.

'Flown before?'

'Never,' she shook her head. 'My dad was a pilot though,' she added, as she always did after a few drinks. She had followed him to Osprey in the hope of finding him, find out something about him, but so far all she knew was that he didn't work here anymore, that he hadn't been employed since 1992 according to the nice lady in HR, the same year that her mum had seen him last.

'Ah, so it's in your blood,' Andre smiled. He was looking straight into her eyes, and yet she didn't feel awkward.

'We're moving on, guys. Drink up.' The captain's voice interrupted them as he emerged from the door, the rest of the crew spilling out behind him.

'Coming,' said Andre, holding up his half full bottle of beer before draining its contents in one go. Bea followed his lead with her cocktail, putting the empty glass down on the table behind her.

'Who did he fly for?' he asked as they followed the others along the street. They were far behind them now as they continued the conversation.

'Us,' she answered. Andre turned and raised his eyebrows at her. 'A long time ago,' she said, knowing that he was far too young to remember him, as was every pilot she had met so far. She was dying to meet someone who did.

They turned a corner and the others had disappeared. Bea looked up at Andre.

'Don't worry, I know where they went,' he said. 'Although, if you want, we could go somewhere else?'

Bea laughed at his nerve. She liked him, but he would wait until later, for now she was enjoying the company of the others too. She held his elbow and pushed him gently forward. 'That's okay, we should stay with the others for now I think.'

Andre smiled and shrugged his shoulders, turning into the first bar on their left. Inside, the rest of the gang were already at the bar ordering drinks.

'There you are,' said the captain to Andre when he saw them. 'We thought we'd lost you.'

'Not this time, I'm afraid.' Andre turned to Bea and looked up at the ceiling, making her laugh. She rolled her eyes back at him and walked over to the safety of Stephen.

'We thought you two had snuck off,' Stephen said quietly, nudging her with his elbow as she tucked herself in next to him.

'Not yet,' she grinned. Maybe it was the daiquiris, but Andre really was growing on her.

Chapter Fifteen

Megan: Just been practicing my ditching commands in the shower lol

Maddie. Haha, I'm weirdly looking forward to the rigs, love a bit of role play

Paul: Me too luv ;)

Chloe: I hate it! I know I'm going to go blank the minute it's my turn.

Megan: I know I'm going to end up shouting commands from my last airline ha! Someone dig me in the ribs if I do!

Jen: Just gotta get through this resit in the morning

Megan: Whaaaaaat? No way did you fail?? You were out before me?

Jen: Afraid so, I didn't think I'd done too bad so finished with time to spare FML. I didn't tell anyone.

Chloe: You should have told us :(

Jen: It's ok, I just made some stupid mistakes as I was so tired I think. I feel ok about it now. Pray for me lol

Paul: Good luck babs, you'll smash it. I'm surprised more of us didn't fail tbh

Darren: It's been a tough week, that's for sure

Chloe: Nearly over. Good luck Jen xxx

Megan: Yes, good luck girl, sending positive vibes your way.

Jen: Cheers guys, just gonna run myself a bubble bath and get an early night. Hopefully see you in the morning!

Chloe: Don't say that, we WILL see you in the morning xxx

Despite it already being Thursday the weekend seemed so far away, and it seemed the days got longer as they got harder. It was nearly over though, and the second week of safety training was almost done. Soon these endless nights of revision would be over.

Chloe shook herself, trying to keep herself awake, practising her commands.

'Open seatbelts, leave bags, get out! Open seatbelts, leave bags, get out!' she repeated, over and over.

Tomorrow was going to be the worst day for her, role playing in the rigs. She knew that her mind was going to go blank, that she would forget everything the minute that it was her turn to evacuate everyone. Her eyes were heavy, but it was only nine o'clock and she lay back, feeling defeated.

The sound of the alarm confused her at first; it felt as if she had only been asleep for an hour and her head was groggy as if she had been drinking. She felt the back of her forehead with her hand, sure that she had a temperature, her throat stinging when she swallowed.

She heaved herself up; this was not the time for her to be coming down with a cold, she thought angrily, not the time at all. She reached into the drawer of her dressing table and pulled out some paracetamol and a tube of Berocca, hoping that she could fight it off before anyone noticed. No one would thank her for going in with a cold and giving it to them, since the pandemic people were just a little more touchy about it.

She put on her dressing gown and shivered. The house was cold this morning, and she was yet to find the thermostat. She suspected that the landlord kept it hidden and controlled it remotely from wherever he was so that they didn't waste the gas. She pictured him in her mind, recalling what he had looked like at their only meeting. *Yes, he has definitely hidden it,* he certainly looked the type.

Downstairs she put the kettle on. Bea was still away and she hadn't heard Kathryn at home. She hadn't seen her for a couple of days, now she thought about it. A knock at the back door made her jump, and her hand shot to her heart. She stepped back from the window and looked, terrified, out into the dark.

'It's me,' said a voice, and Kathryn's white face appeared at the window.

'Oh my God,' Chloe said, unlocking the door and letting her in. 'You scared the living daylights out of me,' she said. Her heart was still racing.

'I'm sorry, but I've been outside for hours,' Kathryn said, brushing past in her padded coat and pulling her hood down. Chloe felt the coldness of it on her skin. 'Since when did the door get locked? I forgot my key, but it's never *usually* a problem.' She looked at Chloe through accusing eyes, her voice annoyed.

It dawned on Chloe that she hadn't seen Kathryn to tell her that she had found the key, and that she was locking the door at night now.

'Oh, Kathryn, I'm so sorry,' she said, feeling suddenly awful. Her nose was red and she stood visibly shivering despite her coat and knitted scarf. 'I forgot to tell you I found the back door key the other day. Here, sit down, let me make you a hot drink. You poor thing.'

Kathryn sat hunched over at the table. 'I got home at three, tried every window. Didn't you hear me throwing stones at yours?'

Chloe shook her head guiltily. 'I was out cold.'

'Clearly.'

'Where did you sleep?' she asked, putting a cup of herbal tea down in front of her and sitting down opposite. She was determined not to let this undo all of the progress she had made with her.

'Sleep?!' Kathryn asked, raising her voice. 'Could you sleep out there?!'

Chloe hung her head. 'No, I guess not.'

'I sat on the bench and read a book on my phone, until the battery died about an hour ago.'

'I'm so sorry,' Chloe said again.

'It's okay,' Kathryn said eventually as she drank her tea. 'My fault for forgetting my key, I guess.'

'No, but I should have told you I was locking the door at night now. I didn't like the idea of anyone coming in.'

'That's fair enough. Where did you find the key though, that was lost years ago?'

'Under the step.' Chloe looked over to where she had found it, noting that Kathryn had just said that she'd been here for years. In some ways that explained her indifference to other housemates, she must have seen lots come and go.

'Wow, I thought we'd looked everywhere.'

'I've watched too many crime programmes,' Chloe said with a smile. 'I don't give up easily.'

'No, it seems you don't,' Kathryn said, tipping her head back to drink the last of her tea. 'Well, I'll be off to bed,' she said, standing up and putting her empty cup in the sink. 'Thanks for the tea.'

'You're welcome, and sorry again,' Chloe apologized. Her stomach still had that sinking feeling at what she had done. She liked Kathryn, even with her slight oddness, and really didn't want to upset her.

'Don't worry, it was kind of okay. I'll make sure not to forget my keys in future,' she said as she climbed the stairs.

Chloe pulled her dressing gown around her as she rinsed their cups at the sink. Her next mission was to find the thermostat...

Chapter Sixteen

Bea

Bea pressed the code on the keypad and waited for the light to go green. It was the middle of the night, the cabin was dark and it seemed that everyone was asleep. She was tired, and the hours until her break were the longest she had ever experienced.

Inside the flight deck Tom, the captain, sat in the left-hand seat, and Pete in the right. She had known that Andre was on break, he had come to see her and let her know.

'Hey,' said Tom. 'How are things back there?'

'All good, everyone is asleep.'

She pulled the door shut behind her and sat on the seat behind them. It was dark outside, and she could see nothing but black beneath them; Sydney was behind them now, and Singapore seemed such a long way away. The lights from the displays and buttons were just enough to be able to see each other clearly.

Pete shifted in his seat and turned to face her. He crossed his arms across his chest and her heart jumped as she panicked about what he was going to say. She was under no illusion that they didn't know about her and Andre spending the night together, but what exactly *had* Andre told them?

'So,' he said, a serious look on his face. 'Andre mentioned your dad used to fly with us?'

'Oh, right,' she said, relieved that *that* was going to be their topic of conversation. 'Yes, but a long time ago.'

'How long, I'm old you know.' Tom grinned.

'His last flight was over thirty years ago,' she said. That was all she knew. Her mum had seen him that one last time and then he had just disappeared, left the company as far as she knew, because when she had called them in her last-ditch attempt to get hold of him after giving birth, the lady on the phone had said that he was no longer on the payroll.

'Ah, *that* long. He'd have been old to have been your dad?' he said. Bea nodded, she'd done the calculations too when she'd found out, he had been much older than her mum, but to a poor girl growing up in Ireland a fancy uniform and promise of a great life would blur a lot of lines.

'Yep, you'd be right there,' she said. 'I never actually met him.'

'That's a shame,' said Tom. He shook his head, a thoughtful look on his face. 'I never get these guys who can walk away.'

'Do you have kids?' Bea asked. Pete stifled a laugh.

'Alright.' Tom shot him an amused look. 'A few. I was married in my Air Force days, and then married again in later life. I was a bit of an older dad too, but I don't think I could have walked away from any of my kids.'

Bea nodded, she couldn't understand it either, but she had built a wall many years ago to stand behind so that she didn't get hurt by things too easily. To be fair, the thing that had messed with her head more was her 'dad' pretending that he was her biological father for all these years when he wasn't, but she had made a decision to try to understand that too, she knew that it had never been done to hurt her.

As for him, her *real* dad, in some ways she was grateful to him, for even without being around she felt as if she owed all of this, her new life, to him somehow. If she had never known that she was a pilot's daughter she would never have considered it possible.

'What is your second name again?' Tom asked.

'O'Neill, why?' she asked.

'Nothing, I started here around the time your dad left, thought I might recognize the name that's all.'

'Oh, right,' Bea said. 'He didn't have the same name as me, I didn't even know about him until a year ago.'

They both looked at her now, and she didn't like the sympathy that she could read in their faces, they didn't need to feel sorry for her. She smiled, 'It's okay, I like O'Neill anyway, it's better than McGhee.' She didn't know why she said that, neither name was bad really. It was just an attempt to find the funny, the positive side, but by the looks on their faces she had just made things worse. Even in the low light she could see the way Tom's face paled and the way he and Pete held a look just a little too long. She sensed something between them, but whatever it was, was not for her to know, it seemed.

'What did I say?' she asked with a small laugh.

'Nothing,' Tom said. 'McGhee, you said?' He stroked his chin now. Pete had turned back to his controls and was looking at the displays intently.

'Uh-huh,' Bea confirmed.

'Interesting.' A voice crackled over the radio and he turned back to the controls too. 'We'd better check in with radar,' he said to Pete.

Bea sensed it was time to leave. 'Nice to chat,' she said, getting up.

'You too.' Tom looked back at her. He gave her a smile, but his eyebrows were drawn together and his forehead lined as if his thoughts were a thousand miles away. 'Sorry, gotta get this done,' he said, 'but nice talking to you.'

Chapter Seventeen

Jade: Can someone remind me where we go during the Initial PA?

Rasia: to your jump seat.

Jade: Thanks babe

Megan: It's Friiiidaaaaaaayyyy!

Chloe: Yesssssss! Just one little exam and a load of drills to get through first :/

Megan: Don't be such a buzz-kill Chlo lol!

Chloe: Sorry, just being realistic. Once that's all over then it is definitely Fridaaaay!

Paul: I can almost taste the beer! Jen are you oot yet?!

Megan: Yes Jen, let us know how you get on. Got everything crossed for you!

Paul: Heading over in five if anyone is coming.

Megan: Wait for me.

Liv: Guys I'm going to be late again, bloody traffic hasn't moved on the M23. So stressed!

Maddie: Don't worry babe, we'll let them know... it's not your fault.

Liv: Thank you, doesn't look good though, late twice in two weeks. Moving a bit now... might make it yet!

Jen: I passed!!!! You aren't getting rid of me yet!! Pass the champagne!

Paul: Bloody great news, definitely passing the bubbles tonight now!!

Megan: Well that has just sealed this Friday Feeling! Well done Jen! xxxx

'Group 352!' Paul called, holding his shot glass in the air, prompting a chorus of 'Group 352' and a synchronized sinking of the liquor.

''I *hate* tequila,' Megan said as she shook her head, her cheeks pinched in.

'Same,' said Chloe, wiping her mouth with the back of her hand. She was unsure that anyone *actually* liked the stuff. 'Rude not to though, right?'

'Yep. Any plans this weekend?'

'Just chilling at home,' said Chloe. 'I might catch up with some friends,' she added, realizing that she hadn't spoken to anyone much since she had started training. She made a mental note to message Laura and Beth in the morning and see if they were around. 'You?'

'I'm helping out on the farm,' Megan grinned. 'Knee deep in shit and freezing for the weekend.'

'That actually sounds amazing,' Chloe cooed.

'Well, you are welcome to come and help out anytime.'

'Really?'

'I was joking, it's not everyone's idea of a fun weekend,' Megan laughed.

'I would love it,' Chloe breathed. 'Honestly,' she added, feeling that she needed to convince her.

'Well, come along then,' Megan said with a big smile. 'Bring your wellies and I'm sure we can find you some stuff to do.'

'Can I?' Chloe felt suddenly excited. 'But...' she realised a problem. 'I don't have any wellies.' She hadn't had any since she was a child jumping in puddles, there wasn't much need for them around town.

'I'm sure we can find you some. If you don't change your mind, then how about next weekend?'

'Deal!' Chloe smiled and clinked her glass with Megan's to seal the deal. 'I definitely won't be changing my mind.'

'So did you see Jo's Insta reel?' Paul said, dropping into the seat next to Chloe. They both shook their heads and he pulled up her page on his phone. They leaned in to watch as Jo's pretty face smiled at them, words appearing on the screen...

If at first you don't succeed...

Try, try again...

She held up a letter to the screen and they all leaned in, heads touching, trying to read it.

'Oh wow, amazing!' said Chloe as she realized it was an offer of employment from another airline.

'Love it,' said Megan. 'She'll smash it this time, I'm sure.'

'That's my girl,' Paul said, putting the phone back in his jacket pocket. 'I'm taking her out tomorrow night,' he added quietly. Chloe looked at him and raised her eyebrows. 'We get on,' he shrugged, an uncharacteristically shy smile on his face.

'Good for you.' Megan gave him a friendly punch on the arm.

'Love it,' said Chloe. 'Wish her good luck from us with the new job, won't you?'

'Yes,' said Megan, 'tell her we are waiting to see those layover pictures,' she winked.

'I will,' he said, a dreamy expression on his face that made them both laugh. He coughed and sat upright when he noticed that they were watching him. 'Anyway,' he said, looking past Chloe at the rain lashing down the window behind her, 'nice weather we're having.'

****

Chloe's head throbbed as she pushed up the garage door. It stuck every few centimetres, groaning in protest at being opened after so many years. Flakes of paint danced downwards and blew away in the wind.

'Just. MOVE,' Chloe said impatiently as she shoved it upwards. All she wanted to do was put this bike inside and get herself home, into her pyjamas and onto that sofa, but this stupid door was holding her up. Finally, she got it to just above her head, but it wouldn't go any further. That would do though, she thought.

She looked at the wall of boxes that stood uniformly the whole way across the entrance. *Whoever had put them there liked being in control,* she narrated the scene as a detective in her head, ready for her evening binge-watch with her mum. They were piled four high, above her head, and she counted seven along. Twenty-eight boxes of 'stuff', all the same size, brown cardboard with a faded red logo in the top right corner of some. *But not so controlling that they had noticed the logo, failing to ensure that they were uniform, too.*

She stood back, hands on her hips and considered her next move. The boxes were set just inches back, not deep enough for the handlebars of the bike. She would need to move some, and she tried to work out which ones would be best.

Her eyes fell to the ones at the bottom and she noticed how some buckled, their bases shredded by mice, it seemed, or *rats*. She shivered. They were worse on the left-hand side, quite untouched on the right, and her decision was made as she walked over and put her hands either side of the top right box. She slid it forward, finding it was surprisingly light, pulling it down onto her chest. Sideways she shuffled, pushing it back up and on top of the pile further down. The next one was slightly heavier and she struggled under its weight, just managing with a lot of huff and puff, to get that on the top too.

She stood for a moment in front of the gap in the wall that she had created and peered into the grainy darkness. At the far end she could make out the faint light from the window at the back, and between her and it, the silhouettes of a past life. Gone was the uniformity of the boxes, now she could make out sheets draped over objects, a wardrobe, an old bike with a basket on the front leant against the wall just in front of her. As she leaned in she could smell the musty air, and feel the chill of it on her face. It was full, that was for sure, but she could make out that there was space on the floor in front of where she stood and so she knelt down and nudged the two remaining boxes in her stack, one inch at a time into it.

The shooting pain in her head reminded her that she was hungover, and she stood up, waiting for the wave of nausea to pass. Taking one last look into the past she turned and retrieved Zac's bike from the side of the garage. It fit, the handlebars turned into the space she had created, and she pulled the door closed over it. In her head she made a mental note to bring back some oil from her dad's shed, she really could do without having to fight like that with the door every morning and evening.

She slipped the key into her back pocket and picked up her backpack from the ground, brushing off the paint that had landed on it. She slung it over her shoulder and took a deep breath. One bus, one train with two changes and she would be home. She had had a great evening, but next time she would decline the tequila, that was for sure.

Chapter Eighteen

Bea

The call had come as a surprise that morning, the first one that she had woken up alone without Andre next to her on this long trip. They were back in Singapore, but after the night out in Sydney and the flight back here she had only managed a couple of glasses of wine at the bar before admitting defeat and calling it an early night. She knew that it wasn't Andre, he had her phone number, and she had a momentary panic that she was meant to be checking out.

'Hello?' she said, hearing the grogginess in her own voice as she pulled herself up.

'Bea?' She recognized the man's voice. 'It's Tom.'

Suddenly awake, Bea sat up. 'Am I late?' she asked in panic.

'No, relax,' he laughed.

Bea looked at the clock on the bedside table; it was 11am.

'Did I wake you?' he asked.

'Um, yes, but it's fine,' she said. She had wanted to get up and see the city in daylight anyway, before they left for home this evening.

'Oh, I'm sorry. Go back to sleep and I'll call you later.'

'No, honestly, I wanted to get up, you're fine. What's up?' she asked.

'I have something I wanted to talk to you about,' Tom said. He paused as if he didn't know how to proceed. 'I don't suppose you could meet me for a coffee sometime today?'

Bea looked at the handset and put it back to her ear. 'Sounds ominous,' she said. 'I can be ready in half an hour?'

'Great, meet me at the coffee shop in the lobby,' he said.

'Okay.' Bea was so confused as she hung up the phone. She tried not to think as she showered and got ready. Whatever it was would become clear soon enough and she wouldn't know what it was before then!

Downstairs Bea smiled at Tom as she approached him at the table by the window.

'Bea, thanks for coming,' he said as he jumped up. His quick movements were in contrast to her sleepiness. 'What can I get you?'

'Oh, a latte with an extra shot,' she said and dropped into one of the velvet bucket chairs. She watched him at the counter, holding some papers under his arm. When he got back to the table he put them down in front of him.

'So, what's up?' she said brightly, feeling that he needed a weight taken off his shoulders.

'I don't know if I'm doing the right thing or not,' he said, leaning back, not looking at her.

Bea leaned forward, and suddenly it dawned on her. Was it Andre? Was he going to tell her he was married? She felt a giggle rising up from her stomach and wanted to put him out of his misery. She didn't care if he was married, she wasn't *that* naïve.

'It's your father,' he said, and the giggle dissolved in a second. Now he was leaning forward, looking straight at her.

'Oh,' was all she could say.

'I didn't say anything on the flight deck the other night because I didn't know *what* to say, or if I should. It wasn't fair to say anything when you had to work, either.'

Bea was speechless, just nodding, but she had a feeling that whatever he was going to tell her was going to open some door into finding more out about her dad.

'Was this your dad?' He showed her a picture of a middle-aged man in a pilot's uniform. He was handsome, but he looked like any other middle-aged pilot if she was honest.

'I don't know, my mum never had any photos,' she shrugged. It was a long time ago, before smartphones or digital cameras.

'Oh.' Tom held the picture by its corner as it lay on the table. 'Well, this was Captain McGhee from Osprey.'

Bea felt her heart stop for a moment.

Leaning forward Bea felt her hand tremble as she took the picture from him. She sank back, trying to keep the picture still as she studied his face. Did she have his nose, his eyes? Her mum had said that she did, but she couldn't see it. 'Wow,' was all she could say, because her throat was caught, and her eyes pricked at the back.

'I'm surprised you have never heard anyone mention his name before,' Tom said. Bea looked up from the picture at him and shook her head.

'Why would I have?' she asked. He had left so long ago she had assumed he would have been forgotten.

'Captain McGhee, your father, is somewhat of an urban legend at Osprey, Bea,' he said, wringing his hands together as he looked at her.

'Why?' What had he done? she wondered.

'In 1992 he never showed up for his flight.' Now he was laying another piece of paper with a photocopy of an old newsletter on it on the table. The same picture was at the top, and the headline said: 'Missing.' The newsletter was dated 12th September 1992 and titled *Osprey News*. Bea had Googled his name a few times, but he had disappeared before the internet was much of a thing, and yet here it was on an old company newsletter. 'No one ever knew what happened to him,' Tom carried on. 'He landed back from Hong Kong and no one ever saw him again. The last people to have seen him were his crew, apparently.'

'He just disappeared, never came back?'

'People use his name when someone leaves the company never to come back, "like Captain McGhee, done a Captain McGhee", I never met him, but I've heard his name a thousand times. I asked someone one day what they meant and found out all of this,' Tom said, sweeping his hand across the papers. 'He just vanished into thin air.'

Bea was stunned, she had presumed he had just decided a new family wasn't for him, and that's what her mum had thought, having just told him that she was pregnant. 'Didn't the police look for him?' she asked quietly. Surely they had tried to find him?

'I suppose they did,' Tom said. 'I think that they found his car in the crew car park at Heathrow, someone told me once, but I'm afraid that's all I know.'

Bea nodded. She felt inexplicably sad, although she knew there could be lots of explanations. He would be in his early eighties now, but maybe he was still out there somewhere? Maybe somebody knew what happened to him?

'I hope I haven't overstepped the mark,' Tom said. 'Telling you all of this. I wasn't sure whether I should or not, whether it was my place.'

'No, no,' Bea said quickly to reassure him. 'I'm so glad you did. My mum just thought he had moved on, she just never heard from him. They weren't married or anything, he would just come to Ireland once a month and see her.'

'You don't sound Irish?' Tom smiled.

'No, she met my dad, stepdad,' she corrected herself, feeling instantly mean downgrading the man who had brought her up as his own, 'and we moved to England.'

'Ah, that explains it,' he nodded. He looked up as Andre approached them and beckoned him with his hand.

'She knows,' he said to him. Andre nodded and looked down at her, his brow lined with concern. 'I hope you don't mind, I ran it past the other pilots last night, to see whether I should tell you.'

Andre rested his hand on her shoulder. 'Are you okay?'

Bea sucked in a deep breath and pulled her shoulders back. 'Ab-so-lutely,' she smiled, seeing the lines on his forehead disappear with relief. 'Thank you, Tom,' she said as she turned to him now. 'It's kind of cool, actually,' she said at the same time as she realised. 'I'd presumed he would be long forgotten, but the fact his name lives on is nice.'

'Who'd have thought we'd be flying with Captain McGhee's daughter,' Andre smirked and shook her shoulder gently. Bea felt a strange sense of pride at her inherited infamy.

'You're not wrong there,' Tom said. He was finally smiling, his job done. 'Right, I'll leave you two to enjoy the day, I didn't sleep a wink last night thinking about this, and I need to get a few hours before the flight.'

'Thank you,' Bea said, getting up and giving him a hug. 'Thank you so much.'

He hugged her back. 'I hope you find some answers.'

Chapter Nineteen

Megan: I wonder where we will all be going next month?

Jen: Nowhere if my referencing isn't done... they are still waiting for one to come back and I've chased it twice!

Darren: Mine only just came back today, now I've got to get my ID appointment, I won't be going anywhere until 2050 at this rate.

Paul: I've ordered meself a four night Vegas :)

Megan: Treat yourself man!

Paul: Ay, I will pet ;)

Rasia: I want a San Francisco to visit family, I wish we could request. Do you think I could email someone?

Megan: I don't know, would it come across as cheeky?

Rasia: Probably, maybe I'll leave it until after I'm out of training, don't want to be getting a name for myself already!

Jen: I really need time off in Feb for a party, I'm definitely going to email rostering beforehand, they are hardly gonna sack you for asking, hey?

Megan: True babe xx

'So where are you taking me first?' asked Zac.

'Um, *I'm* going away first,' her mum butted in as they drove her back to the house together.

'*That* will depend on my roster,' Chloe said, 'and it won't be for six months, so you can fight it out between you then.' She couldn't wait to be able to take people away, explore the world with the people she loved most in it, but she hadn't even got her wings, and then she had to pass her probation before they could even plan that. It was getting closer though, that day when she was handed a shiny wings badge that gave her permission to fly.

'New York for me, I think,' said her mum. 'Or maybe Japan, see the cherry blossom...'

'Vegas for me,' said Zac. Chloe smiled; she could just imagine the pair of them in Vegas, gambling money neither of them really had, dancing at pool parties to the best DJs... it would be nice to spend some time with her brother just hanging out, like they had done years ago, only on another level.

'Sounds good, just let me pass these exams first,' she said as they drew up at the house. The lights were on in the front room for a change, and she wondered who was home. 'See you in a couple of weeks,' she said, grabbing her bag from the footwell and leaning over to give her mum a kiss on the cheek. She looked confused. 'I'm going to the farm next weekend, remember?'

'Oh yes, of course,' she smiled as she remembered.

'Good luck with that, sis,' snorted Zac as he got out of the back seat and hopped into the front passenger seat that she had just vacated, moving it back to accommodate his extra-long legs. He had been unable to see the appeal of the farm when she had told him earlier, a city kid through and through.

'See ya,' she said, undeterred, and pushed the door shut on him. He put his fingers on his head as horns, imitating a cow as they pulled away. She laughed and shook her head at him, forever a child.

Chloe opened the front door gently, not wanting to disturb whoever was in the front room. She heard a door shut upstairs and knew that it must be Kathryn as Bea was away until Tuesday, but she was still surprised when she poked her head into the front room and saw that there was no one there. She walked in and looked around for a clue as to what she had been doing; she had never seen Kathryn come in here before, *ever*. Perhaps Bea had come home early, she wondered.

She felt herself drawn over to the table, where her puzzle lay partly done. She couldn't be entirely sure, but it seemed to her a little more complete than it had done on Friday when she left. Had Kathryn been doing her puzzle? Had she *actually* just run off when she heard her pulling up? Chloe laughed inwardly at the awkwardness of her housemate. She had absolutely no aversion to someone helping with her puzzles, in fact she positively invited help, there really was no need for her to hide it.

She went up the stairs to her room and put her bag down, unpacking the fresh washing. She had also thrown in some old clothes that she didn't mind getting ruined at the farm... *The farm...* she thought as she hung up the old hoodie. Only one week until she would be 'knee deep in shit,' as Megan had so nicely put it, and she couldn't wait!

She put the can of oil her dad had given on the dressing table, ready to tackle the garage door one evening in the week, but rain was forecast tomorrow so she would be taking the bus. In fact, it was forecast all week, but the weatherman had been known to get it wrong before, and he might well do again. Lastly, she pulled the Yankee Candle she had got for her birthday out of her bag and put that on the other end of the dresser to the oil, lighting it with the lighter she had 'borrowed' from Zac. The room was slowly beginning to feel like hers.

There was a knock at her door and she opened it to see Kathryn standing there in her pyjamas.

'Oh, hi.' Chloe gave her a big smile to counter her awkwardness.

'Hi,' said Kathryn. 'I just wanted to apologise, I might have done a little bit of your puzzle.' She looked at the floor as she mumbled the words quickly. 'I don't know what came over me, I don't normally touch other people's things, but I do love a puzzle.' She looked up now; the middle-aged woman had the look of a guilty child and Chloe just wanted to hug her.

'I thought it was coming along,' Chloe said kindly. 'Thanks for the help.'

'Really?' Kathryn looked unsure.

'Honestly, I love that you are helping me with it!' Chloe said as brightly as she could, to reassure her. 'I usually do them with my mum, I hate doing them alone.'

'Oh phew. I thought you would notice, I would have if someone had meddled with mine,' she said with a half-smile.

Chloe nodded and smiled back. She hadn't seen this side of Kathryn before, but the insecure woman that stood before her was easy to like. 'We can do it together,' she said. 'Hopefully that way it will be finished before the end of my course.'

'Deal,' Kathryn said brightly. 'Better get to bed, earlies this week.'

Chloe waited a moment before shutting her door, smiling to herself. She had a wine friend and a puzzle friend in the house now... she might actually be sad to leave.

Chapter Twenty

Bea

'The captain says we can get off,' the Flight Manager called over the PA. 'Thanks for a lovely flight, everyone, I've got a train to catch so I'm going to run. Enjoy your days off.'

Bea stuffed her duty-free gin into her wheelie bag and zipped it up. When she stood up she looked around the empty cabin; rubbish littered the aisles, crumbs were trodden into the carpet next to where the children had been sitting at the bulkhead, blankets discarded on the floor. It never ceased to amaze her what a mess people could make in a relatively short space of time.

She was the last one to leave by the looks of things; they had all said goodbye at the end of the flight, knowing that, even though they had just spent the last week together, once they were allowed off each would be on their own private mission to get home as fast as they could. Not Bea though, not today. Today she was happy to go at her own pace, her legs were tired from the long flight.

She put her handbag over her shoulder and raised the handle on her wheelie, pulling it up the aisle behind her. She was surprised to see Andre at the door waiting for her. Even though he had chosen to stay with her again on their last night, she had still expected him to rush off now, home to whoever was waiting for him.

'Hey,' she said. 'You needn't have waited.'

'I wanted to,' he smiled. 'Do you mind?'

'Of course not,' she smiled back. 'Thanks.'

They walked along in comfortable silence, alongside the stream of passengers that were heading in the same direction.

'So, do you have plans for your days off?' Andre asked as they emerged into the immigration hall.

'Not really,' Bea said. She wasn't lying, she had made loose plans with Shane, but Shane was always a loose plan. He was good fun, but a real rough diamond with whom she knew there was no future. He made her laugh though, and took her out, and sometimes that was just what she needed.

They walked down the staff aisle and flashed their badges at the officer to be let through.

'Do you want to come out for dinner with me?'

'Oh.' It wasn't often that Bea was taken by surprise, she preferred to be in control, but he had just got her. 'Um,' she stumbled, thinking quickly. Did she want to get into something that might get messy? She liked him, and she could possibly *really* like him, but therein lay the problem.

'I don't bite,' he said with a grin, stopping to let her onto the escalator in front of him.

'Maybe,' she said as they got off at the bottom and headed together to the baggage belt. 'I hope you don't mind me asking, but are you married?' There, she had asked it. After a week of stopping herself, telling herself that it didn't matter either way, now it did.

Andre looked at her and threw his head back as he laughed. 'No, I am not married, neither do I have a girlfriend or children,' he said, visibly struggling to keep a straight face, but looking at her directly in the eye, in a way that made her believe him.

'Oh,' Bea smiled. She was sure he thought that was what she wanted to hear, and mostly it was, but whatever he had said would have thrown up problems. Without a wife or ties, he should behave in a different way, be a gentleman, and when men were under that pressure they often didn't. It was easier with someone like Shane, she would never want more from him and could never be let down.

'Here,' he said, and he took a pen out of his jacket pocket. He leaned over, pulled a small notepad from his flight bag and wrote a number onto it. 'I would really love to see you again,' he said, 'and I have no plans tomorrow if you would let me take you out.' He handed her the piece of paper, just as she was about to say okay anyway, but she held it in. It wouldn't do him any harm to wait a few hours. If she was going to do this, she would need to keep the balance right from the beginning. She looked at him and gave him her best enigmatic smile, tucking the piece of paper into her handbag just as her case appeared on the carousel. As she stepped forward to lift it Andre's arm reached past her and lifted it for her.

'Thank you. Excuse me but I have to catch a bus,' she said, pretending to look at her watch. She knew that she still had plenty of time before the next bus left Heathrow for Gatwick, but she *really* needed some fresh air, and a bit of space from this handsome, almost perfect man.

'Call me,' he said, and waved as she made off. She held up her hand and rushed towards the customs channel. She would call him, she was quite sure, but she definitely needed to get herself in check before she did so.

****

At home in her room Bea opened her case on the floor and started to take out all of the things she needed to. She put the new, fluffy, white dressing gown from the Singapore hotel on her bed, and threw her laundry bag next to her door. Closing the case she slid it under her bed, out of the way for the next four days. She opened her smaller wheelie bag and took out her makeup and toiletries, and then reached inside the front pocket, pulling out the carefully folded sheets of paper. She closed the bag and slid that, too, under the bed, before climbing onto it and holding up the two pages in front of her.

'What happened to you?' she asked out loud, looking from the photo to the other sheet and reading the article once again. 'Where did you go, Dad?'

She leaned back and tried to think of ways she could find out, but her brain was tired, and sleep won.

Chapter Twenty-One

Liv: I hope you all had a great weekend! Sorry I couldn't join you, fun stops when you get married and have kids!

Megan: You'll be able to let your hair down when you're away soon Liv :)

Paul: She'll be drinking us all under the tables!

Maddie: Liv I bet you can't wait to have some proper 'you' time

Liv: I literally cannot wait. A big bed all to myself with no kids or dogs on it haha! And wine of course... I'd love to indulge in a hangover too.

Jen: Do you think you'll miss the kids?

Liv: Probably, but they'll be with their dad so they'll be ok. I have got one friend who thinks I'm very selfish but she always has an opinion!

Megan: Don't listen to her! Loads of mum's do this and it works really well... bet she wouldn't judge if your hubby was going away.

Liv: You're so right!

Megan: And think of the holidays you'll be able to take them on!

Liv: Exactly!! My eldest just wants me to get to America and get her some sweets so she can show off to her friends... and those drinks that are all over TikTok?

Maddie: Prime! Yes, my nephew is on at me for them too lol. Guys did we need to do anything other than the eLearning for Aviation medical?

Megan: No babe, just that. Will be so nice not to have an exam every morning, hey?

Paul: Damn right

Aviation Medical was not turning out to be the easy ride they had all been hoping for after the two intense weeks of SEP.

'So, what is the time of useful consciousness at thirty-five thousand feet?' They had new trainers for the week, both ex-nurses, and Fi, as Fiona liked to be called, stood now covering the answer on the whiteboard with her palm.

Maddie shot her hand up; she was proving to be the know-it-all of the group. 'Thirty-five seconds,' she said.

'Correct,' Fi nodded, her hand still over the answers. 'How about forty thousand feet? Someone different this time,' she said as Maddie's hand went up again. Chloe felt as if they were back in a school classroom, with Maddie in Georgia Harper's seat.

'Eighteen seconds,' Megan said next to her.

'Cor-rect,' Fi said, removing her hand to show all of the answers. Chloe quickly scribbled TUC, short for 'time of useful consciousness', onto her notepad, reminding herself to get them in her head before the exam at the end of the week. She was relieved that there wasn't a daily one for medical, but it did mean more to learn at once... 'Now, the reason you need to be aware of these times is because if there is less oxygen than you need for useful consciousness then you need to be getting on portable oxygen as quick as you can, before you become hypoxic.' She clicked the remote in her hand and the word HYPOXIA came up on the board. She clicked it again and the subtitle read: "Signs and Symptoms". 'Make sure you learn these.'

Chloe wrote them down as they appeared, and then the treatment, her pages filling up along with her brain. By the end of the afternoon she could deal with burns, cuts and faints, and knew the physiology of altitude...

'At this rate we'll be qualified paramedics by the end of the week,' she said to Paul and Megan as they left the building.

'I love it,' Megan said. 'Much better than SEP.'

'Astrophysics would be better than SEP,' quipped Paul.

'See you in the morning, guys,' Chloe said as they stepped outside. It was dark already, and although it wasn't raining the ground was wet, telling her that it had been earlier. The air was fresh and crisp, and she wished that she had risked bringing the bike this morning as she boarded the crowded bus and stood in the aisle holding on to the pole for the entire journey.

As she walked up to the house, she tried as usual to guess who might be in. Kathryn was on earlies, so she should be back, and Bea should have landed today, shouldn't she? The pair of navy heels at the bottom of the stairs confirmed that she had, but there was no other sign of her. A smell of spices lingered in the air, stronger as she walked into the kitchen, but they were left behind from Kathryn's earlier cooking, as she was nowhere to be seen either.

Without the pressure of an early exam, Chloe took her time making herself a stir-fry for dinner and carried it through to the front room. The puzzle was coming along quite quickly, at this rate she would need to get another if she was to have one going until the end of the course. She heard the back door open and close, followed shortly after by Kathryn standing at the door looking at her.

'Mind if I join you for a bit?'

'Not at all.' Chloe decided not to ask her why she had come in the back door again, making a mental note to lock it when she went to bed later.

Kathryn sat to her left and they worked in comfortable silence, Chloe eating her dinner in between pieces. It was just like at home, she and her mum would sit just like this and say nothing, just switch off and focus on the jigsaw pieces.

She heard footsteps coming down the stairs and looked up as Bea passed the door.

'Hey,' she called out. 'Good trip?'

Bea stopped in the doorway and smiled; she looked tired, wrapped up in a bathrobe, wet hair bundled in a towel on her head. 'Brilliant, thanks.' The smile dropped when she noticed Kathryn. 'Oh, hi,' she said to her, her voice reluctant.

'Hi,' Kathryn said without looking up, back to the awkward stand-offish Kathryn that Chloe remembered. Bea rolled her eyes at Chloe and carried on her way to the kitchen, walking back a few minutes later with a glass of wine in her hand. This time she didn't even look in the living room as she passed.

Chloe opened her mouth and closed it again, not knowing what to say. She had managed to break the ice with Kathryn herself, but she couldn't do it for Bea, they would have to work it out themselves, if they even wanted to. She did wonder what they actually thought of each other though, both so totally different that had they not ended up sharing this house they absolutely wouldn't have been in each other's lives out of choice, she was quite sure.

'Right,' Kathryn said, slotting a piece into place. 'Thanks for that, I'm heading up.'

'Goodnight,' Chloe smiled up at her.

'Night,' she said back. She didn't smile, but that was okay, it was just her way, Chloe had come to realise.

Chloe stood up and took her empty bowl into the kitchen, putting it on the side next to Bea's half-full wine bottle. She walked to the back door and opened it, breathing in the fresh night air through her nose. It smelt of bonfires and rain. She closed it again and turned the key, wondering again what Kathryn had been doing out there. Perhaps she just liked the night air, too?

There was a knock at the front door; she waited a moment to see if anyone else was going to answer it before she did. There was no sound of footsteps, just some music playing in an upstairs room, and so she shuffled along the tiled floor in her slippered feet. In the patterned glass she could make out a tall silhouette and she slipped the security chain across before she opened it. A man with wavy hair and a huge smile greeted her.

'Hey, is Bea home?' he asked, a hint of an accent in his voice.

'I'll just get her,' said Chloe, giving him a smile back before shutting the door on him again.

Should she have asked him his name, or invited him in? she wondered as she climbed the stairs.

She knocked Bea's door, lightly at first and then when there was no answer, hammered it loudly with her knuckles.

'Bea, you have a visitor,' she called over the music.

The door opened and Bea stood there, her hair now dried and makeup on, looking beautiful.

'Hi,' she said. 'Sorry.' She left the door open as she walked over to a speaker on top of a wooden chest of drawers and turned the music down. Chloe noticed that the same red carpet was in this room too, though much more worn than hers was, and Bea's had a double bed; the walls were faintly blue, with navy curtains and a faded border ran around the walls with pictures of steam trains on it. She imagined a boy had slept in here once, although why the landlord hadn't removed the childish decoration before renting it out was a little odd. On top of the drawers she saw that Bea had a whole collection of photos standing in frames. There was also one, an old picture of a pilot, pinned alone on her wall.

'Sorry,' Chloe said, stopping herself from being nosy. 'But there's a man at the door for you.'

'Oh, heck,' Bea said, still in her dressing gown. 'Can you let him in and tell him I'll be down in five minutes?'

'No problem,' Chloe said as the door shut on her.

'She said to come in and she'll be down in five minutes,' she said to the man outside, opening the door wide now that she knew he could be trusted.

'It's okay,' he said, 'I need to make a call, I'll wait out here.'

Chloe was relieved, wondering how she would have made conversation with him while they waited. Minutes later Bea's heeled shoes clip-clopped down the stairs.

'He's waiting outside,' Chloe called from the kitchen as she put away her bowl.

'Wish me luck,' Bea said. She was checking herself in the mirror by the front door.

'You don't need it,' Chloe assured her. Bea looked stunning in her trouser suit.

'This one's special,' she grinned. 'He's a pilot.'

'Ahhh,' Chloe said as Bea opened the front door and left. Yes, she could see that now, could imagine him flying a plane. She had thought Bea was all about having fun, though? Maybe she had got that wrong, didn't every girl want to find the perfect partner deep down after all? 'Have fun,' she called after her.

Chapter Twenty-Two

Paul: Week Three nearly over guys and gals :)

Megan: That makes me sad :(

Paul: are you mad?!

Megan: Sad to leave you all, not sad to finish training!

Paul: Ah, fair enough. I can't wait to see the back of you all tbf

Paul: Joking!

Darren: I think we all deserve a week in the Caribbean after this I have to say!

Jen: I think you should put that idea forward Dazza, I'm sure they'll go for it haha

Darren: Honestly, I don't think my police training was this intense, although it was a long time ago :/

Jade: I know right? I lit can't believe all the stuff we need to know... I'm never going to remember it once we are through! Childbirth? Really? Anyone starts labour on my flight and I shall be locking myself in the furthest toilet. Actually, I'll be doing that for vomit too, I'm too squeamish for bodily fluids!

Megan: Dead! Great help you'd be on the farm when the calves are being born.

Jade: Yes well birthing calves is luckily not going to come up in my future, unless it takes a peculiar turn!

Chloe: I would love to birth a calf :)))))

Megan: None due this weekend, sorry Chlo! xxxx

Chloe was starting to feel as though Annie was an old friend. The rubber torso with the eerie girl's face had been her companion all day as she learned how to resuscitate and provide Immediate Life Support to unfortunate passengers.

'Make sure you are using enough pressure,' Fi said as they did compressions for the umpteenth time. 'Remember, you will probably break ribs, but carry on regardless, your priority is to keep that blood pumping.'

The whole room bounced up and down in unison, the sound of the Annies clicking as one.

'Twenty-nine, thirty,' Fi said. 'Now breaths.'

They all shifted to the doll's head and clamped the plastic mask down with their hands before delivering two breaths. Annie's chest rose as the air went in.

'Now, hopefully someone is on their way with the medical kit and defibrillator. Meanwhile, you keep going with compressions and breaths.'

Chloe put her hands back in place, one on top of the other, and resumed compressions, trying to ignore the pain in the bottom hand as the pressure continued.

'Great job, everyone, you can stop now. Who's tired?' Chloe sat back on her heels and put up her hand along with all of the others. Fi smiled. 'Well, you did a great job, and *that*,' she looked up at the clock, 'is a good place to finish.'

It was coming up to four o'clock, an hour before they normally finished; were they letting them go home early? The door opened and in came a man she hadn't seen before.

'Guys, this is Adrian, and he has come to take you for a behind-the-scenes look at Ops,' Fi said.

'Ooh,' said Megan. Chloe smiled; now *that* was something she had been dying to see.

They followed Adrian down stairs, along corridors and up more stairs. Chloe felt disorientated, lost in the maze. Finally he flashed his badge at a reader on the wall and they followed him through a set of double doors... a huge room opened up in front of them. The lights were dimmed in here, and it was just as she had imagined; screens lit up everywhere and huge whiteboards had codes and times scribbled across them. Low chatter provided the background music as heads poked up behind low, screened-off desks.

Adrian pointed out each department, people looking up occasionally when their names and roles were mentioned, friendly faces that Chloe tried to store for future reference. They all followed him through the room in silence. No one wanted to disturb what was obviously *very* important work.

The buzz of Ops tailed off as they emerged out the back and into a room that said Rostering over the door.

'Now this is who you need to make friends with,' Adrian said.

A middle-aged lady looked up from her desk and gave him a tight-lipped smile.

'Carmel here is the one to thank, or blame,' he winked at her, 'for those wonderful rosters.'

'I promise I do my best to keep everyone happy,' she said, rolling her eyes at him before smiling at the group.

Adrian laughed. 'Just teasing, she's amazing, just bear in mind you can't all have a roster full of five-night Caribbeans, hey?' Carmel nodded in agreement.

'Well, that's just not on,' Paul said. 'Do you take bribes?'

'She has a penchant for Gucci handbags,' Adrian said with a suggestive nod.

'I was thinking a nice bottle of wine more like?' Paul shuffled on his feet and put his hands in his pockets.

'Sorry, I don't drink.' Carmel shook her head, a small smile on her face. 'What's your name?'

Paul hesitated. 'Darren,' he answered, his face straight. Chloe clutched Megan's arm and tried to keep her laugh in as she watched the real Darren shake his head in disbelief and stare hard at Paul.

'Well, Darren, our Carmel is expensive, you'll have to up your game, I'm afraid,' Adrian said on her behalf, his eyes laughing. 'Anyway, we had better let her get on with her work,' he said, giving her a small wave of his hand. 'The other friends you need to make, if you follow me,' Adrian continued as he led them away and down another corridor, 'are in my department, Crewing.'

'I swear if I get a rubbish roster I'm coming for you,' said Darren, giving Paul a playful punch in the arm as they followed him.

'Sorry, mate,' Paul laughed. 'Not sure where that came from.'

Adrian held another door open for them up ahead and ushered them through.

'My housemate works here,' Chloe said hurriedly as she passed him. 'Kathryn.'

'Oh,' said Adrian, drawing his eyebrows together thoughtfully.

'Red hair,' Chloe prompted.

'Ah yes, of course. Quirky,' he said, giving Chloe a knowing smile that made her laugh. 'Yes, she's an assistant, very quiet. I think she's finished for the day though?'

Chloe nodded; she could imagine that Kathryn just came in and kept her head down while she did her work, not drawing attention to herself, being a little awkward sometimes. 'Yes, she's on earlies this week,' she said, feeling slightly smug that she was in the know about their mutual quirky acquaintance.

The hour passed quickly as Adrian explained how requests were processed, the rules around flight hours and constraints to rosters. Chloe took it all in as he showed them how each flight had to have a minimum number of crew, and how they dealt with crew phoning in sick, replacing them with people on standby. Before they knew it, it was five o'clock and he was leading them out, along another corridor and towards a flight of stairs at the end. The walls here were filled with photos that seemed to tell the history of the airline. A black and white picture of an old plane and smiling, achingly glamorous crew sat above a plaque that told her the airline's first flight had been in 1966. She scanned the other pictures as they walked quickly, noting the changes of uniform and the new planes, the way the airline's logo evolved...

Then pictures of more planes and people, one in particular catching her eye. She had seen it before, and she stopped in her tracks for a moment as she tried to remember where.

'Come on, Chlo,' said Megan, tugging her arm. The others were ahead of them now, and if they didn't keep up they might never find their way out.

'Coming,' Chloe said, distracted by thought as she followed her. Where had she seen that picture?

'Bea's room!' she said suddenly as they reached the main door of the building.

'Huh? Megan said, confusion written on her face.

'Oh, nothing,' she said, realising that she had said her thoughts out loud. Megan turned back to talking to Maddie. *The photo was the same one in Bea's room,* she thought. She wondered why Bea would have an interest in the old photo and wished she had managed to read what was written beneath it. What was the connection between this pilot and a crew member who had only joined the airline a few months ago? Chloe laughed at herself, at the narration that was becoming so common in her head lately. Maybe Bea just liked old photos? Perhaps she had an interest in history? Perhaps she knew who he was? Maybe flying was not really the career for her, Chloe laughed to herself again as she headed for the bus. Perhaps she should have been a detective after all? One with an interest in insignificant connections?!

Chapter Twenty-Three

Bea

Hello,

I was really hoping someone could help me out, forgive me if you are not the right department, but it was suggested that I try you first.

Bea sucked in a deep breath. It was Andre who had suggested that she try crew records, that they would possibly know more than HR, and since she had no better ideas of her own she figured she had nothing to lose.

It has come to my attention recently, she continued, *that my father, Anthony McGhee was a pilot for this airline many years ago. My mother had lived in the belief that he had just left us when he found out that she was pregnant as she never heard from him again, but I have been given reason to believe that he actually disappeared and that the circumstances were mysterious. I am attaching a copy of the company newsletter from the time that was passed to me just last week.*

I was wondering if records from as far back as 1992 would still be held anywhere as I would love to find out some more information about him. When I contacted HR previously they confirmed that he had not been on the payroll since then.

I would really appreciate any help you can give me with my investigations,

Best wishes

Beatrice O'Neill

She hesitated before sending the email; would they think she was mad, rambling on like that? Did companies keep records of employees from that far back?

She hit SEND and leaned back on her bed. It was Andre's fault, he was the one who had told her to do it. She smiled as she thought about him and their evening together; he was definitely giving out all the right signals, but she was holding back on planning a future with him just yet. She opened up the internet on her phone and put 'storage,' into the search bar. Mum and Dad were off to the Algarve next week, leaving her behind as they headed for retirement in the sun, and leaving her with just a week to find a home for all of her stuff. Sure, she'd had a month to sort it, but she had been hoping to find that damn garage key.

She looked around her room as the page loaded. She could possibly fit the rest of her clothes in here, but it was the bits of furniture that she needed a home for, the pieces from when she had her own house, the small things that meant something... like the coffee table she had coveted and saved up for months for. Maybe she could put it in the living room? But where would she put the dresser?

She clicked on the first advert for local storage, baulking at the cost. There was no way on earth she could afford *that* on her wages. No, she had one week to come up with something or her beloved furniture would have to be sold, and the thought of that made her sad.

Bea looked at the photos on her dresser. She was looking forward to going home this weekend, seeing the family one last time before they left. But the thought of the weekend made her sad, too, knowing that her childhood home was going to be someone else's, that she and her two younger sisters wouldn't have a base anymore. She turned to the picture of her real dad on her wall, the one she saw last thing at night and first thing in the morning now. She had wondered if she should take it back with her, show her mum, but decided it was the last thing she needed when she was already dealing with everything else. No, she would wait until she had more to tell her before she opened that can of worms.

She leaned over and turned off the bedside lamp.

'Night, Dad,' she said, rolling over and letting her mind drift off to somewhere where they were together. Tonight they were out in Singapore with their crew and he was buying her drinks, proud that his daughter was with him at work...

Chapter Twenty-Four

Jade: Anyone who's staying down want to go to Brighton tomorrow?

Paul: Not really beach weather?

Jen: I'd have loved to but I've got a few shifts in the bar so going home, need to get some money ££

Jade: Oh babe I'm so broke, but I have good overdraft

Megan: Champagne lifestyle, lemonade income this job. You'll never be rich

Paul: But will be rich in other ways :)

Jen: Cheesy

Chloe: We'd love to join you, but Megs is taking me farming :))))

Liv: Amazing, have fun! Obviously I am tied to the family all weekend or would love a jaunt to Brighton!

Jade: Anyone else?

Darren: I'm in

Maddie: I'm in too

Jade: I'll look at some train times. Sure we'll find somewhere fun when we get there!

The weekend had come around quickly, and Chloe felt so excited she could barely contain herself. The train that was taking them out of London and to the Kent countryside was packed, but they had managed to find two seats together, and room overhead for their bags.

'Here,' Megan grinned as she handed her a can of something. Chloe looked at it, smiling when she realised that it was prosecco.

'Amazing,' she said, pulling the tab to open it and taking a sip as it fizzed out. The bubbles felt good on the back of her throat.

'We deserve it,' said Megan.

'We certainly do,' said Chloe. Avmed was done, everyone had passed, and she felt ready to deal with all sorts of medical problems now. Next week was service training, and somehow that felt as if it was going to be much more fun than what they had covered so far.

'Here's to a week without exams,' Megan said, raising her can.

'A week with no exams,' Chloe sighed.

Chloe watched out of the window as the city started to fade, the buildings becoming fewer and fewer, giving way to fields and open spaces. She had been to Wales once as a child with her mum, to visit an old family friend, and could still remember the sense of freedom she had felt getting out of London and into the country. She could definitely see herself moving out of the hustle and bustle of the city one day.

'You are so lucky to live out here,' she said to Megan as the train raced along. The sun was almost set now and the sky looked like an orange and red watercolour painting, the vibrant colours washing into each other. Chloe had never seen a sky like it.

'It can get a bit boring sometimes, but that's why flying is good, mixes it up.'

'I love it,' Chloe said, turning back to the window to catch the last of the view before darkness descended. Before she knew it almost an hour had passed and she felt Megan tap her shoulder.

'We're here!'

Chloe snapped out of her trance and looked up to see her taking their bags down. She passed her down the overstuffed backpack that she had managed to squeeze everything into. Megan was waving now, and Chloe looked out of the window to see a very handsome man waving back at her as the train rolled slowly past him.

'Right, ready?'

'Yep,' Chloe said, slinging her bag over her shoulder and following her to the door. The train came to a stop and the door whooshed open. The handsome man was in front of them now and Megan had walked quickly over and thrown her arms around him. Chloe held back, uncertain whether she should hug him too.

'Chloe, this is my brother Matt,' Megan said. 'Matt, Chloe.'

Matt pushed his flat cap back a little on his head and leaned forward, his hand outstretched. Chloe felt her cheeks flush as she shook it.

'Pleased to meet you, Chloe,' he said. Chloe smiled back, no words forthcoming. Was it the country clothes, the flat cap and practical waxed jacket, the rugged, weathered features, or the prosecco that was making him so achingly attractive to her? Whatever it was it was ridiculous, and she was embarrassed by her own awkwardness. Besides, she would be meeting his wife very soon no doubt, and so she had better get all such thoughts out of her head. Right. Now.

****

The farmhouse was almost exactly how she had imagined it to be as they drove down the pot-holed drive towards it. Red brick, cosy-looking, with a yard opening up to the side where she could just make out the silhouette of a tractor in the pitch darkness. As they got out of the mud-splattered Land Rover she couldn't help but notice just how much darker night was out here, without the city lights adding their permanent glow. She followed them both along a pathway around to the back of the house.

'Come on in,' Matt said, holding the door open for her. She smiled and walked past him into the warm kitchen, where half a dozen pairs of wellies stood on the flagstone floor by the door. Chloe's cheeks were starting to ache but she still couldn't stop smiling; this place was the stuff of dreams to someone like her.

'I'll order a Chinese, shall I?' Megan asked, dropping her bag on the enormous oak dining table.

Chloe blinked, the story-book perfection momentarily fractured. She had been expecting a hearty stew simmering on the Aga, wasn't that what you cooked in farmhouses? Followed by apple pie made from the fruits of the orchard? She laughed inwardly. 'I love Chinese, sounds great,' she said, taking off her trainers and setting them down next to the wellies.

'You know my order,' Matt said. 'I'll be back in half hour, I just have a couple of bits left to do.'

'Okay,' Megan said, pulling her phone out of her bag. 'Right, let me get this ordered first, they take forever to deliver out here, and then I'll show you your room. What do you like?'

'Anything veggie,' said Chloe, taking a seat at the table, running her fingers over the worn wood. Megan nodded as she concentrated on her screen.

'Right-oh,' she said. 'Prosecco is in the fridge, glasses on the dresser over there.'

'Fabulous,' said Chloe, getting back up. *Who knew farming could be so much fun?*

****

Chloe was in a happy haze when she sank into the guest bed that night. It was early, apparently farmers were 'early to bed, early to rise,' Matt had told her as he said goodnight at nine-thirty. Now, at ten-fifteen, she knew that she would need to set an alarm if she was to meet him downstairs at six am as she had promised; she didn't want to miss out on *anything* by staying in bed. She reached into her bag on the floor and dug around in it until she found her phone; she had been having such a lovely evening she hadn't even looked at it since they had arrived.

On the screen she saw the missed messages from her mum, asking how she was getting on, a missed call from her, and then another from a number she didn't recognize.

Strange, she thought. She was used to missed calls in the day, always someone that she didn't really want to speak to as they invariably wanted to sell her something, but this had come through at nine-twenty on a Friday night. Surely offices were closed by then?

'Hmm.' She shrugged; whoever or whatever it was it couldn't have been important or they would have left a voicemail. She opened up her messages, eager to share her farm experience so far with her mum, and sank back into the feather pillows. Tomorrow couldn't come soon enough.

Chapter Twenty-Five

Jade: Train at 1210, does that work for everyone?

Darren: Good with me

Paul: Works here

Maddie: Perfect, meet outside?

Sophie: Hey, sorry I don't usually speak up on here, but can I join you all?

Maddie: Sophie!!! Good to have you join us, I know this group can be a bit mental to keep up with

Sophie: That's ok, I'm the odd one out being a local girl, you all look like you've been having fun though! Having a few problems with the fella and have the night off work so could do with a reason to get out of town.

Maddie: You can tell us all about it on the train girl, so glad you're coming :)

Sophie: Thanks. I don't think he is going to deal with me doing this job, but I'm not giving it up, I want to fly so bad!

Liv: No man should want you to give up your dream sweetheart, you let him deal with his issues and go have yourself a good weekend.

Paul: Yes Sophie! We'll cheer you up! Megs where ya at?

Megan: On the farm I'm afraid, and I have Chloe with me... she's out milking the cows with my bro

while I keep warm lol! Sophie you be careful with those lot... especially Paul, he's a terrible influence!

Sophie: Oh dear, what have I let myself in for haha

It was cold the next morning, and Chloe could see her breath in the air as she rushed to get dressed, layering all of her clothes one on top of the other. Downstairs in the kitchen Matt was already there, pulling his boots on by the back door.

'Good morning,' he said cheerily.

'Morning,' Chloe said back, brighter than she had ever felt at this time of day.

'Ready?' he asked.

'Uh,' Chloe stumbled, as there obviously wasn't going to be a cup of tea or briefing before they headed out. Where was Megan? 'Er, can I borrow some wellies?'

'Help yourself,' he said, opening the back door, 'meet me outside.'

Chloe listened for any sound of her friend coming downstairs. Nothing. She walked over to the boots and pulled on the first pair that looked roughly the right size. Maybe she wasn't coming? Come to think of it, she couldn't remember Megan saying anything about joining them when she had asked him if he would take her with him.

Well, she thought, *looks like it's just me and the handsome farmer.* So far there had been no sign of a wife. She'd had worse mornings.

The milking shed was at the far side of the farm, and Chloe felt quite useless as she watched Matt expertly herd the cows in and attach their machines. She counted twenty in total, beautiful beasts who seemed quite content, chomping away on their food while their udders were emptied. She had a million questions but kept quiet as he worked quickly.

With the final pump attached he stood back and stopped for the first time.

'How much milk does each one produce?' Chloe asked, aware that she sounded like a child on a school trip.

'Varies,' he said, his hands on his hips as he watched his wards carefully. 'We take less from them here though, as we like to keep their calves with them for longer, on other farms they take them away after a couple of days.'

'Oh.' Chloe thought about it; she had read a little about it on her journey to being a vegetarian, but as she still enjoyed dairy, she hadn't delved too much into that area in case it made her feel bad.

'Means the milk is more expensive,' Matt said. He was having to talk loudly over the machines now, 'but people seem happy to pay it if it's been kinder to the cow.'

Chloe smiled; she loved the idea.

They didn't speak much as the morning went on. Occasionally he would give her a job to do, but mostly she watched and took it all in. Every last wonderful bit. Reuniting the cows with their calves in the shed was perhaps the most beautiful thing she had ever witnessed, and cleaning up the poo hadn't bothered her a single bit. As the last of the hay was distributed she noticed that it was now broad daylight, and her stomach was growling.

'Sounds like someone needs breakfast,' Matt laughed as he appeared next to her. 'Come on.'

They climbed back into the car and drove along the track that they had come along this morning. Chloe could see the fields either side now, the grass on one side lush and green after all the recent rain, and muddy on the other. 'We alternate the fields,' Matt said. All morning it had felt as though he could read her thoughts, explaining things just as she was wondering about them. The way he seemed to be in tune with her really wasn't helping with her growing crush.

The smell of bacon coming from the kitchen hit Chloe as soon as Matt opened the door. Inside the table was laid with plates and glasses, with orange juice, toast and butter in the middle.

'Ah, I do love it when you're home,' Matt said to Megan, who was still in her fluffy dressing gown and slippers, cooking their breakfast at the stove.

'I know,' she grinned. 'Morning, Chlo, how was that?'

Chloe smiled as wide as she could. 'Amazing,' she said. 'Totally amazing.' She caught sight of herself in the mirror that hung by the door above the boots. Her cheeks and nose were pink and her eyes were sparkling. She *felt* amazing too, full of fresh air and nature. 'I would love to be a farmer,' she said, joining Matt at the table as Megan put a fried breakfast in front of them both.

'No meat,' Megan said with a wink. Chloe smiled, grateful that she had remembered, but secretly jealous of the bacon and sausages that they both had. It smelt delicious.

'So, what have you got in store for us girls this afternoon?' Megan asked. Matt gave her a devilish smile and pushed his fingers together menacingly.

'Well, there's a wall that needs fixing and the hay needs sorting. I need to get some of the high bales down.' He raised his eyebrows at Megan.

'Nope, not doing it,' she said firmly, looking down at her toast as she buttered it a little bit harder.

Matt laughed. 'Megan hates heights,' he explained to Chloe, who thought it sounded great.

'So do you!' Megan exclaimed.

Matt shuffled. 'I don't *hate* them, I just prefer not to risk a broken neck.' The way he looked down gave Chloe the impression that he actually disliked heights as much as Megan did.

'But you'll happily risk your little sister's,' Megan scowled.

'I'll do it,' Chloe offered without hesitation. There was nothing she would love more than climbing hay bales and throwing them down. Matt and Megan looked at each other and then at her. They were both smiling now. 'Honestly, I'd love it. Although, Megan,' she added in amused afterthought, 'isn't a fear of heights a slight contradiction to your career choice?'

Megan pulled her lips into a tight smile, while Matt leaned back, nodding smugly as he chewed his breakfast. 'Exactly what I've been saying all along,' he said.

'Thanks, Chloe, now he thinks he's won the argument,' Megan said, rolling her eyes. 'It's different, a different sort of height.'

'Oh, right,' Chloe said, nodding now too. She looked at Matt. 'Of course. A different type of height.'

'You two, stop ganging up on me, or... or you can make your own breakfast next time.'

'Sorry, sis,' Matt laughed.

'Yeah, sorry, Megs,' Chloe said, stifling her own laugh. Megan shook her head at them both.

'Children,' she said in exasperation, but with a smile on her face.

****

'Right, I'm off to see Tony,' Matt said as the two girls sat in front of the wood burner drinking hot chocolate with Baileys in. Gone were the farmer clothes and in their place was an outfit that wouldn't have looked out of place in any London bar. He looked HOT, and Chloe knew she was staring.

'Have fun,' Chloe called, blowing her hot chocolate to cool it down.

'Chloe,' Megan said slowly as the back door shut behind him.

'Yeah?'

'Do you fancy my brother?' she grinned at her over the top of her mug. Had it been that obvious?

'No!' she protested, too loudly.

Megan giggled. 'He's gay, Tony is his latest boyfriend.'

'Oh, really?' Chloe tried her best to stop the disappointment showing on her face and sound indifferent.

'He's a good-looking man, but definitely not for you, babe.'

'I didn't fancy him, just thought he was handsome...'

'Uh-huh,' Megan nodded knowingly. 'Still getting up at six tomorrow?'

'Yes,' Chloe laughed now. She could hardly cancel just because Matt wasn't available to her, could she? Besides, he was still nice to look at, and she loved the farm enough to get out of bed early once again...

Falling into bed later, Chloe was pleasantly exhausted from the afternoon in the hay barn. Reluctantly she picked up her phone. She hadn't missed it all day, only now feeling that she should probably check it. It was amazing that the WhatsApp group was still so active, but there was, as usual, too much to catch up on. The missed call got her attention though, the same number as last night, and again no voicemail. She was intrigued, but it was too late to call it back, and what if it was someone she didn't want to talk to? She texted her mum and put the phone back down, feeling sleep coming as soon as she shut her eyes. It really had been the best day.

Chapter Twenty-Six

Jade: Guys start sending me your pics and videos of the past three weeks, I'm going to start working on the video for our wings.

Megan: {image}

Jade: Omg, DEAD!!!! Brilliant Megan. Keep them coming, I need enough for a good five minutes. Suggestions of music too?

Darren: I'm leaving on a jet plane?

Maddie: Don't know that one?

Darren: Showing my age lol. Busted?

Megan: What have you been Busted for Dazza?

Darren: Never mind :/

Megan: Only pulling your leg... Of course I know the Busted song hahahahah 'Air Hostess, I like the way you dress lalalala'

Sophie: Something about 'new starts' for me. Think I'm single :(

Maddie: Oh babe, I'm so sorry.

Sophie: Not sure how I'm going to get through this week if I'm honest

Jen: You will babe, we'll get you through it. No pressure of exams, so we can just concentrate on having fun. Sorry to hear that though, never easy breaking up with someone.

Chloe: So sorry Sophie. I feel your pain, but I'm a few months on... this job will be the best thing for us though, and they obviously just weren't the right ones for us. Big hugs xxx

Chloe was in a deep sleep when her alarm went off on Monday morning. For a moment she lay there and tried to figure out where she was, having been back on the farm in her dreams all night, but not with handsome Matt, or with Megan, she had been with Lucas. She tried to ignore the sinking feeling in her stomach as she looked around, her eyes falling on the dressing table that told her immediately where she was.

She stood up slowly, her head a little thick after the amount of wine that she and Megan had had in the pub on the way home, over their Sunday roast. It had been the best weekend, and she really hoped that they would invite her again soon. She pulled open the curtains; it wasn't quite light and there was a low fog that made her want to get outside and breathe it in. She was going to cycle today, she decided, her love of the outside reignited after the farm.

The house was quiet, and she opened her door carefully, not wanting to disturb anyone if they were home. In the bathroom she noticed Bea's toothbrush lying on the windowsill; there was a small pool of water underneath it, as if it had been used recently.

Downstairs she looked in at the living room. More of the puzzle had been done, she noticed, but that only told her that Kathryn had been home at some point over the weekend, and not the exact time... her inquiring mind carried on like this, entertaining herself as she looked for clues while she made herself a coffee. A bowl on the draining board... was it Kathryn's or Bea's? she wondered, deciding that Kathryn would have put hers away...

By the back door Chloe slid her hand across the shelf, looking for the key to the garage. It wasn't there. She stood, perplexed, for a moment and tried to think where it might be. She *had* put it back, hadn't she? She reran the day that she put the bike in there, but it was a week ago now, and she could just about remember locking it, not what she did with the key after. If she hadn't put it back, where would it be?

She took the stairs two at a time, wondering if her hunch was right. She had been wearing her stonewash jeans, and she hadn't worn them since. In her wardrobe she pulled them down from the top shelf and dug her hand into the back pocket, feeling the key as she did so. She smiled at her success. Turning around she reached down and picked up her backpack from the floor, opening it and pulling out the clothes from the weekend. In their place she put in her iPad and notepads, looking around for a pen. There was no pen to be seen and she pulled open a drawer in the hope of finding one in there.

Something stopped her in her tracks, and she stood looking into the drawer blankly, wondering what it was. Something wasn't right.

Inside the drawer was a random collection of things that didn't belong elsewhere... stationery, hairgrips, a torch, plasters... It wasn't so much what was in there though, as how it had all been moved around. She had been in this drawer when she packed for the farm, and distinctly remembered giving it a bit of a sort-out as she looked for her gloves. She remembered putting the hair stuff in the front so that she could find it more easily, as it had all become a bit of a muddle, and now they were more in the centre. Also, the battery pack for her phone, she was quite sure that had been on the far right-hand side... hadn't it?

Had someone been in there?

She opened the other drawers, but although it was possible their contents had been moved around, she couldn't be quite sure as she hadn't taken so much notice of *them*. A look at her phone told her that it was time to leave if she was going to get to training on time, and she closed the drawers, picturing Bea or Kathryn in here when she was away, pulling them out and rifling through them. Who was it, and what had they been looking for? Should she ask them when she saw them, or was there a chance they would lie? Should she wait and see if they just told her?

Chloe cycled fast along the paths, the fog lifting and giving way to a bright winter morning by the time she arrived. She hadn't much noticed it though, her mind mulling over the fact that someone had been in her room. That someone had been going through her things. She had nothing to hide though, maybe they had just wanted to borrow something? Yes, she decided, that was what it must have been, they had just needed to borrow a pen or something, and *really* she didn't mind at all, she told herself over and over until she was almost convinced.

She forced a smile as she locked up the bike in the glass-covered rack at the back of the building. *Not everything unusual is part of a crime scene, Chloe.*

Chapter Twenty-Seven

Jade: Guys I'm running late, go without me, having a hair nightmare!

Paul: We can wait, no rush this morning.

Jade: No, honestly, go on, I'll leg it over at the last minute. I was practicing a new style for when we are in uniform and I've got the comb tangled...

Megan: Nooooo! Right, what room are you in, you can't do this alone!

Jade: 316, thank you so much, I think I might cry :(

Megan: Coming. Paul go on and cover for us, say we got stuck in the lift or something if we're late lol

Paul: Will do. You girls, glad we don't have long hair eh Daz?

Darren: or any

Jade: You don't know how lucky you are!

Sophie: I'm running late too. Can someone put on here what room we are in, don't think I'll make it in time to meet in the cafeteria.

Liv: I'm here, I'll find out. Hope you're ok Sophie, see you in a bit for a hug. Jade be brave haha

Jen: I'm stuck in traffic too fml! I left so early as well, do the schools start an hour earlier down here or something?!

Jade: I hope we have some nice trainers for service… we are not getting off to a good start group 352!!

'Would you like a drink, madam?' Megan asked, her face serious, her eyes laughing.

'Ooh, a glass of your finest champagne please.' Chloe went along with the role play, disappointed to be handed a glass of water.

'Sir?'

'Sex on the Beach, please,' said Paul.

'Barbados or Jamaica?'

'Both.' He too was handed a glass of water, with a hint of a smile from Megan as she pushed her trolley on to the next row.

'Well done, guys,' said the trainer as they reached the back row of the fake aircraft. 'You can pop the cart away, and then if we can have two volunteers to do Business Class main meals please.' Paul shot Chloe a look and grabbed her arm, thrusting it skywards along with his. Her stomach dipped; she had been quite enjoying her flight so far.

In the galley Chloe looked at the metal boxes and carts, trying to read the labels and work out what was in them. Some of them seemed to be in another language with words she had never used before.

'Can you all see us?' George, the trainer, poked his head out of the galley and into the cabin. Chloe knew that they were now on the screen at the very front of the small cabin, and Paul gave a cheeky wave to the camera that was bearing down on them. 'Great. *Sooo…*' He flicked a red latch up and stepped on the cart's brake release pedal, pulling it out between them. 'Business Class main meal service. First, we need to set up the drinks. Chloe, next to you is a bar cart. If you can open it and find a tray of wines for me.'

Chloe froze for a second. Despite all of the safety training she still didn't feel as if she was really crew, and it didn't feel like her place to be opening carts and rummaging around in them. George raised his eyebrows and smiled at her, and she felt her heart rate quicken as she turned to look at the carts, relieved that the first one had 'BAR' written clearly on its label. She flicked up the handle and pulled it open, but it wouldn't move, and she felt her face flush as she pulled it again, harder this time.

'Don't forget the latch,' George prompted.

Chloe moved her hand up and slid the red metal latch across, trying to forget that everyone was watching her, and tried the handle again. This time the cart opened to show her the trays of drinks inside.

'Right, so we need a tray of wines,' George said. 'Remember your manual handling, Chloe.'

Chloe corrected her posture, bending her knees, and pulled out a metal tray full of cute little glass bottles. She laid them down on top of the cart.

'Now we also need some still and sparkling water,' George carried on. 'In this galley you will find it in the fridge, but remember when you get on board just to check all of the carts as things are in different places on each of the aircraft.'

Paul opened the fridge and pulled out some water. Chloe wished she was as confident as him, but this kind of role play, when she was a lead character and people were watching, was her worst nightmare, and she was trying so hard to remember everything that she knew she was forgetting to smile. She fought the urge to kick him hard in the shins for volunteering her to do the biggest part of the whole service.

George talked them through loading the hot meals into another box and finally she was in the aisle, on the end of a cart, delivering them to her 'passengers'.

'Smile, Chlo,' Megan laughed when she handed her the tray. The glasses rattled together as she put it down on the table, her hand shaking.

'Still or sparkling water?' Chloe asked, trying her hardest to pull the corners of her mouth upwards.

'Still please, babe,' Megan said, the sympathy on her face making Chloe feel even worse. 'And white wine.'

Chloe handed her the water-filled bottle and stood back up straight, watching Paul for a moment as he seemed to be thriving in the aisle on the other end. Why couldn't she just be natural like him? Why did it all seem difficult when she knew that it wasn't?

'What would you like to eat, madam?' she asked Jade in the next row, looking over her shoulder to see how many people were left. It was lunchtime and she could see eager faces waiting for her to get to them.

'The chicken, please,' Jade said quietly. 'With still water and white wine.' Chloe took a deep breath and forced a smile onto her face. In no time she would have to serve a whole aircraft, so there was no point going to pieces now.

'Well done, guys,' George said when they had served the last person. 'Take your own meals and I'll pop the cart away.'

Chloe sat down with Paul, putting her tray on the table in front of her. She wished that it was real wine in the bottle, she could really do with that right now.

'Is this what they have on board today?' someone asked.

George's head poked out from the galley. 'It certainly is,' he said. 'This is the exact same meal that crew will be serving up there today.' There were murmurs of approval, and despite the fact that she had completely lost her appetite, Chloe regarded her tray with a new appreciation. She had never flown in Business Class before, never had metal cutlery and real china on a flight, and she felt suddenly privileged. 'But remember,' he said, walking out of the galley now and standing in the aisle in front of them, 'it's as much about *how* you are serving something as *what* you are serving.'

Chloe sank back in her seat, sure that he was making a dig at her awful attempt. She was going to be terrible, she just knew it, was going to drop things on people, say the wrong things, not be able to find things....

'But you guys just did a superb job, well done, Paul and Chloe,' he said, clapping his hands together. The others joined in and Paul nudged her with his elbow. Her despair subsided just a little; had she really done okay? She turned to Paul, who was relishing the applause as he buttered his bread roll. Perhaps she had? 'Now, who wants to volunteer for the most glamorous part? Clearing in?'

****

'Well done for today, guys.' They were back in the classroom and George walked around the room handing them each a booklet. 'Everything you need to know is in here,' he said, setting one down in front of Chloe. She picked it up and flicked through the pages, pleased to see that it had a lot of pictures. The door knocked and they all turned their heads to see an older lady walk in. She was dressed casually in loose camel trousers and a patterned blouse, Chloe felt sure that she had seen her somewhere before.

'Ahhh, *Carmel*,' George greeted her. 'Guys,' he said as he gave the last booklet out and walked over to Carmel, who stood in the doorway holding a pile of paper, and kissed her on the cheek. 'I had forgotten that today was such an important day for you all!' He grinned at them and rubbed his hands eagerly together. 'The lovely Carmel is here to make your dreams come true, people.' He took the papers from her and waved them in the air. '*These*,' he said, 'Are your very first rosters!'

An excited murmur rose up around the room.

'Usually, you wouldn't get these before the last day of training, but since it is the most important roster of the year...' He paused and looked around at them. 'The Christmas one,' he nodded to check they understood,

'Carmel here has done yours early so that you can plan your celebrations around your flights.'

'Enjoy,' she said, giving them a small wave and retreating through the door. Chloe sensed that she was definitely more of an 'office' type, not comfortable on centre stage. She reminded her a bit of Kathryn.

'So!' George studied the top sheet. 'Maddie,' he walked over to her as they all watched eagerly. 'Looks like you'll be in Miami for Christmas, my lovely.' He handed her the sheet. 'Megan, you'll be at home for Christmas, but a nice little New York and Boston to get all your shopping done beforehand...'

The wait for hers was excruciatingly painful and Chloe scooted forward on the edge of her seat, absorbing everyone else's excitement. 'Jade, standby for you, the world is your oyster as they say. Hope you get called for something nice... Paul, curry for you. Delhi Christmas Eve.' He delivered the news and the papers quickly, finally reaching her. 'Chloe...' She held her breath when he said her name. 'You'll be at home for your Christmas dinner before heading to Singapore that night, you lucky thing.' He put the A4 piece of paper down in front of her and she picked it up eagerly. Down the left-hand side were the numbers 1-31, and next to each a code. She scanned down to 25 and saw the SIN that denoted her flight to Singapore, and her heart skipped a beat. She was going to Singapore, HER! Chloe! Singapore! The rest of the page was a blur that she couldn't quite understand.

'Guys,' George called above the excited chatter. 'I had meant to cover roster codes with you before you got your rosters, but here is a quick summary of what it all means.' He leaned over his laptop on the desk at the front and a page of codes appeared on the board along with their meanings. 'Take a picture of that with your phones and I'll go into it in more depth in the morning, but I'm conscious that we have run over today.' Chloe looked at the clock; where had the last hour gone? She snapped a photo of the board and folded her roster, putting it carefully into her bag. Maybe she would get it framed, her mum would love that.

'And, guys,' George called loudly after them as they gathered up their belongings, the first of them almost out of the door. Everyone stopped and looked back at him. He smiled as he drew his brows together, as if pleading. 'Please all be on time tomorrow!'

Chapter Twenty-Eight

Megan: Here's my roster guys {image}

Anyone on any of my flights?

Darren: I think I'm on your New York! {image}

Megan: Amazing! We can explore together!

Darren: That's if my ID gets sorted so don't hold your breath

Jade: {image}

Jen: {image}

Paul: {image} Still not sure what it all means!

Rasia: Paul we are on the San Francisco together :) {image}

Paul: So we are babs, the poor crew who have to carry us newbies!

Rasia: Speak for yourself :)

Maddie: True though, must be annoying for the crew to have new people on board that don't have a clue, don't you think? I'm a bit worried now.

Megan: Most people will just remember they were new once themselves, don't worry about it, I'm sure they will love you all xxx

It was freezing. December had arrived along with plummeting temperatures, but as she rode her bike back to the house her mind was so distracted with the excitement of Singapore, and what had turned out to be a Cape Town just before it, that she barely felt the wind biting at her cheeks. She took the last small hill without any of the usual huffing and puffing, and arrived feeling on top of the world. It was dark and the lights were all on in the house; she hoped that it meant Bea was home.

Dropping her bag on the floor she fumbled with numb fingers through the front pocket for the garage key, quickly flinging the door up and parking the bike in front of the boxes. The door moved freely now since she had oiled the mechanisms. She pulled it down and locked it again, looking up at the house just as the curtain to Bea's room moved. She was excited to share her roster with her and walked quickly to the front door.

'Bea,' she called out as she shut it behind her.

'I'm here,' Bea answered straight back; she was already hanging over the wooden banister, her hair falling either side of her face.

'I got my roster!' Chloe put her bag down and tugged the zip open. 'And I got bubbly to celebrate!'

'Well.' Bea stood up straight and appeared with a huge smile at the top of the stairs a split second later. 'If you're sharing then I'm up for a celebration. What did you get?!'

'Singapore!' Chloe sang the word as she galloped into the kitchen. She handed her roster to Bea when she appeared behind her.

Bea sat down at the table and studied it. 'That Cape Town is a bit harsh,' she muttered, 'but I wouldn't mind a Singapore Christmas Day.'

'What does the rest of it mean?' Chloe asked, pouring their drinks and sitting down with her. 'They didn't really go through it.'

Bea laid it down between them. 'This is your Cape Town,' she said, pointing to the CPT. 'This is your report time, and this is the take-off time. This is the flight time.' She pointed along the columns.

'Uh-huh,' Chloe nodded, trying to take it all in. 'What is Cape Town like? Is it amazing?'

'Yes, but you only have one night, so expect to be tired.'

Chloe still smiled; one night was better than no nights, surely?

'And this is Airport Standby.' She pointed to the three days. 'So pack for every eventuality, bikinis and winter clothes, it's a tough one but you could get something really nice.'

'I'm *soooo* excited.'

'I'm excited for you,' Bea grinned, holding her glass up in the air. Chloe lifted hers and clinked them together.

'What did you get?'

Bea's smile dropped just a little. 'I'm off,' she said. 'We got our rosters last month. My parents are moving to Portugal so I'm hoping to go out there.'

'Oh, how lovely,' Chloe said, although she would have hated for her own parents to move away.

'Hmm, it will be different, that's for sure, but they are going whether I like it or not so I am trying to see the positive side.'

'I think I would miss my folks,' Chloe said. Bea looked thoughtful and she felt bad for her. 'But I guess it's not too far, and lots of cheap holidays,' she added brightly.

'You're right.' Bea took a deep breath in and smiled as she exhaled. 'I'm sure it will be fine. *Anyway*... changing the subject, have you been keeping a secret, missy?' She leaned forward and looked at Chloe so seriously that she let out an involuntary giggle.

'What?' she said, darting her eyes left and right, racking her brain for what it might be.

'Did I just see you shutting the garage door?' Bea asked slowly.

'Oh. Yes!'

'You have a key?' Bea's eyes were wide now.

'Um, yes, I found it the other day. Didn't I tell you?'

'Er no, you certainly did not!'

Chloe felt as if she was being told off, but Bea was still smiling and she felt utterly confused. 'Why?' she asked.

'You are an absolute genius, that's why!' Bea beamed, putting her glass down and clenching both of her hands into fists. 'You absolute bloody star!' She shook her head. 'What's it like in there? Is there any room for a few small things?'

'Er, I think so.' Chloe still hadn't had a proper look. The days were so short, dark when she left, dark when she arrived back. 'There's a lot of boxes at the front but there seems to be some room behind. Why?' she asked, curious as to why Bea was so excited.

'Well, Mum and Dad need me to take all my things, and I had nowhere to stow them until now... you may have just saved them from the charity shop, that's what!'

'Oh, how wonderful!' Chloe felt Bea's joy. 'Well let me know and I'll leave you the key, I just need it for the bike.'

'Sunday night would be amazing, Dad can drop it all here when he brings me home.'

'Cool, I'll leave it on the table Friday night when I leave.' Bea topped their glasses up; it seemed that they both had reason to celebrate. 'I haven't found a light switch in there yet though, so you might want to do it in daylight,' she added as an afterthought.

'Noted,' Bea said. 'I'm going to miss you when you leave, Chloe. I can't believe it's only next week.'

Chloe felt a thud in her chest. Bea was right, next Friday was her very last day of training, and she would be moving back home. She felt inexplicably sad, hadn't considered that she would form any kind of attachment to the house or the people in it when she first arrived. She would even miss Kathryn and her funny ways. 'I'll miss you too,' she said, watching her prosecco dance as she twirled the glass in her fingers, 'but hopefully we will fly together,' she added, looking up.

'Yes! Let's request something!'

'Definitely,' said Chloe, thinking it was a great idea. 'Will we get it?' She had no idea how these things worked.

'Maybe, depends what mood Carmel is in, she can be a bit of a bitch,' Bea shrugged, smiling as she drained her glass. She picked up the empty bottle and rolled her eyes. 'Good job I've got some more in the fridge, hey?!'

Chapter Twenty-Nine

Bea

Dear Beatrice,

Thank you for your email. I regret to inform you that we don't keep records of employees going so far back other than dates of employment, and I have been unable to unearth any details for you other than the newsletter that you already have.

I wish you the best of luck and do hope that you are able to find the answers that you are looking for somewhere.

Kind Regards

Marlae

Human Resources Executive, Osprey Aviation Ltd

Bea sighed. She had refreshed her emails at least ten times a day for days now, hoping that when the reply *did* arrive, it would give her something to go on. But there it was. Nothing. Nada. Zilch.

She sat back in her bed and contemplated her next move. Should she go to the police? Could you just walk into a police station and ask for files? Would they still have them, and if they did, would they let her see them? Would she need a lawyer to do it for her? Anyway, even if they did, however unlikely that was, if the police hadn't been able to find out what happened to him, she was hardly going to be able to, was she?

Her mind raced around and around, but every time she found her resolve to pursue it, she turned a corner and realised it was futile... but how could she just leave it there? Not know anything about him? Yes, maybe she would never find out what happened, but it would be nice to know *something* about him. Anything.

She looked at the time on her phone; it was nearly time to leave, and her disappointment faded slightly as the prospect of flying to New York with Andre on the flight deck tonight put a smile on her face. He had checked with her that it was okay before he swapped onto her flight too, forever the gentleman.

Downstairs in the kitchen she made herself a coffee and ordered an Uber. She really should sort out her driving soon, she thought as she poured in the boiling water; it was about time she got over her fear and grew up. The front door opened and an icy blast blew along the hallway, making her shiver. Chloe appeared, her face almost completely covered between the cycle helmet and the scarf pulled up to her eyes. She pulled her gloves off in the doorway and wriggled out of her padded coat.

'Hey,' Bea called out. 'Cold out there?'

'Bloody freezing,' Chloe said, pulling off her scarf. Her nose and cheeks were pink underneath it.

'How was your day?'

'Good,' Chloe replied, finally free of the coat, which she hung on the pegs by the door. She took off the helmet and put it on the floor underneath. 'Disruptive passenger training.' She had spent the day learning how to deal with disruptive passengers and how, in the worst cases, to handcuff them and strap them to a seat. They had laughed a lot, and Megan had cried when Paul almost broke her wrist, but it had been a fun day... although she hoped that she never needed to use any of it.

'Ah,' Bea said knowingly. 'Reckon it would work on a twenty-stone man after ten cans of Stella?'

Chloe laughed. 'Probably not. Where are you off to?'

'The Big Apple, with Andre.' She gave a shy smile.

'Ooh, handsome pilot Andre?'

'Yep.'

Something came back to her, the picture on Bea's wall, the one she had seen at training. She had never asked Bea about it, indeed it had completely slipped her mind until now. 'You like a handsome pilot, hey?'

Bea looked confused. 'What makes you say that?'

'The picture on your wall,' Chloe grinned. 'I saw it over your shoulder when you opened your door the other day.'

'Oh, that!' Now Bea laughed and sat down at the table. She rummaged through her bag that was sitting on the table. 'That man was my dad.'

'*Whaaat*?' Chloe stood open-mouthed. How had she not known that Bea's dad was a pilot? She'd never mentioned it, and why was his picture on the wall at the office?

Bea held out a copy of the newsletter to her. She had made a few copies and had put some in her bag to show around at work in the hope that one of the older pilots might know something.

'But I thought you were seeing your dad at the weekend?' Chloe asked, taking the paper from her.

'He's not my biological father,' Bea explained. 'My mum thought my real dad, Anthony, didn't want to be with us, so she planned to bring me up alone and then met my other dad. I know it sounds a bit messed up. I just found out recently that Anthony went missing the day, or the day after, she told him she was pregnant and was never seen again. He worked for us, but that's all I know.'

Chloe felt the hairs stand up on her neck as she read the article. 'They never found anything?'

'Nope.'

'Do you know where he lived?'

'Local, it says there, but no one can tell me any more than that.'

Chloe shook her head. It was a cold case, as cold as they got, but one thing she had learned from hours of watching her programmes, was that even the coldest of cases could be solved.

'Can I take a picture of this?' she asked.

'Keep it,' Bea said, standing up as her phone beeped. 'I've got more copies. My cab's here, enjoy the rest of the week, I might not see you as I get back on Friday night. Are you going home on the weekend?'

'Yes,' Chloe answered her as she walked to the front door. 'Have a great flight.'

'Thanks,' Bea called back as she closed the door. 'Oh, and don't forget to leave me the garage key.'

'I won't.' Chloe sat down and reread the newsletter, taking in every detail. She pulled a pen from her bag and started to underline any little thing that might have meant something.

Here in front of her was a real mystery, and her mind desperately wanted to help Bea solve it.

Chapter Thirty

Jen: I'm actually scared I might cry when I see you all in your uniforms!

Jade: Same, I'm welling up at the thought of it

Jen: We've got to get loads of photos and videos... we'll be viral on TikTok by the time I'm finished lol

Sophie: I so cannot wait to post a picture of me in uniform and show someone what he is missing!

Jen: And we need to get some before pics so that we can see the transition!

Maddie: Just learning how to do this hairstyle {Image}

Jade: Love a French twist but I'd look like a hard-boiled egg if I wore one

Maddie: LOL

Megan: {image}

Jade: OMFG how do you do that?! I need a step-by-step guide... my skills end at one of those doughnut bun things!

Megan: We can have a hair tutorial at lunch tomorrow :)

Darren: Can you do anything with mine?

Megan: Sorry Dazza you're a lost cause my friend!

'Was that *ever* a good look?' Megan asked, curling her top lip. Mannequins lined the wall, wearing all of the company uniforms from the very beginning. The one she was referring to was from the 1980s, paisley print scarf and shoulder pads upon shoulder pads.

Chloe smiled, but she actually quite liked it, liked *all* of them. She imagined how glamorous the wearers must have felt at the time, when the styles were fashionable and the job even more enviable than it was today.

'Right, we can take three at a time,' a lady said as she came out from behind the long desk at the back of the room. 'Who wants to go first?'

The others were too busy taking photos to hear her so Chloe shot her hand up and stepped forward, pulling Megan with her. The lady beckoned them towards her, along with Maddie. 'Follow me, ladies.'

Through a door at the back of the room was another, bigger room. A younger girl smiled at them and stood up from where she was unpacking boxes at the back. Along the wall on the left were rails of clothes, and on the right a row of curtained changing cubicles. Chloe breathed in deeply, the smell of new fabric making her skin tingle.

'Size ten?' she asked, smiling at Megan. Megan nodded in reply. The girl walked quickly along the rail pulling out a selection of clothes on their hangers. 'You can try them on over there,' she said, handing them to her.

'Twelve?'

'In some things,' Chloe answered, wishing that there was a size eleven, as that was what she really was, she was sure.

'Try these,' the lady said as she handed her a skirt, blouse and jacket. 'We can always take them in if they're too big.'

'Thank you.' Chloe almost snatched them from her and headed quickly to her cubicle. Inside she pulled off her clothes, letting them drop to the floor in an untidy heap. She wriggled into the pencil skirt and buttoned the short-sleeved blouse with clumsy, nervous fingers. The jacket felt loose, but she didn't care, the silk lining felt good against her bare arms, and she fastened the three silver buttons, swishing the curtain back as she did so.

She turned to the full-length mirror on her right and studied the smart person who looked back at her. Something was missing though, she didn't quite feel the part, could have been working in an office in the businesslike suit. She fought the disappointment that she felt in her stomach.

'How does it feel?' The lady came over to her and pulled at the back of the jacket, immediately giving Chloe a waist. 'I think we can go a size down on this,' she said, walking off again and returning a moment later with another one. Once Chloe had changed the jacket she held up a scarf and placed it around her neck, tying it in a cravat at the front and tucking it into the open collar of the blouse. As she stepped away Chloe looked in the mirror again and this time her reflection caught her breath. It was amazing what difference a waist and a scarf could make. She LOVED it!

'You look amazing,' Megan said, appearing behind her.

'You too, and you,' Chloe said as Maddie came out too. They ALL looked amazing, like real air hostesses.

'Would you like photos?' the lady asked once she had finished tying Maddie's scarf.

'Yes please,' Chloe said without hesitation, 'I'll just grab my phone!'

****

You've just made me cry!

Chloe had known that the photo would do just that.

Do you like it? she asked, shamelessly digging for compliments.

You look absolutely amazing! Send it to your Dad!

Will do. Is he at work?

Yes. Are you home Friday night?

Yes! Crime Scene?

Sounds perfect. Love you, so proud xxx

Thanks! Love you too Mum xxx

Chapter Thirty-One

Bea

'Can I get a hot dessert please?' called Elaine as she squeezed behind her in the galley with a tray full of dirty plates.

Damn! Bea's stomach flipped as she realised that she had forgotten to put them in. *What was wrong with her today?* She was usually so alert and organized, knew exactly what she was doing, but today her mind seemed to be made up of cotton wool.

'They'll be a few minutes,' she said, hastily opening a cart and taking out the foil-wrapped puddings. She made room in an oven and turned them on high. Ten minutes would have to be long enough for them today, even if they usually had fifteen.

'Do you have any more clearing-in drawers?' the Flight Manager called from where she was relieving Elaine of her dirty tray at the opposite door.

'Um…' Bea looked along the carts, trying to guess which one had spare drawers in. 'Yes, here,' she said, relieved to find some in the first one she opened.

'Can I get two chickens please?' Scott called as he too walked into the galley with a tray of dirty starter plates.

'No problem,' Bea answered, fixing a smile on her face and hoping it masked the fact that she felt as if she was drowning. She took a deep breath, opening an oven and pulling out two chicken dinners. Was there anything else she had forgotten? she wondered as she plated up the meals.

'Here you go.' She handed him the plates, turned her back and took a deep breath to calm herself. *You've done galley plenty of times*, she told herself, *you know what you're doing.*

'Two veg and that's my mains done,' Elaine called.

'Mine are all done too,' Scott said, disappearing back into the aisle. Bea wiped her brow with the back of her gloved hand.

'Are you okay?' Julie, the Flight Manager was next to her now, a look of concern on her face.

'Yes, just a bit out of sorts.' Bea felt her voice wobble.

'Do you need to take a moment?'

'No, honestly I'm okay. I just have a lot on my mind, but nothing serious. Sorry, I was a bit of a disaster there,' she apologised as she plated the last two meals.

'Not at all,' Julie smiled kindly at her now. 'You did a great job, you just looked like you were miles away just then, that was all.'

'Ah, yes, I probably was.' She'd felt as if her brain had been miles away since the Singapore trip, going around and around in circles most of the time. She'd shown the pictures to at least a dozen people at check-in this morning, but nobody had been in the company for long enough to be able to tell her anything. It was starting to make her feel a bit unhinged if she were honest, and she didn't like it.

'Everything okay out here?' The other half of her problem appeared in the galley, the other person that was using up space in her brain. She had only seen Andre in passing this morning, the pilots checking in just after them. When they boarded he had winked at her across the aisle as he walked to the flight deck, but there was always someone around and they were yet to speak properly.

'All good, do you want some dinner, we've almost finished?' Julie asked.

'Sounds good,' he grinned and rubbed his stomach. Bea concentrated on tidying the galley side and not looking at him. They had agreed not to let on to the crew about them, or rather Andre had agreed when Bea had insisted. She wasn't ready to risk people knowing, only to fly with them six months later and have to explain how it hadn't worked out. Also, she wasn't sure that she knew him well enough yet... how did she know that she wasn't one of many? Somehow, deep down, she felt that he was honest, but she wasn't quite ready to leave herself too open just yet.

'I'll grab you a menu,' Julie said and left the galley.

'Hey.' Bea felt his hand on her shoulder and she turned around, looking up into his lovely face. They were finally alone for a moment. 'How about a show tonight? My treat?'

'That sounds good,' she smiled. It sounded perfect in fact, losing her mind to a Broadway show, getting off the Dad-roundabout for a few hours. She had expected him to want them to go out drinking, for her to have to be fun and interesting... and yet it was as though he could read her, know exactly what she needed. She felt relieved of a burden that she hadn't even realised she was carrying.

'Great.' He moved his hand as Julie came back in and handed him a blue folded menu. 'I'll see what el Capitano wants first,' he said, holding it up and heading back to the flight deck door.

'He's a nice guy,' Julie said as he closed the door behind him.

'Yes, he is,' agreed Bea as she busied herself again.

'Handsome too,' Julie added, still looking at the door.

Bea didn't look up, just nodded, acknowledging the small dig of defensiveness that she felt and pushing it quickly aside. Did Julie fancy him, or was she onto them? Did it matter either way?

'I don't suppose the coffee machine is working for a cappuccino?' Scott appeared behind them.

'What do you think?' Bea let out a dry laugh. The espresso machine was *always* broken.

'Nope,' he rolled his eyes. 'Always worth an ask, you just never know. White coffee will have to do then.'

'White coffee coming up.' She felt suddenly better, her mind calm and clear once again since Andre had touched her shoulder. He really was what she needed right now.

Chapter Thirty-Two

Paul: What are we doing tomorrow guys? What is HF when it's at home?

Megan: Human Factors

Paul: cheers for the detailed explanation Luv

Megan: LOL, sorry, it's just stuff about communication and things that affect you, could be anything really, they used to change it every year at my last airline.

Paul: Oh okay, we'll wait and see then. No exam though, right?

Megan: Right.

Paul: Ace. Who's up for the pub then?

Sophie: Did someone say pub? Count me in, just dropped all the scumbags stuff off at his door and I'm sure there was a girl in there! Fuming!

Megan: Better angry than upset girl. Count me in too, might get dinner there, I could do with a decent meal!

Jen: Guys if you're on TikTok drop your names here and I'll tag you... this video is the best, cracking myself up!

'Do you fancy coming to the farm this weekend?'

Chloe looked up from her salad at Megan, who was sitting on her left. They were in the canteen, at their usual table. 'I would have loved that, but I've already promised Mum I'll go home,' she said sadly. It was too late to cancel now, her mum would have been planning meals and looking forward to her getting there tomorrow since she had confirmed that she would be.

'Ah that's a shame, another time.'

'Definitely,' she nodded hard. 'Next weekend?'

'Straight after our wings?'

'Good point.' Chloe thought about it. Yes, that probably wouldn't be a great idea as her family would all be coming along to the ceremony to see her graduate and they would probably expect to celebrate with her afterwards too. 'Maybe not,' she said. 'The weekend after?'

'I'm flying then.'

'Oh, me too,' Chloe said, smiling at the realisation that her first flight was so soon. She reached into her bag for her folded-up roster, determined to get a weekend at the farm booked in before the opportunity was gone. 'The seventeenth?'

Megan looked thoughtful for a moment. 'Yep,' she said slowly. 'That could work, I'm pretty sure I have a flight on the nineteenth so I'm off that weekend... I'll double-check later when I have my roster.'

'Fabulous,' Chloe said, feeling tingly inside at the thought of so many good things to look forward to.

'Time to go back.' Paul's chair scraped loudly across the floor as he stood up.

Chloe looked at her watch, and saw that the thirty minutes had flown by. 'Crikey,' she said as she put the lid back on her salad and stuffed it back into her bag. 'That went quickly.'

In the classroom the tables had been stacked at the back and chairs were set in small circles around flip pads on easels. A man in casual slacks and shirt welcomed them in. 'Don't look scared,' he said as they came to a halt in the door behind Paul. 'Sit anywhere you like, just leave one chair spare at each station for one of the pilots who will be joining us shortly.'

Megan, Paul and Chloe stayed close to each other and headed to the station at the back. Within a couple of minutes the door opened again and a small group of older men came in, all holding coffee mugs and seeming very relaxed about being there. Chloe recognized one as the pilot that had come to the house to see Bea and was relieved when he sat in a different group. She felt inexplicably embarrassed about talking to pilots, let alone one that was dating her housemate. She wondered what could be so important that they were being dragged away from the much more important things they must have to do, to spend time with trainee cabin crew.

'Right,' the man at the front clapped his hands together and the chatter died down. 'Now that we are all here, let me introduce myself. My name is Mike and I'll be taking you today for Human Factors training.' He paused and looked slowly around. 'Now, I know many of you haven't flown before, and might be wondering what this is all about, so I'm going to start off with a few short videos that will explain to you just why we need to get together, just like this once a year...' He walked over to the door and dimmed the lights on the switch. A picture of a crashed plane came up on the screen at the front, and the room fell completely silent.

Chloe was glad that the room was dark as they watched the re-enactment of what had happened to the doomed flight at the start, the real voices of the pilots playing over the sound. Over three videos they watched as three planes crashed and countless lives were lost, unnecessarily.

She dabbed the tears from the corner of her eyes as the final scene finished and Mike turned the lights back up. Turning to Megan, she laughed at her friend's wet face, glad that she wasn't alone. Even the pilots looked sombre.

'So, in your groups, if you can write down some of the reasons why you think Human Factors may be important,' Mike said to the silent room.

The pilot who had by default ended up next to the flip chart picked up the marker pen and smiled at them. He was younger than her dad, maybe in his late thirties, quite short with a round, friendly face. 'Who wants to go first then?' he asked.

'Better communication between pilots and crew,' said Paul.

They waited as he wrote it down, with handwriting that reminded Chloe of her old maths teacher – almost illegible.

'Understanding our limitations,' said Megan.

'Understanding how important our knowledge and drills are,' Chloe added, making a mental note to make sure she was 100% sure which engine was which number when she got out on line.

Mike appeared behind them. 'Yes, brilliant,' he said. 'That top one,' he spoke louder and addressed the whole room. 'Better communication between pilots and crew. In 1991 when that first crash happened, a lot of pilots had a God-complex,' there was a knowing snigger from the pilots in the room, 'and so most crew would have been nervous to approach them, let alone correct them on anything. We needed to get away from that, and from every incident that happens we try to learn something that might stop it happening again. If that crewmember hadn't presumed that the captain was right and he was wrong, or had been brave enough to check with him, the outcome could have been very different. Do we all agree?' They all nodded their heads, some muttered 'yes.' Chloe could understand it though, how he would have been intimidated, she felt it now even when they were so outnumbered in the room. 'Now we like to think the divide has been broken down, that we are all very much on the same team.'

Mike walked over to the next group. 'I'm Russ and I don't have a God-complex, I promise,' their pilot put up his hand to them and smiled.

'That's not what I heard,' teased Megan. Russ's face dropped and he looked genuinely worried. 'Kidding,' Megan laughed. Chloe felt bad for him, he seemed like a nice guy.

'Phew,' he said, wiping pretend sweat from his brow.

The afternoon session turned out to be quite fun, and as it went on Chloe felt her levels of intimidation subside. They, the pilots, really were just like them, but maybe just a bit smarter than her and with a much higher level of responsibility. She quietly watched Bea's date as he blended in with everyone in his group; he was funny and self-deprecating, and she made a note to tell Bea that she approved. At the end she was sorry to see the pilots leave, having quite enjoyed their company.

Ben shook hands with Mike as they handed over at the door. 'Right, Group 352, how did you all find that?'

'Well, apart from the scary crashes it was good,' said Maddie.

'Yes, hard to watch, hey?' They all nodded. 'But it was good for you to spend some time with the pilots, and I hope you will take something away from it.' He walked over to the desk and picked up some papers. 'Before you go, I just want to give you all this telephone list. It's got every department you could ever want to speak to on there, and all of their extensions. So store them in your phones, especially Crew Scheduling and the Medical number, in case you should ever need medical help downroute.' He walked around and handed them all a sheet.

Chloe looked at the list, and down to Crew Scheduling. Landline numbers always seemed slightly alien to her, they didn't even have one at home. She noticed the number started with 01293; she'd seen it somewhere before, but where? She thought hard. She didn't know anyone around here, did she?

'Coming, Chlo?' Megan prodded her, and immediately jogged her memory. The weekend at the farm, the two missed calls!

'Yes,' she said, grabbing her coat from the back of her seat and following her out. She was distracted, opening her phone and going into her missed calls. The numbers matched, both had come from Crew Scheduling. But why? Why would they have been calling her?

Kathryn.

It must have been Kathryn, she realised... but she had seen her since and she'd not said anything?

'Chlo, you're miles away,' Megan laughed.

'Oh. Sorry. Yes,' she stuttered. 'Sorry, I was just trying to work something out.'

'We said we are going to grab some dinner at the pub, are you coming. Curry and a pint night?'

Chloe folded the piece of paper and put it in her bag. 'Yes. Yes, I am,' she said definitely. No exams tomorrow, and only six more days with her friends, she was definitely going to the pub for dinner. She made a mental note to ask Kathryn about the call when she saw her next, although whatever it was couldn't have been that important if she hadn't brought it up since. Could it?

Chapter Thirty-Three

Jade: Is anyone else around this weekend?

Paul: Sorry, got to go back up to Manny and see Jo ;)

Megan: Ahhhhh Pauly is in love :)

Paul: Steady on, I never said that!

Megan: Pulling your leg, say hi to her from us! Sorry Jade, brother needs me on the farm, but I'll be back Sunday night.

Jen: I'm heading home too... need to get some washing done.

Chloe: And me, sorry Jade x

Darren: And me, it's like an exodus!

Sophie: I'm around but I picked up some shifts so working both evenings, need to get some money££

Jade: Well that made my mind up then, I'm going home for a bit of my mum's cooking, see you all Sunday eve if you're around. Crew room for a catch up?

Megan: Of course. Reckon I'll be back at the hotel about 8 xxx

'...and then you push down on the fingers...'

'Ow!' Zac yelped as she pushed his hand over, fingers into his palm. She kept the pressure on the back of his wrist as she nudged him towards the dining table.

'Seriously, that hurts,' he protested. 'You can stop now.'

Chloe wasn't done yet though, she had waited years to be the stronger sibling and he had outright challenged her. 'There,' she said as she pushed him down onto the seat. He snatched his hand away from her and rubbed it, his face red and unamused. Chloe stood back, hands on her hips and threw her head back in laughter.

'Stop bullying your brother,' her mum said as she came in carrying a basket full of clean laundry to fold, setting it down on the table.

'He said I wouldn't be able to restrain him, so I was just showing him he was wrong.'

'Alright, little sis, so you're not just going to be a waitress in the sky, you'll make a good bouncer too.' Zac shook his hand out.

'And nurse, don't forget nurse...'

'And nurse,' Zac nodded submissively.

'Firefighter,' she prompted him, although she hadn't done that training yet, but he didn't need to know.

'Firefighter.'

'And I'll save your ass if the plane crashes.'

'Jeez, my little sister is a badass,' he said, eyebrows raised in amusement.

'And don't forget it,' Chloe laughed. She joined her mum at the table and started to fold the washing alongside her.

'So what time is your wings next Friday?' her mum asked.

'Six, will Dad be able to make it?'

'Yes, he's taken the night off.'

Chloe smiled; he always worked Friday nights, but it wouldn't have been the same without him there.

'And you, little sissy, I mean brother?'

Zac looked up from his phone. 'Well I was planning on it, but any more of that and I won't be.'

Chloe stuck her tongue out at him playfully. 'Perfect.' She couldn't believe how quickly the time had gone, and that in just a week she would be a certified air hostess, cabin crew, flight attendant, trolley dolly or whatever else you wanted to call her, she would accept any of those titles. She would be licensed to fly, and she would be travelling the world at somebody else's expense. A tingle of excitement ran through her, making her shudder. 'I'm so excited,' she said, her voice coming out as a squeak.

Her mum put her arm around her and squeezed her. 'I'm so proud of you,' she said.

Chloe turned and hugged her. 'I wouldn't have done it without you, Mum. Thank you.' It was true, if her mum hadn't shown her the advert she would probably have still been working at the supermarket deciding what she wanted to do with her life, while moping about

Lucas. As it was she had barely given him a thought since she started training, and now she couldn't imagine him in her future at all. When she thought about her future it was all about her, and it felt good.

'Right, that's that done,' her mum said, patting her on the back as she pulled away. 'You get the hot chocolates sorted while I pop this away quickly. Are you joining us, Zac?'

'What for?'

'*Crime Scene*, of course.'

'Er. No,' he said, getting up from the table. 'I have a date with my Xbox.'

'Not with your girlfriend?' Chloe asked.

'No, she's working tonight so I thought I'd stay home.'

'Because she won't let him take his Xbox to her place,' her mum called back from the stairs, where she had headed with the folded clothes.

'I don't blame her,' said Chloe, split between admiration that she was so firm, and concern that her brother might end up a little submissive.

'When we get somewhere together I'll put my foot down, don't you worry.'

'I'm sure you will, brother dear,' she patted him on the back, 'I'm sure you will.'

He shoved her gently out of the way as he headed off to his room. 'You just go and watch your old people's programmes, sister dear.'

'Ouch, that hurt.' Chloe put a hand on her chest and laughed. She walked over to the kettle and flicked it on, leaning backwards to stretch out her back. Her hands slid down past her back pocket and she felt a small lump on one side. Her stomach dropped. 'Oh, crap,' she said aloud, pulling out the garage key. She had totally forgotten to leave it out for Bea. She thought hard for a moment, breathing out loudly when she remembered that she had taken Bea's number just the other day. She looked around for her phone, seeing it on the table.

Hey, she texted. *I completely forgot to leave the garage key out. What time are you planning on coming back Sunday? I'll make sure I'm back, and give you a hand with the stuff too xxx*

A text came back before she had finished making the drinks.

No problem. Should be there about three, so we have time before dark. Sorry you have to come back early.

My own fault! See you then xxx

'Ready?' Her mum appeared, taking the two mugs from the side.

'Right behind you, just getting the biscuits.'

Chapter Thirty-Four

Bea

Bea felt detached from everything that was going on around her, sitting on the sofa in the conservatory watching everyone party while she was consumed by the overwhelming need to tell her mum what she had found out. She knew that she couldn't though, that she really, *really* couldn't do that right now, if ever. The subject of her biological dad had been off the cards since the day she had found out. There had been nothing to talk about after that, the facts were as they were and she hadn't wanted, when pushed, to go any further into their time before, even when Bea had told her that she had got a job at the same airline as he had flown for… even then the news had just seemed to wash over her, as if it didn't matter, but Bea was sure that it must have.

'Bea, can you give me a hand?' her mum called from the far end of the open plan kitchen diner.

She put her prosecco down on the side table. 'Coming.' Bea scanned the room for her sisters; Sophie had gone upstairs to get little Jacob to sleep a while ago now, but Kayla and her latest boyfriend Mike were nowhere to be seen. They weren't drinkers though, and a kitchen full of drunk 'adults', as she still thought of her aunts and uncles despite being a grownup herself now, had probably driven them to the sanctuary of the living room.

'Can you just pop these on the table, love.' Her mum handed her a tray of canapes.

'They might need something a bit more substantial.' Bea nodded towards Aunty Bev and Uncle Mike, who were dancing erratically to the music.

'Your bloody father and his punch, stay away from it,' her mum laughed and looked upwards to heaven.

'Oh don't you worry, I'm staying firmly away,' Bea reassured her. She had seen the glint in her dad's eye when he had proclaimed his *'great idea'* about how to use up all the part-empty bottles of booze that weren't worth 'lugging all the way to Portugal'. She could handle her booze, but she wasn't stupid.

'Bea, have some punch,' he called right on cue as she passed him with the tray.

'Okay, Dad,' she said, putting the tray down. She knew better than to say no, she'd played this game before. He beamed as he passed her the plastic cup of rocket fuel. She took a tiny sip, feeling the burn immediately on her throat.

'Mmmm,' she said, raising her eyebrows. 'That's good,' she lied, touched by how proud he looked with himself. 'Cheers.'

'I'm gonna miss this house,' he slurred, dropping a heavy arm on her shoulder and looking wistfully around the room.

'Me too.' Bea wished so much that they weren't going.

'But we aren't far away.'

'I know.' She looked up and smiled at him, the man who had brought her up as his own for all of these years. She had never felt different to her sisters, he never treated her any differently to them, in fact she had always felt like the favourite if she were honest. 'Love you, Dad.'

His lip quivered and he squeezed her shoulder. 'I love you too, my girl,' he said and kissed the top of her head.

Bea sucked in a sharp breath and blinked to stop the stinging at the back of her eyes. What was she thinking these past weeks? Why was she so desperate to find out about her biological dad when her *real* dad, Brian O'Neill, was right here, had always been right here by her side? For weeks she had been so focused on Anthony McGhee that she had almost forgotten that she already had the best dad in the world. 'Cheers, Dad.' She held up her glass.

'Cheers.' He knocked her cup with his and they both sipped their punch together, screwing up their faces immediately after.

'Rough.' Bea pulled her lips into a thin smile.

'Yep,' agreed her dad, making them both laugh before they drank some more.

'Don't mind me, you two just get drunk while I do all the work,' her mum teased as she carried another tray past them.

'We won't,' they said together, always united in amusement at her martyrdom. She rolled her eyes at them, a smile on her face.

Bea waited a moment before turning to give her dad a hug, sneakily putting her cup down on the side behind him. 'I'm going to help Mum,' she said.

'You always were a good girl,' he said, squeezing her tight before letting her go. 'Don't forget your punch,' he called after her, her cup in his hand. He raised his eyebrows knowingly.

'I'll come back for it,' she grinned, *in a couple of hours*.

Chapter Thirty-Five

Paul: Whoop whoop, one week to go!! Just heading back down now, see yous all tonight!

Sophie: Anyone mind if I join you in the crew room?

Jade: More the merrier, bring wine!

Megan: Second that. Be heading off soon. Safe travels everyone, hope the traffic is kind to those of you driving, and be careful on those roads, it's slippery out there.

Liv: Sure you're not a mum like me Megan?!

Megan: Ha!

Liv: Just dishing up the roast, see you in the morning.

Paul: Maybe we should all go to Liv's?

Megan: Good idea!

Liv: Like I would give you my address LOL

Paul: I have means... listen out for me knocking the door in five hours!

Liv: Oh heck :))))

Chloe waved her mum off from the end of the drive and waited a moment. It was just before three and there was no sign of them yet, but it was too cold just to stand here waiting. She picked up her bag and walked up to the house, Megan was right about the icy ground and she trod carefully, opening the front door and dropping the bag just inside before closing it again. It was a nice day, the sun was shining, but the December temperatures were still struggling to get above freezing. She was dressed for it though, hat and gloves on ready for some work in the fresh air.

She walked over to the garage, pulled open the big metal door and stood back, deciding where to start first with the sea of boxes. Without knowing what exactly Bea was coming with it was hard to tell how many she would need to move, but she was sure that she had mentioned 'furniture,' and that probably meant something sizeable. She pulled the bike outside and then one by one lifted the boxes that were behind it, stacking them in a pile at the far end. The first couple were so light she wondered if they even had anything in them, but as she got lower down they got much, much heavier.

She crouched down, remembering what she had been taught about manual handling, trying to use her legs to lift the weight, not twisting her body. Slowly she made an opening, but it was barely enough for a person to get through, and she moved along. Another stack and she felt warm with the exertion; she pulled down the zip of her jacket just slightly to let the air onto her neck. There was still no sign of Bea.

Chloe stood and tried to decide what to do. Should she move more, or wait, just in case it wasn't necessary? She stepped forward and peered into the garage, and then another step, and another, until she was inside.

Daylight shone through the gap in the boxes along one side of the room, dust dancing in its light. The far end and the other side were still quite dark, but her eyes adjusted quickly and slowly she could make out some of the things around her. All along the right-hand wall, in the light, was some kind of workbench with tools hanging above it. Others lay on it as if they had only just been put there, an offcut of wood still held in the vice at the end. Behind it were drawers upon drawers of screws and such like.

She turned to the other side, where sheets partly covered a huge wooden wardrobe, and more boxes sat haphazardly against it. An old floor lamp with a yellow tasselled shade that was disintegrating stood over a wooden child's kart. Chloe pushed it with her toe and it rolled forward, its front wheels moving from side to side as it went. She looked back at the workbench, wondering if it had been made there, by whoever had worked on it. An open box to the side showed a collection of gardening magazines, and she picked the top one up, squinting in the dim light to read the front… it was dated 1991, before she was born.

Curiosity tempted her further back, where the room was darker still. The light didn't quite reach back here, and she only had the tiny amount that could penetrate the cobwebs on the far window to show her the way. She watched her warm breath send a thin white fog wisping away until it was swallowed up by the dark.

Surely there must have been a light in here once? Where would be the most likely place for a switch? she wondered. A thought came to her and she walked carefully over to where you could just make out the wooden door, her hands sweeping side to side in front of her in case she walked into something. She wished that she had her phone for its torch, but it was in her bag inside the house, no good to her right now. Reaching the door, she ran her fingers over the wall slowly until she felt what she was hoping to find.

'Bingo!' She flicked the switch and fluorescent light flooded the room.

Chloe inhaled sharply, catching her breath as she took it all in; she felt as if she had just stepped, uninvited, into somebody else's life. So many things, so many memories, for someone, and she stood frozen to the spot, looking from one thing to the next, moving just her head, arms crossed across her chest; Bikes, three of them, a big one, a medium one with a basket on the front, and a child's one. A tricycle. There was a sewing machine on a wooden table, clothes in plastic wrappers hung on a rail. Old pictures and photo frames were stacked upright, facing the wall so that she couldn't see their subjects, but she was sure that they would have hung in the house once. Chloe's heart started to beat faster. She had an overwhelming feeling that she didn't have the right to be there, that she wasn't allowed.

The sound of a car pulling onto the driveway worked to snap her back into reality and she walked quickly outside to meet Bea, trying to slow down her breathing as she did so.

'Hey,' Bea waved as she got out of the passenger seat of the small white van.

'Careful,' warned Chloe. 'It's a bit slippery out here.'

A man with a friendly face smiled at her and gave a wave as he walked around and opened the vehicle's back door. 'Thanks,' said Bea. 'This is my dad. Dad, this is Chloe.'

'Nice to meet you, Chloe,' he called out.

'You too.' Chloe followed Bea and watched as her dad started to unload their cargo.

'Is there much space in there?' Bea asked.

'Some, but we might need to clear an area,' Chloe replied, noting that the van was quite full. 'I'll give you a hand.'

'You're amazing, we'll start making room while you unload, Dad.'

'Right you are,' he replied, staggering backwards under the weight of a glass-topped coffee table.

Back in the garage Chloe watched as Bea took straight away to picking things up and moving them around. 'Do you not find it, you know, creepy in here?'

'No. It's just a load of old stuff,' Bea answered without turning around. 'I think if we move some of this right to the back we'll make enough room.'

Chloe regarded the back wall for the first time. On the left it was literally piled to the ceiling with boxes of all shapes and sizes, with none of the uniformity of the ones at the front. To the right was a tall filing cabinet, and next to that a collection of gardening equipment; lawnmower, strimmer, piles of pots, and tools hanging on the wall behind, next to the window.

Bea worked quickly, passing Chloe with the largest of the bikes, which squeaked as it was dragged across the concrete floor on its flat tyres. She leaned it up against the things at the back and headed straight back for the others. Chloe looked around, her eyes falling on an old armchair with worn fabric on its arms and a sunken cushion. She picked it up, surprised to find that it was quite light, and moved it to the back too. Next a box with 'KITCHEN' written in capital letters on its top.

'Where am I putting this, girls?'

'Over here,' Bea called her dad forward. In no time at all they had cleared a sizeable space on the floor.

'Crikey, bit of a time warp in here,' he said, putting two old suitcases down at the side of the space. He walked over to the workbench, running his fingers over its well-worn surfaces.

'Uh-huh,' agreed Chloe with a nod of her head. 'It certainly is.'

Bea, it seemed, had none of their sensitivity. 'Can someone give me a hand with the table?' she called from the van.

'Coming,' Chloe called back, leaving her dad to admire the tools for a moment longer.

In no time the van was empty, and the garage fuller than it had already been.

'That's it, thank you so much, both of you.' Bea put an arm around each of them as they started to put the boxes back along the front.

'Ah, the light,' Chloe said, suddenly noticing that it was still on. She squeezed through the remaining gap and walked carefully over to switch it off. It was getting dark outside now, and with the boxes blocking most of the door she was in almost total darkness. She shuffled slowly back, knocking her shin on something, and then the other. 'Damn,' she cursed.

'You okay?' asked Bea.

'I'll live,' Chloe said as she reached outside, leaning over to rub her legs. 'I'm glad I don't need to go back in there for a while though. Right, if you don't need me I'll be off. Bea, can you leave the key in the kitchen so I can get the bike out in the morning?'

'Sure,' Bea answered.

'Nice to meet you, Bea's dad.'

'You too, love,' he said. 'So,' he turned to Bea, 'does the owner ever come back for any of the stuff in there?'

Bea shook her head. 'I hope not,' she said. 'He might not be too pleased about my things being there.'

'Well it's not hurting him, I'm sure he'd be okay,' said her dad.

'Mmm,' said Bea, quickly changing the subject. She hadn't told her dad that the agent had come back with a flat 'no' when she had asked if she could use the garage. 'What time is your flight Sunday?'

'Early, why?'

'Nothing, I was just hoping to catch Mum before you go, that's all,' she said. 'I'll give her a call later.'

'Right you are. Anything else you need me to do while I'm here?'

Bea shook her head sadly. 'What will I do when you're in another country?'

'You'll save a big list up for when I come back, I'm sure,' he smiled, wrapping her in his arms.

Chapter Thirty-Six

Maddie: Megan, what is this smoke training like? I've just watched the video and now I'm thinking of calling in sick!

Megan: I won't lie, it's not nice babe, but it's got to be done, so don't call in sick. Just think of it as five minutes of your life. Once it's done that's it for three years. Jen, that wings video, I have such a RBF LOL

Maddie: Wish I hadn't watched it this morning. Okay, putting my big girl's pants on. Are we meeting downstairs?

Jen: You do not Megs! I'm telling you it's gonna go viral!

Paul: I'm down already.

Megan: Of course you are! Those things will kill you Paul.

Paul: I know, I'll give up after training, promise. Am I in the video? I better be!

Jen: Yep, stood outside having a fag... it's how we will all remember you haha

Paul: Not for my good looks and lightening wit?

Jen: Oh yeah, that too! Sorry Paul, love you really xxx

'I don't think I can do this.' Maddie turned around to Chloe, panic in her eyes. Chloe didn't know how to help her, she was concentrating so hard on keeping herself calm, her own anxiety that had haunted her teens threatening to come back after staying at bay for so long. She put her arm around her nonetheless and decided not to mention that she was struggling too.

'It'll be fine, we'll get through it together.' She counted back in the line, working out that it would be her, Maddie, Sophie and Megan going into the smoke- filled cabin together. Going in and putting the fires out had been easy enough, they were controlled and she hadn't been in the least bit worried. When it had been her turn smoke had appeared in the hat rack, and so she had known to open it slowly and squirt her extinguisher inside before closing it again. Others had got seat fires, toilet fire and entertainment, but the drills were easy to remember and the instructors had been there with them. Now though, as they all stood looking through the window, the mock cabin filled up quickly with dense smoke and all conversation subsided.

'Right, first four, smoke hoods on,' Ben called from where he was stationed at the right-hand end of the metal structure.

The first four shuffled forward like prisoners in their oversized navy boiler suits. Oversized on all except Paul that was, whose suit barely skimmed his ankles. Reaching Ben, they stood in an arc and each held out their hood, shaking it until the rubber formed a dome, and then pushed their heads through the tight rubber seal. They reminded Chloe of astronauts now, with their silver hoods and wide, clear visors.

Chloe couldn't hear what Ben was saying, but along with the others she watched as Paul stepped in front and the others formed a line behind him, each with their right arm on the person's shoulder in front. They all copied him as he demonstrated walking forward waving his arm from side to side in front of him.

Finally, Ben opened the door, letting out some of the smoke... and then they were gone, Paul leading them in to find the fire that they had been tasked with putting out.

Through the window she could just make out her classmates, moving forward slowly, somebody's left arm coming close to the window, making a sweeping motion as it checked for obstacles. It reminded Chloe of herself in the dark of the garage yesterday; she wished she had done this training beforehand, it might have saved her a few bruises.

'Don't forget to check down low,' Ben called in to them.

'BCF to row forty four,' someone called.

'Here.' Chloe recognised Paul's voice.

'I'm testing it now.' There was a short pause. 'Discharging at the flames.'

'Is it out?' asked Ben.

'Yes, it's out,' Paul shouted back.

'So what will you do now?'

Another voice. 'Dampen it down.'

'Brilliant,' said Ben with a clap of his hands. 'Stunning work, you guys, you can make your way out now.'

The four firefighters emerged in a cloud of smoke from the door at the other end. They each pulled their smoke hoods off quickly, relief on their faces as they took deep breaths.

'Give them a wipe and pass them to the next four,' Gemma called after them.

The four in front had already gone and Paul walked over, handing his hood to Maddie.

'Gee, thanks. How was it?'

'It was fun,' said Paul. Chloe looked at the faces of the others. They all just looked glad it was over, not as if they had been having fun.

'It was awful,' said someone else, handing hers to Chloe.

'I really, *really* don't think I can do it,' Maddie said quietly.

'Babe, you'll be fine.' Megan stepped forward and put her arm on her shoulder, looking her straight in the eye. 'I'll lead, just stay behind me and keep talking. Okay?'

Maddie nodded, and Chloe thought she might cry. 'Feel the fear and do it anyway,' she said, as much for her own benefit as Maddie's. It was what her dad had always said to her when she wobbled and said she couldn't do something. He taught her *never* to let her anxiety take control, that she was the one who controlled *it.*

When their time came Chloe pushed her head, bun and all, through the rubber neck seal, emerging into the smoke hood with stray hairs pulled across her face. She tried to reach inside and move them, with little success. She took a deep breath, but there didn't seem enough air in the hood to fill her lungs and she pulled the neck seal back to let some more in. She knew that in reality they would have had oxygen in them, but the classroom ones didn't work like that.

'Remember, you're a team,' Ben said, as he opened the door for them.

They formed their line and shuffled slowly inside. Chloe could hear her own breathing and feel the pulse in her head. She could feel Jen's hand on her shoulder and gave Maddie a gentle pat on hers as they took one small step at a time. In her mind she transported herself back to the sofa at home, watching TV with her mum. It was a technique she had learned years ago to calm herself, taking herself off to somewhere she was at her most relaxed. On the TV she could see the investigator flicking through a big phone book trying to find someone's address. It wasn't the episode they had watched at the weekend, but it was familiar, one they had seen on repeat a few times.

'Everyone okay?' Megan's voice sounded muffled. A noise made Chloe turn and she saw a flashing red light behind her, above the toilet door.

'Toilet fire,' she said loudly so that they all heard, her heart rate rising once again.

'I'll get the extinguisher,' Jen called, letting go of Chloe's shoulder and leaning down to remove it from the bulkhead just in front of the toilet.

'You found it so you fight it, Chlo,' Megan said. Chloe was so grateful for Megan's calm direction as the hood and the smoke were making her increasingly claustrophobic. She felt the cold, hard extinguisher against her hand as Jen passed it to her.

'Feeling the door with the back of my hand,' she said aloud. The drill was in her head now, as if she was reading it from the page. She knelt down, relieved that the smoke was thinner near the floor and she could see much better. 'Kneeling down and cracking the door open. Discharging extinguisher.' She flipped up the catch and squeezed the trigger hard until all of its contents had been emptied. 'Closing door.'

'Right, waiting for thirty seconds,' said Megan. 'Count with me, Maddie.'

'...twenty-seven, twenty-eight, twenty-nine, thirty,' the four voices counted together. Chloe could hear the trembling in Maddie's voice and feel it in her own.

Chloe pushed the door open now. The light was on inside and most of the smoke had gone. She checked all of the stowages for the source of the pretend fire. The thin smoke still coming from the waste bin told her that it had come from there.

'So what are you going to do now?' Ben's voice came over the speaker.

'We are going to dampen it down,' answered Megan on behalf of them all.

'Well done, team, you can come on out now.'

In the fresh air Chloe didn't care about her hair as she wrenched the hood off. Only Megan was smiling, and Maddie was visibly shaking.

'You did it, girl.' Megan squeezed Maddie, evoking a small smile. 'We aren't losing anyone else.'

'No, we're not,' said Sophie. 'That was pretty horrendous though, I'm glad we don't have to do it again for three years.'

'I might have to take a Valium next time,' said Maddie.

'Whatever it takes,' Megan laughed. 'Are you okay, Chlo?'

'Yes, yes,' Chloe said with a big smile, bringing herself back from a million miles away. The anxiety and tension of the exercise had completely gone and now she was buzzing with excitement at what had just occurred to her...

Chapter Thirty-Seven

Darren: Four more days guys!

Sophie: And in uniform from tomorrow. This shit is getting reaaaal!

Darren: Does anyone mind if I write a speech for the Wings?

Rasia: I think that would be lovely Darren :)

Liv: Oh Darren, what a lovely thought xxx

Paul: Only if you say nice things buddy, I feel a bit bullied lately

Megan: Oh Pauly :(

Paul: Only joking you melt LOL

Megan: Phew, I thought you had feelings for a minute there!

Paul: See what I mean!

Liv: I'll pick up the wine and thank you cards tonight, I'm doing the food shop anyway. Will let you know how much each it comes to tomorrow x

Megan: Thanks for sorting that Liv xxx

Jen: Video almost done, I just want to get a bit of us all in uniform tomorrow to finish it off. It looks great though!

Sophie: I've seen other groups have cupcakes with their names on. Do Osprey provide them?

Jade: Apparently not, I asked someone on the week before us. I'll try and find out where they got them done and see if we can get some last minute.

Megan: As long as there is champagne then we are good :)

Jade: Second that. Cheers!

Darren: I might just read out our conversation on here LOL

Megan: Then everyone would be asleep and we wouldn't be getting out until next year!!

Jade: And we'd probably not get our wings hahahah

'Hey,' Chloe said as Kathryn came in the back door.

'Oh, hi,' she said, looking at the floor as she closed the door and locked it.

Chloe took her eyes off of her stir-fry for a moment and searched for something to say. *Did you forget your key?* wasn't going to work, as she was clearly in her pyjamas and dressing gown, but she didn't feel that she could ask her outright what on earth she had been doing outside in the cold and dark either. She waited and watched as she wiped her slippers on the mat. 'Cold out?'

'Uh-huh.' She gave Chloe a small smile and passed behind her. 'I just needed a bit of fresh air,' she said, keeping her head down as she left the room and headed upstairs.

Chloe shook her head, turning back to her dinner. *Fresh air*, she thought, amused; *freezing cold fresh air in your pyjamas.* She smirked at her housemate's likeable weirdness, deciding to ask her another day if it was her that had phoned her from crewing, as she didn't seem very talkative tonight.

In her room after her dinner Chloe took a moment to admire the new uniform that hung on the back of her door, smoothing down the material. Tomorrow was the first day that they got to wear it, and she couldn't wait. Any other night and she might have been trying it on, giving it a little more attention, but she had things to do that were more important right now.

She sat on her bed and propped her iPad up on her knees. Her mind had been so distracted from the moment it had hit her, and now that she was finally here in her room, alone, she felt her skin tingle with excitement. She took two deep breaths to slow down her brain and set to work.

Half an hour of searching and a small subscription fee later she was there, at the place that she knew existed but hadn't been sure she would find… she was in the online archives of the BT phonebook. It was something she had seen so many times on those programmes where people tried to trace their ancestors, but when she had seen it in her mind earlier, it was as if she was being sent a message, as though someone had just given her a hard shove in the right direction for solving Bea's mystery.

The telephone book had been around for over a century, before her time indeed, but not by much. Her mum remembered it well and told her so every time it came up on the TV. Now though they were no longer fat paper books that listed the names and addresses of all and sundry, and they were confined to museums and digital archives... the latter of which was now in front of her, inviting her to explore it.

She read the introduction, taking note of the fact that the records were only public up until 1984, hoping that this was recent enough to shed even a glimmer of light on her investigation. If Anthony McGhee had lived locally in 1984 she was determined to find out where, to give even the smallest amount of information to Bea as her parting gift to her friend. She typed 'Crawley' into the small search box at the top.

Searchword not found

Hmmph

The website was basic, and she struggled to find the right terms. Her fingers worked quickly to keep up with her mind, trying keyword after keyword until she finally found what she was looking for... a sense of jubilation as she followed one link after another to reach it.

On the screen now was the telephone directory for Crawley dated 1984. She paused on the front cover for a moment, imagining it as a real book, with its thousand-plus pages, and felt as if she was stepping back so much further than thirty-nine years in time. She scrolled down, scanning the first few pages as she did so, noting the adverts for things that had changed so much. The pages moved quicker and quicker and she watched as the Cs merged into Ds, then E, F, Gs, until surnames beginning with M appeared. She slowed down, past those that began with Ma until she reached Mc… and now she leaned in close in case she missed it.

McGhee! There it was! Chloe jolted up, focussing hard on the page now. Her search was suddenly over, and it had been simpler than she could possibly have imagined it would be… especially since Anthony was the first of just three McGhees there. She looked across at the address that preceded the phone number.

6, Addison Road. Crawley.

'Shit,' Chloe said aloud, reading it again and again, but it stayed the same. She felt a cold chill run up her spine and shivered. This house had been his home, and Bea had been living in it all along. How the hell was she going to tell her *that*?

Chapter Thirty-Eight

Bea

'I think that I'm just going to leave it in the past,' Bea said as she curled into Andre on the sofa. 'I don't know what else to do.'

'Well keep asking around, somebody will remember him, I am sure.' He pulled her closer and kissed the top of her head.

It was Bea's first time in Andre's apartment and she was pleasantly surprised by how homely and un-bachelor-like it was. Sure, it could do with some soft furnishings perhaps, but she liked it, a lot, about as much as she liked him.

'I'm going to tell my mum on Thursday when I get back,' she said, sitting up now. She knew that it might upset her, and that it wasn't great timing, but it was too much of a burden for her to carry on her own anymore. She needed to share it with the only other person she knew who cared.

'I think she will be comforted to know that he didn't just leave you both. You know,' Andre paused and looked at her, 'I think your dad would have been very proud of you.'

Bea smiled, feeling a warmth that made her unsettled. Her first heartbreak at the tender age of nineteen had toughened her up, and she had stood behind her wall ever since, always keeping a little bit back for herself, trying to set a good example to her younger sisters so that they didn't get hurt like she had. Something about Andre was different though, it was as if he could just reach through that wall and into her soul, and it didn't hurt.

'How about a glass of wine?' Andre asked. Bea nodded; he always seemed to be able to read her, know when not to push her. She was strong, she would work everything out in her head eventually, she just needed time. 'Just the one,' she said, conscious that she needed to be up early.

'One large one,' he said, ruffling the top of her hair and pushing himself up from the sofa.

Bea smiled as she smoothed her hair back down, leaning forward to pick her phone up from the table. She scanned down through the notifications on her lock screen, tapping on the message from Chloe that had come through during their film.

Hey, are you home tonight?

No, she typed back, *staying at Andre's. Miami in the morning, back Thursday in time for your wings.* She added a bunch of aircraft emojis, knowing how excited Chloe must be.

Ah, ok, have a great time. See you when you get back x

Bea felt a twinge of guilt; she really should have stayed home this week for Chloe's last few days, shared those last bottles of wine and the excitement with her. All she had at home was Kathryn, and she was about as exciting as the news. She would make it up to her though, goodness knew she would need a glass of wine after she saw her mum Thursday afternoon.

****

Chloe put her phone down and lay back, steepling her fingers and tapping them together. She couldn't tell Bea over a text what she had discovered, that was for sure, and now she wouldn't be able to tell her until at least Thursday. How on earth was she going to get through the next few days knowing what she did and not being able to tell anyone? So far, she hadn't talked to anyone on her training course about any of it, there hadn't been much to tell, and now it was all a little too much to blurt out over their morning coffee. One thing was for sure though, she couldn't just lie here like this, she needed to DO something. But what?

Chapter Thirty-Nine

Sophie: Is anyone nervous about their first flight. Like how to get to the car park and finding the crew room etc?

Maddie: Me! Honestly I'm not stupid normally, but I feel like I don't know anything!

Paul: How about we drive to Heathrow together tomorrow night after training? I've got room for four of you in my car?

Maddie: Paul I love you X

Darren: Count me in!

Megan: Here's the directions they sent us: {image}

Jade: I've booked a hotel the night before my first flight so I don't have to panic about the traffic

Jen: Me too, after you told me that earlier. Fab idea!

Liv: Guys who do I send a picture of my visa to? It's just arrived!

Megan: Crew records babe x

Liv: Thanks Megs, you literally know everything :)

Sophie: I've just burned a hole in my shirt trying to iron it for tomorrow... got distracted :(

Liv: Oh sweetheart! Good job we have spares!

Chloe pulled up the garage door and stepped inside quickly. She shivered despite the layers of clothes she had thrown on, the air feeling even colder inside than it was out. She knew that she must be mad, but told herself that it only seemed like that because it was cold and dark; had it been eight o'clock on a summer's evening it would have seemed perfectly acceptable to be out here.

She moved Zac's bike and enough of the boxes to let her through. This time she had come prepared and she shone the torch on her phone at the floor ahead of her, tracking a path over to the back door and the light switch.

Standing once again in the garage she felt less overwhelmed than she had done yesterday. She knew what to expect this time, and she scanned the room deciding where to start. The frames drew her to them and she walked over, crouching down and pulling the first one backwards. It was a painting of a landscape somewhere in England, it looked like... a cathedral set amongst rolling hills. She set it aside and checked the next one. This time a black and white photo of a couple in Victorian clothes, the stern-looking lady sitting in front of the wiry man with a handlebar moustache. Next a vintage coloured photo of a baby, chubby cheeks, smiling with two pearly white teeth that he seemed so proud of. Then a family photo. She picked this one up, standing to look at it closely. She recognized the man, in his pilot's uniform, as Bea's dad. The boy aged eight or nine stood in front, wearing short trousers and a blazer, the shoes on his feet catching the camera's flash in their polish. Chloe leaned in, trying to see what she could remember of the landlord in his face. The eyes perhaps, but she couldn't be sure, although it must have been him. The wife stood smiling, her hands on her son's shoulders. She was pretty, small and slim, obviously where her son got his height from. She wore a wrap dress with a pattern on it, and her hair was set in a wavy bob. Chloe tried to read her eyes; was she happy? Did she know that her husband was a cheat? Did she think that she deserved more or was she grateful for what he gave her? Chloe found it hard to believe that any woman could honestly not know that their husband was cheating, although maybe in those days, before mobiles and social media, it was much easier for them, especially for a pilot.

The next photo showed the boy again, a few years older with that teenager awkwardness, holding a young baby girl with a bow around her head. A cousin, perhaps? She put the pictures back down, feeling that they weren't going to tell her much. What was she hoping to find though? Would she know it when she saw it? She ran her hand over the Singer sewing machine, wiping the dust from the black lacquer and tracing the hand-painted flowers with her finger. There was a pile of neatly folded materials on the shelf underneath. Had she planned to make something with them? she wondered.

What did she need to find out? What would Bea like to know? What did anyone need to know about their dad? She put herself in Bea's shoes, as someone who knew nothing about their dad other than where he lived, not that she even knew that yet, and what he did for a living. Hobbies, family…

Her eyes fell on the far wall, and she pictured the family out on the bikes that were there now. She wondered if they went out together often, and if they enjoyed each other's company when they did? The child's bike was small, didn't he get a bigger one? Was it a short-lived activity for their family, like it had been for hers when mum had decided one summer that they should all go out cycling together? The few times they went Dad and Zac would always get competitive, cycling off too fast for them to keep up, and making Mum mad. She smiled at the memory and looked along the wall...

The filing cabinet!

Chloe felt a rush of adrenalin, which got stronger when she saw that the key was in the lock. She walked over, dragging the boxes that stood in front of it out of the way with no regard to the manual handling techniques she had practised yesterday. She twisted the key ninety degrees and pulled the top drawer out...

It was all there, everything... Chloe thought she must have felt just like Howard Carter when he discovered the tomb of King Tut. File after file, every detail of their lives, all here for Bea when she got back. For a moment she hesitated. Should she stop there, was it any of her business? She had found the information, but did she need to know the details?

She couldn't help herself though, couldn't fight her curiosity. Nosy, her mum would have called her, although she'd have done the same... they both loved a mystery.

Her fingers flicked through the first divider; piles of bank statements, some up until just last year in the name of Mrs Jean McGhee. From what she could see she had several accounts, one with over two hundred thousand pounds in it. Chloe wondered if, if she had time to trace back far enough, she had received a life insurance payout when Anthony never turned up? She looked at her watch; nearly nine, and too late for such a high-level investigation… besides which, what would it tell her?

She moved on to the next drawer, thumbing through Anthony's flying logs and licences. She took each one out and looked at it, being careful to put them back in the same order so that Bea could look through them herself.

Chloe caught herself. Maybe she should stop there, leave whatever was to be found for Bea. After all it didn't matter to her, it was immaterial. She was moving out in just a few days and would never have anything to do with the landlord or his garage again. She closed the drawer, but before she stood up she quickly opened up the one underneath, just for a split second. This one didn't have the dividers hanging from its rails, just a pile of stuff, a picture of laughing, elderly people on the top. She reached down, taking the brochure out just for a moment. 'Oaklands Retirement Home,' was written across the top. A single piece of paper fell out from between the pages and landed lightly on the floor. Chloe picked it up and read it.

Dear Mr McGhee,

We are delighted to be able to offer your mother a room at Oaklands Care home, with availability from March 1st…

Chloe looked at the top of the letter. It was dated February 2nd 2022.

Chapter Forty

Jade: Don't laugh when you see me, I look totally ridic

Jen: Oh babe, I know you don't, it's just different for us, that's all!

Megan: My skirt is soooo tight, too many pub dinners haha

Sophie: Same here, I know I've been comfort eating but surely you can't put on this much weight in just a few days??

Megan: I think the ones we tried on were probably a little stretched perhaps?

Liv: Good point, you're probably right. I'll bring a needle and thread in case of any accidents LOL

Megan: Oh Liv, you're such a mum, I love it!

Jade: Can you imagine, bending over and bursting your skirt…

Sophie: Even worse, what if it happens onboard EEEK

Jen: DEAD! That's it, I'm carrying a spare skirt, just in case!

Sophie: I'm going to practice leaning over on the aircraft visit today. Anyone want to have a quick run over Boeing this morning?

Chloe almost didn't recognize her group in the cafeteria.

'Chloe, you look amazing,' said Megan, patting the empty seat next to her. Chloe knew that she didn't, she had hardly slept a wink last night thinking about the McGhees, and her tired eyes had been watering so much it had been impossible to apply her eyeliner. Then her hair just hadn't wanted to go up in the style she had planned and so she had been forced to use the foam doughnut that they recommended to fix it in a bun. With her hair pulled back harshly against her head she reminded herself of Miss Trunchbull from *Matilda*, her favourite childhood film, when she looked in the mirror... and then there was the red lipstick, which seemed to drain any colour from her face. There had been no time to do anything about it though, running for the bus as she couldn't possibly cycle in this skirt, and she had resigned herself to making more of an effort tomorrow.

'Thank you,' she said nevertheless, looking now at her friend. 'So do you.' Megan genuinely looked beautiful with her soft hairstyle and flawless makeup. 'So does everyone,' she added, looking around the table. Paul looked smart in his three-piece suit, and the girls all looked so professional, the neck scarfs complementing their painted faces, all of their hair so much nicer than hers. She wished so much that she had managed to sleep last night, that she was able to enjoy this day that she had looked forward to so much.

'Are you okay?' Megan asked, her hand still on the seat she had saved for her.

'Yes, I just need a coffee,' Chloe smiled weakly. 'Do you want anything?' Megan shook her head. 'Won't be a sec.'

She didn't notice Kathryn in the queue until she spoke. 'Wow, you look nice,' she said, her smile and the simple compliment taking Chloe by surprise. She looked as if she meant it, and Chloe believed that she did, that this smart look was indeed something she would like, whether it made Chloe look her most pretty or not.

'Thank you,' Chloe said. 'Sorry, I was in a world of my own then,' she apologised, realising that her reply had come with a delay.

'Yes, I heard you come in late last night,' Kathryn said over her shoulder as she paid the cashier.

Chloe just smiled again, deciding this wasn't the place to be explaining what she had been doing. Kathryn was already walking away.

'Have a good day,' she said.

'You too,' Kathryn said without looking back.

'What can I get you?' asked the cashier, stopping Chloe from calling Kathryn back. She still wanted to ask her if it had been her that had called her when she'd been at the farm, and her opportunities were dwindling now with just a few days left in the house.

'A latte please, extra shot,' Chloe said, distracted. She was sure she would see Bea again, but she wondered about Kathryn... which was a shame because she quite liked her, found her calming to be around. Perhaps she would catch her tonight, she wondered, after all she must be home if she was working now, mustn't she?

'Chlo, are you sure you're okay?' Megan interrupted her thoughts as she sat back down, and Chloe suddenly realised she didn't remember the lady giving her the coffee or having walked back to the table.

'Sorry, I didn't sleep well last night,' she apologised, blinking to get the water out of her eyes and wiping it away with her finger. 'There's a few things going on at the house,' she offered by way of explanation.

'Anything you want to talk about?' Megan was frowning at her now, her face serious. Did she really look that bad?

'It's a long story,' Chloe smiled, 'too long for now.'

****

The plane looked as if it had been the scene of a riot. A riot in India, judging by the pungent smell of curry and spices. The carpets were covered in rubbish and crumbs, the seats with blankets and left-behind carrier bags and wrappers. Chloe was sure that she had never left anything like this mess behind her when she got off a plane, but she would certainly make sure that she didn't in the future.

'Do we have to clean the plane after?' someone asked, echoing what Chloe was wondering.

'Thankfully not,' Ben laughed kindly. 'Any of you that have come from short-haul, breathe a sigh of relief as you are no longer responsible for cleaning. Your day finishes when that last passenger gets off.'

'Music to my ears,' said Megan.

'Right, we'll have to be quick, Group 352,' Ben said with a clap of his hands to stop their chatter. 'This plane is being towed in an hour. Group one, you're with Janine.' He pointed to an instructor Chloe hadn't seen before. 'Pilot incapacitation in the flight deck. Group two, you're with me, and group three, if you could head down to the back where Dan is waiting for you in the galley to take you all to bed.' A few of the group giggled at his suggestion. 'By that I mean the crew rest area,' he added with a cheeky wink.

Chloe had been assigned to group one and so followed Janine to the front of the aircraft. She could feel the effects of the coffee slowly working to make her feel more alive, or at least less dead than she had done.

'So, what is your emergency access code?' Janine asked, getting straight to work as they gathered around the cockpit door. They all recited the code. 'Corr-ect,' Janine smiled, pulling it open. 'But since there are no pilots in there today we won't be trying that out. Come on in,' she said, beckoning them with her hand.

The four of them followed her, squeezing in behind the two pilots' seats.

'So, in the event of pilot incapacitation, what are our primary objectives?' Janine asked as she sat herself in the captain's seat and fastened the lap belt.

'Remove them from the controls,' they all said together, all except Chloe who was picturing Captain McGhee sitting there, where Janine was. Would he have kept his hat on? His jacket?

'Cor-rect,' Janine said. 'And how will we do that?'

'Push down on the horizontal,' they all said, together again. This time Chloe joined in, fighting to keep her mind in the present. By now they had already sat the exams and learned the facts, but the act of seeing it in real life was the final step to making sure that they *really* understood, and Chloe wanted to make sure she knew *everything* before she was out on line.

'So would someone like to do just that?' Janine asked.

Chloe leaned forward to look at the controls on the inside edge of the seat. She could picture the photo from the manual and reached out to point at the lever marked 'H'. 'There,' she said.

'Do it then,' Janine said, leaning back in her seat. Chloe leaned over, pushing the lever and pulling the seat back with her other hand. It slid easily backwards on its tracks.

'Well done,' said Janine. 'Next?'

One by one they carried out the procedure, reclining the seat and tucking her crossed arms behind her harness, locking it to keep them in place. Chloe imagined having to do it up in the air, how scary it would be. 'I'm glad we have two pilots,' she said.

'Yes, and two engines,' Janine grinned, releasing herself from the seat. Yes, Chloe was pleased about that too, a spare pilot and a spare engine were a great idea.

'Have you ever had anything bad happen on board?' Jen asked.

Janine looked thoughtful, leaning over, facing them now behind the seat. 'Nope,' she said eventually with a small shake of her head. 'In my fifteen years the worst I have had is some pretty rough turbulence. Touch wood,' she added, tapping her own head. 'And I hope you all have the same luck. But if things do go wrong at least you will know what to do.'

A murmur from outside made them turn to see the next group patiently waiting. 'Time's up, group one,' Janine said, looking at her watch. 'If you can lead the way to the back of the aircraft, let's have a look at Boeing crew rest,' she said.

****

'Right, tell me what's going on,' Megan demanded, sitting down in the seat next to Chloe. They were back in the cafeteria having a quick break before returning to the classroom.

'What do you mean?' Chloe asked, confused by her abruptness.

'You have been a million miles away all day,' Megan scolded, before taking a deep breath. 'What's happened, Chlo?' she asked, her voice softening. 'Are you okay?'

'I'm fine,' Chloe smiled, touched by her concern. 'Honestly. I just didn't have enough sleep, I was investigating something until late last night, that's all.'

'Investigating?' Megan repeated, her top lip curling. 'You're training to be cabin crew, babe, not a detective,' she grinned. 'Go on though,' she prompted her to continue with a curt nod.

Chloe organised her thoughts, twirling her thumbs around each other as she set about trying to explain everything as briefly as she could. 'My housemate is trying to find out about her dad, who was a pilot here. He went missing over thirty years ago, and I found out he used to live in the very same house we live in now. So, last night I went into the garage and was looking through some old stuff and....'

'*Jeeeeez.*' Paul's voice cut her off and Chloe looked up. Megan was looking at her, eyes wide and mouth open, and Paul was leaning in from where he had been sitting listening on the other side of her.

'Sorry, I know it all sounds a bit nuts,' she laughed, leaning back in her seat.

'Yes, but carry on.' Megan rolled her finger. 'I'm gripped here. What did you find?'

'I found out that his wife is in an old people's home near here,' she said, mindlessly peeling back the lid of her yoghurt and licking it.

'Your housemate's mum?' asked Megan.

'No, sorry I forgot to say, he was married with a son, but was having an affair with my housemate's mum in Ireland, who got pregnant and had just told him before he disappeared...'

Paul exhaled loudly. 'So, what happened to the pilot?' he asked, his upper body wrapped around Megan now as he leaned closer still.

Chloe shrugged. 'My housemate doesn't know, she only found out about him recently. Nobody knows, it seems.'

'She must have been freaked out to find out she was living in his house?' Megan shook her head in disbelief.

'That's the thing,' said Chloe. 'She's crew too,' she said, realizing that she hadn't told them that, 'and she's on a trip at the moment, so she doesn't know yet. She only found out recently that he actually went missing. Her mum had just thought he'd left her when she was pregnant and gone back to his wife.'

Paul blinked hard. 'I'm so confused right now,' he said.

'Sorry,' Chloe apologised, aware that she might have left out some details in her effort to make a long story short.

'So, when she gets back, how the hell are you going to break all of this to her?' Megan was holding her face in her hands, dragging her cheeks downwards.

Chloe took a spoonful of her yoghurt and thought about it. She had absolutely no idea how she was going to tell her. No idea whatsoever.

'No wonder you've been away with the fairies,' Megan said when she didn't reply, shaking her head slowly. 'What do you think happened to him?'

'I haven't got a clue,' Chloe said, shaking her head slowly too.

'What about his wife?' Paul asked. 'Surely she must know something?'

'Yes, Paul,' she said, pointing her spoon at him. 'Yes, she must.' It was what had been on her mind all day, what had had her going around in circles. She had an overwhelming urge to go and visit Jean, but it was equally weighed with her awareness that this was nothing to do with her, and that by visiting her she was undoubtedly crossing a moral line. Should she leave any future investigations to Bea, or should she just do them for her and present her with everything she could find out when she got back? It was a dilemma, but deep down she knew exactly what she was going to do, she had known since the moment she had read the letter from the nursing home...

Chapter Forty-One

Jen: The video is too big to share so here's a link to it guys {link} Hope you like it!

Sophie: OOH, going in!

Jen: SO glad we all went to the airport btw, thanks Paul, feel much better about Sunday now :)

Paul: Welcome Babs

Megan: Any of you who didn't come I put a map further up on here.

Chloe: Cheers Megs… sorry I couldn't come xx

Megs: No worries, hope you get to the bottom of things!

Jen: Sounds ominous?

Chloe: Long story… might have to write a book about it one day lol!

Sophie: Jen this is amazing! You made me cry!!! Love that you got all the trainers in there too.

Jen: Thanks luv. I'm gonna miss you guys so much :(

Paul: Stop it you lot, I'm even getting emotional now!

Darren: Great work Jen. Still working on my speech…

The taxi pulled up and Chloe got out in front of the nursing home. It was a long, three-storey, red-brick building, set back from the road behind high walls. A row of windows stretched out either side of the double doors that had 'Oaklands' carved in huge letters on a wooden board above them. Through the glass she could see a reception desk with a middle-aged lady wearing a lilac nurse's uniform sitting behind it, looking intently down at something. She felt nervous, but she had made the decision to come here and she was determined to follow it through.

To the right of the door was a numeric keypad and a 'Call' button, which she pressed. A buzzer sounded and the door clicked unlocked, so she pulled it open and stepped inside, walking purposefully over to the desk.

'I'm here to visit my grandmother, Jean McGhee,' she said, channelling all of the confidence that she had managed to muster. The lady looked at her blankly, her hand on the open magazine in front of her. She said nothing and so Chloe spoke again. 'Can you remind me which room she is in, please? I've only been here once before.'

The woman studied her for a moment longer, making Chloe's heart race. That was as far as she had got in planning her story to get in. 'Grandmother, you say?'

'That's right,' she smiled. 'She only came here in March, and I have been working away a lot so haven't managed to get in often. I don't think we've met before,' she offered a hand. 'I'm Chloe, and I hear Granny is very happy here at Oaklands.'

'Hmmph,' the woman said, ignoring her hand. 'Room 7. Sign in over there.' She pointed to a computer at the end of the desk and looked back down to the magazine. Chloe typed in her name hurriedly, snatching the visitor's badge the moment it printed out. She stuck it to the chest of her blazer as she dashed to the door. 'Thank you,' she called over her shoulder as it closed behind her.

Safely inside, she turned right, following the sign to rooms 1-15. The corridor smelt faintly of urine, and a waft of vegetables came from where she imagined the kitchen was.

'Nurse, can you take me home to Sheffield?' someone called out as she passed the open door of what looked like a communal sitting room. Chloe waved and smiled at the confused old lady, her heart pulling, but unsure how to answer her plea for help. At the end she took the stairs two at a time to the next floor. Room 7 was directly in front of her. She took a deep breath before knocking on the door gently with her knuckle.

'Hello?' A small voice came from within. Chloe pushed the door open slowly and put her head around to look into the room. It took her by surprise to find a large living room furnished nicely with dark wood and ornate rugs. The TV was on in the far corner and she could make out the back of the occupant sitting in an armchair, elbows resting on the arms of a high-back chair that reminded her of the one in the garage back in Addison Road. Perhaps they had been a pair once, she wondered.

'Is someone there?' The lady's voice sounded frail and unsure.

'Oh, hi, yes.' Chloe stepped inside and closed the door gently behind her. 'Jean?'

'That's me. Who's there?'

Chloe walked over to where she could see her, standing in front of the window and holding her hands together. 'Hi, Jean, my name's Chloe,' she said brightly.

Jean's grey brows pulled into a frown. She was tiny, wasted away by the years, and unrecognisable from the photo of her in the garage. Her thin, white hair was brushed back unflatteringly, her blue eyes sunken deep into her wrinkled face. 'Do I know you, dear?' she asked.

Chloe stepped forward. 'No, no you don't,' she said. 'Do you mind if I sit down?' she asked, feeling suddenly lost for words. Jean nodded and she took a seat opposite her on the only other chair in the room, a wooden dining chair with a tapestry cushion.

For a moment they both just looked at each other, until Chloe remembered how she had planned to go about this and spoke. 'I was doing some research for my airline,' she said, touching her neck scarf, 'Osprey, and I came across the story of your husband, Anthony.'

Something flickered behind Jean's eyes, but her face didn't move. Chloe waited.

'Anthony, your husband,' she prompted, wanting Jean to lead the conversation.

'The name rings a bell, but I don't remember, dear.' She shook her head. Chloe felt her stomach deflate. She must remember, surely?

'He was a pilot, at Osprey?' she prompted. Nothing. 'You had a son together, Andrew.'

Now Jean smiled. 'Yes, I have a son,' she said. 'He's a good boy, a good boy.'

'Yes,' Chloe smiled at her. 'And Anthony was his father.'

Jean stopped smiling now, her face suddenly sad. 'Anthony,' she said quietly, looking into nowhere. 'My darling Anthony.' She wrung her hands together now.

'Yes, Anthony,' Chloe said eagerly, leaning forward. 'What happened to Anthony, Jean? Where did he go?'

'Anthony. Anthony,' Jean repeated, shaking her head.

'Your husband, Anthony,' said Chloe, aware that she was getting distressed but not stopping. 'Jean, he disappeared, remember?'

Jean shook her head, her eyes blank again. Chloe could see that her memories had mostly left her as dementia had taken over and she leaned back, close to defeat. 'I'm so sorry, I shouldn't have come,' she said, aloud but not really for Jean's benefit. 'It's just I was in the garage and came across the photos and the address....'

Suddenly she was aware that Jean was sitting forward, her eyes clear. There was something there, she knew it. 'What is it, Jean, what do you remember?' she asked. 'Was it the garage?'

Jean was wringing her hands together faster now, muttering something that Chloe couldn't quite understand.

'I'm trying to find him, Jean. I'm trying to find Anthony...'

'No, no, no, no,' Jean repeated, her head shaking with each 'no.'

'Do you know where he is, Jean?' Chloe pushed. 'Where is Anthony?'

'NOOOO!' Jean's shout made Chloe jump up. 'Get out! Stay out of the garage!' she shouted, trying to push herself up from her seat, lunging towards Chloe, who shifted her seat backwards... and then it was gone. Whatever window had opened into her past had been closed just as quickly as it had opened and she had glazed over once again, slumping back in her chair and closing her eyes.

'Jean?' Chloe touched her arm, making her flinch and open her eyes again.

'Hello, dear,' she smiled. 'Do I know you?'

Chapter Forty-Two

Megan: Has anyone heard from Chloe?

Paul: No?

Megan: I tried to call her but no answer?

Paul: She's probably still doing her investigations lol

Jen: I am so intrigued about these investigations!

Darren: Er, ex-copper here, why don't I know anything about this?!

Megan: I'm sure she'll fill you in on it all tomorrow Dazza. @Chloe call me!

Chloe felt as if she'd had twenty coffees. Her mind was racing at a hundred miles an hour along with her heart rate, and she could hear the fast thud of her pulse in her ears. She stood in the middle of the garage trying to decide where to start, looking around and narrowing her search by eliminating the things that she had already looked at... not that she wouldn't come back to them later, just in case she had missed something. There was always a chance that she had. Her phone buzzed, another message on the group. She turned it off, eliminating one distraction.

She put her hands on her hips and took a deep breath. *What would a crime scene investigator do?* They would be methodical, that was what. They would start somewhere and work in a set direction so that nothing got left out. With that question answered she was left with the next. Where should she start? Back to front? Left to right? Right to left? She looked around. Most of the McGhees' belongings were now around the edges of the garage, pushed to the sides to make room for Bea's things. Her eyes fell on Bea's coffee table that she had unknowingly snuck into her own dad's garage, fearful that the landlord would find out, fearful of her own half-brother. In fact, everything in here was in one way or another connected to her, and yet she had absolutely no idea… what a bizarre thought that all was, and it wasn't helping her to decide where to start!

She caught sight of the pile of boxes that barricaded the front... boxes and boxes of who knew what. She would start with them, she decided with a nod of her head… surely one of them must hold a piece of this tantalizing jigsaw…

****

An hour had passed when Chloe looked at her watch, and so far her search had come up with nothing. It was strange, as if the lighter boxes that made up the top level had been filled with no thought or reason, a few pieces of clothing in one, a blanket in another. The lightest ones were completely unnecessary in her opinion, and yet someone hadn't thought so, had thought it necessary to put something in every last one. She slid one of the bottom ones, a heavy one, towards her, trying not to get her hopes up after so many disappointments, trying to stay focused…

investigations were rarely straightforward, or indeed quick, she reminded herself.

Stripping back the parcel tape she opened the top flaps enough for the light to get in. A pile of old children's books lay inside, and she took out a few to see if they were hiding anything, but they weren't. A random selection of annuals and comics sat on top of hardback early-readers. They were in perfect condition, as if they had never been read. With a sigh she closed it and slid it along to the pile of boxes that had been checked. Soon she would run out of room and would need to start stacking them up again, but not yet.

The next box was the heaviest so far, and this one made Chloe stop in her tracks when she opened it. Unlike all of the others, inside this one there were no books or blankets, no trinkets or heirlooms, no random household items. Inside this one were three bricks, lying side by side in the bottom, bubble wrap stuffed on top of them to fill the space. It was so odd that Chloe didn't know what to think, and so she just moved swiftly on to the next one, and the next... all of which held exactly the same thing, bricks or stones and bubble wrap. The entire bottom layer of boxes were the same.

Chloe stood back and looked at the opened boxes, completely confused. Why on earth would anyone pack these boxes like this? In fact, why had any of them been filled like they had, when all around the rest of the room things were slung perfectly haphazardly, perfectly normally for a family garage?

She took a few more steps back and cast her eye over them all, imagining them all back where they had been.

There had been something about them that had niggled her from the first day she had opened the garage if she thought about it, something that had seemed odd, but she hadn't given any thought to as it hadn't concerned her. What *was* it about this wall of boxes that was so out of place?

And then she realised... They were a WALL. That was what!

Whoever had put them there, and her money was on the landlord, had been trying to build a wall. She was sure of it, it was the only thing that explained them.

But why? Why had he built a wall? What was it in here—she looked around her—that he had wanted to hide behind the wall?

Deciding that the boxes were going to tell her nothing more than their purpose here, and with an overpowering feeling that there was something that she needed to find, Chloe worked fast along one side of the garage. She picked up the chair, running her hands over its fabric looking for lumps, and shook the pictures in case there was something inside. She pulled each piece of material out from beneath the sewing machine and unfolded it in case it was keeping a secret. On the other side she pulled out every tiny drawer of nuts, bolts and screws, in case there was something small that held the secret, like a microchip... *were they even invented back then*? A box of video tapes, labelled by year, caught her attention and she slowed down as she took them out one by one, hoping that one would say something obvious like 'You've found me!' or 'I hold the secret!' but of course, none did. She put them to one side… there was a high chance that it was them she was looking for, and she punched the air when she found the player just behind on which she could watch them later… but somehow she knew that she couldn't stop there.

She remembered the look in Jean's eyes when she told her to stay out of the garage, the fear and panic in them. There was something in here that was much more obvious. If it were small it would have been easy to hide, to throw away, but whatever it was that she was afraid of her finding was much bigger than that, much more obvious… why else build a wall to hide it?

She passed by the old wooden door at the back and worked her way along the far wall, underneath the window, pulling out the lawnmower and gardening equipment to check behind. She opened the filing cabinet once again, flicking through the files that she had already seen, checking underneath and behind them this time. She pulled the box down from on top and opened it, spreading the files inside across the floor so that she could see them more easily, her fingers working quickly as her eyes scanned each page. Finding nothing, she scraped them up and thrust them back inside. She could feel it in her blood, she knew it was here, and despite the fact that her watch told her it was nearly ten o'clock, she couldn't give up now.

To the left she moved the bikes aside, noticing for the first time an old chest freezer standing firm under its heavy load, piled high almost to the ceiling with 'stuff.' Chloe sighed; this last corner was the one she had put off, the one that she had known was going to be the biggest challenge. She looked around her for something to stand on, pulling over a wooden chair and climbing up onto it; she reached up high to pull the metal toolbox from the very top, almost toppling under its weight, dropping it into the crook of her elbows before stepping carefully down. Laying it on the floor she went back up, again and again, bringing down an old computer monitor, a keyboard, more books, some fishing equipment... it went on and on, a collection of things that had been stuffed on top of and aside each other, balanced precariously and yet firmly at the same time. With just two old drawers left, filled with cutlery and utensils, she took a breather and surveyed the things she had brought down. It was hot now, or at least *she* was hot, but her blazer was long off, and her sleeves short already. She was still in her uniform and she wished that she had got changed, her blouse marked by dirt and dust; the spare that she was reserving for her first flight would have to come out for tomorrow.

On her knees now, Chloe checked each item meticulously. The toolbox only held tools, the fishing box only fishing equipment. The huge plastic container was just crockery, an heirloom she guessed, by how these were carefully wrapped unlike so much of the rest. Nothing, nothing and nothing.

Chloe sighed and looked back over to the box of video tapes. She didn't actually know how to play one, but her mum would, although it would be too late to start now, perhaps it would be something she would have to hand over to Bea. Her stomach sank at the thought. All around her lay open boxes and displaced items, and yet she knew nothing more now than she had when she had started. She looked at her watch; five hours had passed and she hadn't found a thing… and now she would have to put it all back.

She heard the sound of a car on the street, not on the driveway but close, and wondered if Kathryn was home. Maybe she had got a lift? Maybe, if she used her best powers of persuasion, roped her in with the tale of mystery, she would help her to put all of this back?

Chloe took one last look along the last wall. She had been so sure that she would find something, and not just some videos that she would need to watch at a later date. She ran her eyes from left to right, starting at the top, and then going lower, right to left. Left to right, right to left she went until she was at the floor. Right to left…

She hadn't noticed the small green light before, nor had she heard the almost silent hum from the freezer that should have told her that it was still on. Why had she not noticed that before? She walked over, lifting the two drawers from the top and laying them on top of the other things on the floor. She wondered how long whatever was in it had been in there, and braced herself as she pulled the handle up. It stuck at first, the rubber seals frozen together, and so she grabbed it with both hands, groaning as she yanked it open with all of her might.

The fog of cold air that came out cleared quickly, and Chloe took a moment to just stand and look. She couldn't quite make it out, just some colours, dark in places, yellowish white in others. She leaned in closer, focusing on the dark patch, touching it with her fingers.

It moved slightly, hardened but separate pieces, like straw… she ran her hand down, the frost melting under the warmth of her hand to reveal something that looked familiar to her. Was it hair? On a head?

Chloe jumped back as if she had touched electricity, her eyes wide and heart beating hard against the wall of her chest. She could see him, bent over, four gold stripes on his shoulder… the person whose hair she had just stroked… Captain McGhee.

Somehow, she hadn't heard them come in, hadn't heard them until they were behind her, and then it was too late.

Chapter Forty-Three

Bea

London was covered in its usual haze as they flew over it on their approach to Heathrow. Bea tried to distract herself from thinking of the day ahead by spotting as many famous landmarks as she could along the winding River Thames. She picked out the dome of the O2 and then followed it along to the London Eye and the Houses of Parliament. Tracing a route north she found the gardens of Buckingham Palace, and then back down the long stretch of The Mall to Trafalgar Square. She always felt so lucky to see this view, so privileged to see her capital city laid out in front of her like a magnificent map. Soon it was behind them, giving way to the urban sprawl around the city, the plane descending lower and lower as they neared the airport.

Ding, ding.

The flashing of the seatbelt sign twice was their signal that landing was imminent, and Bea leaned back into her headrest, hands under her thighs. She was grateful not to have passengers in front of her today, small talk would have been a struggle when she had a much bigger conversation swimming around in disjointed pieces in her mind.

The passengers were off quickly, no wheelchairs to wait for or last-minute lost belongings to search for.

'Thanks, everyone, you can get off,' the manager called over the PA. Bea changed her shoes, slipping her feet into her heels and stuffing the flats into her wheelie bag.

'Bye, Bea.' Shelley the purser walked quickly past on the opposite aisle. 'Do you want me to wait for you?'

'No, but thanks,' Bea waved. 'I'm going to take a slow walk.' She needed to get all those jumbled thoughts organised in her head so that they came out in the right order, so that they did the least amount of damage possible.

Ninety minutes later she was at her parents'; their cars were in the driveway, they were expecting her last visit before they handed over the keys and flew off. She took a deep breath as she let herself in, immediately hit by the emptiness of the hallway and the echo of her footsteps as she walked along it.

'Mum?'

'Just coming!' Her mum's voice sounded excited as she called from upstairs. 'Stick the kettle on.'

In the kitchen a pile of boxes sat on the floor by the dining table. One was open on the side, next to the tea-making equipment, poised to be loaded with the very final pieces. Bea filled the kettle and switched it on, helping herself to a biscuit from the open packet of Gingernuts.

'Morning, how was your flight?' Her mum was in her dressing gown, rubbing her wet hair with a towel.

'Good thanks. Where's Dad?'

'Just hopping in the shower,' she answered, putting the towel down on the side and taking over from Bea with making the tea. 'Let me do that, I'm sure you've made enough people cups of tea last night.'

Bea laughed. 'Fair point,' she agreed, stepping back to let her mum in.

'Mum, I need to tell you something,' Bea said as they sat at the table, putting the packet of biscuits down between them. There was no point putting it off.

Her mum held her mug in both hands and looked at her, waiting. 'Go on then,' she said eventually, when Bea found the words had stuck in her throat. Bea coughed to release them.

'Dad didn't leave us,' she blurted out.

Her mum looked amused and concerned at the same time, her brow furrowed but her mouth slightly turned up on one side. 'He's in the shower, love,' she said, making Bea laugh, and breaking through her tension.

'No, not *Dad*,' she said. 'Anthony McGhee, my rea...' she stopped herself from saying it, 'my biological father.' Her mum's smirk had dropped now, her brow stayed how it was. 'Apparently he went missing the day that he saw you, he was never seen again.'

'Oh.'

Bea couldn't read her face, it was as if there were no thoughts attached to the blank expression. 'I met some pilots who knew of him, and they told me he was some kind of legend at Osprey. Here...' She opened her bag that sat at her feet and pulled out a copy of the newsletter, handing it to her. It would do a better job of explaining things than she was. She waited as her mum's eyes moved down the page, until she eventually finished, laying it down on the table and taking a deep breath.

'Wow. I hadn't expected that,' she said, and then she smiled.

'Are you okay?' Bea asked.

'Yes, yes I am,' her mum said softly.

'Are you happy to know that he hadn't just left us?' Bea knew that it had made *her* feel better, less 'abandoned'.

'Of course,' her mum said, sipping the last of her tea and putting the mug down. She laid her hands flat on the table in front of her now. 'But that was something I had accepted a long, long time ago, I guess, and I suppose it doesn't really make a difference now. His poor family must have been beside themselves though.'

Bea smiled now; it was typical of her mum to worry more about other people than herself. 'Don't you wonder what might have happened if he hadn't gone missing though?'

Her mum was thoughtful for a second. 'Nope,' she decided with a shake of her head. She leaned across the table and rubbed Bea's hand. 'Maybe he just needs to stay in the past.'

'What's going on here then?' Her *real* dad walked into the room and they both looked up at him, both smiling at the man who would never leave them. 'What have I missed?'

'Nothing, I'll fill you in later.' Her mum picked up her empty mug and walked over to him, giving him a kiss on the cheek. 'Cuppa?'

'You know me, never say no.'

And that was that. Bea smiled, feeling all warm inside as she watched her parents together. She hadn't needed to be worried after all; Anthony McGhee might have broken her mum's heart all those years ago, but her dad had done a great job of fixing it back up. She leaned back and picked up the newsletter, looking at the picture before putting it back in her bag. *Maybe he just needs to stay in the past.*

****

Back at the house Bea carried her bags up the stairs and sat on her bed. She bristled at the sound of Kathryn's sewing machine from across the hall, closing her bedroom door loudly so that she would know she was home. It had been weeks since she'd heard the dull whirring that seemed to go right through her, weeks since she had banged on her door and shouted at her about the noise disturbing her rest on landing day. Kathryn hadn't said a word in return, but the noise had stopped, just as it stopped now. She breathed a sigh of relief.

She took one last look at the picture of Anthony McGhee on her wall before pulling it down and putting it, along with all the printouts of the newsletter, in her drawer. It was already two o'clock, she realised, just time for a short nap before Chloe got home, and she wanted to make sure she had a great last night before her wings tomorrow...

Chapter Forty-Four

Jen: It's like my brain is saying Noooo to studying, like it had enough of that these last weeks!

Sophie: Same, it's not even hard but my brain cells are gone

Jen: And then even after we get our wings, I feel like I am going to have to relearn everything before my first flight, I can't remember anything!

Darren: I've finished my speech {Document}

Megan: Love it, who knew you were such a great writer!

Darren: Cheers :) Any word from Chloe?

Megan: No, she must have her phone off. Sure she'll catch up on here later. Bubble bath and an early night for me. Night all xxx

Paul: Megan it's 9pm

Megan: Farmer's daughter... early to bed, early to rise babe... can't keep up with all these late nights...night xxx

Paul: Tbf you need your beauty sleep

Megan: Ouch. Night Chloe, wherever you are xxx

Chloe's head killed. The sharp pains felt as though someone was stabbing her with a dagger, over and over. Her hip hurt too. Whatever she was lying on was hard, and cold. She opened one eye, but it made the pain in her head worse, so she closed it again. She wanted to hold it, but she couldn't move her arm. Why couldn't she move her arm? Why couldn't she move any of her limbs, come to that? And her mouth, what was that pulling at it...?

Ignoring the pain she opened both of her eyes now and tried to focus, but everything around her was a blur. She held her gaze on the same point until the object sharpened up, pondering what the metal claws were that she could see. She tried to sit up, but without her arms to push with she flailed on the floor, her skirt not offering much comfort between her and what she could now see in the dim light was a concrete floor.

The garage. She knew where she was now. She was in the garage at Addison Road. She was lying on the floor in the garage at Addison Road... and she could not move.

The panic grew slowly at first. Twisting her wrists, she used her fingers to feel for what was holding them together behind her back. Something smooth, plasticky to touch, cut into her wrists, so tight that she couldn't get a finger underneath. When she pulled up her legs moved too, as if they were attached to her arms, tied together somehow...

She was tied up! Her heart jolted before starting to beat so hard and fast she thought she might go into cardiac arrest, struggling to breathe, pulling in short, shallow breaths through her nose.

Her tongue ran over what was in her mouth, some cloth pulled tight, and she presumed tied at the back. She had been 'bound and gagged'... like a hostage in a movie. Chloe blinked hard, over and over. It must be a bad dream, it had to be, and she needed to wake up. This wasn't really happening to her. It couldn't be. Things like *this* didn't happen to people like *her*! The pain in her head didn't go away though, and she didn't wake up.

What the hell was going on? How had she ended up here, like this? She looked frantically around for answers, twisting her neck to see over her shoulder... and then she saw the freezer, and it all came back, a chill coming over her body and making her shiver at the memory of what, *who* was inside it. She couldn't remember who did this to her, wasn't sure she'd even seen him... but she was pretty certain who it was, and if he'd left her here alive she was also certain that he would be back... and then what? What would he do next? Whatever he was planning, one thing she was sure of was that it wouldn't end well for her, like it hadn't ended well for Captain McGhee.

A rush of tears escaped from Chloe's eyes and her whole body started to shake uncontrollably. Her fingers tingled as she struggled to slow down her breathing, knowing that she was at risk of hyperventilating. She tried to shout but her voice was muted behind the cloth.

So, this was what true fear felt like, she thought as she acknowledged every feeling she was having. *This is what it feels like to be terrified.*

Chapter Forty-Five

Megan: @Chloe are you on your way? Where are you girl?

Liv: Traffic is a bugger this morning, I'm hoping to be on time though, maybe she's caught?

Darren: Where is she coming from?

Megan: She either gets the bus or cycles in. Maybe she's on her bike and can't see her phone...

Darren: I'm sure she's fine... not much bad stuff happens around here!

Megan: You're right, I've always been a worrier.

Paul: Walk over with me Megs, we'll check the timetable at her bus stop on the way.

'I'm worried about her,' Megan said to Paul as Chloe's phone went straight through to voicemail once more. It was lunchtime and still nobody had heard from her.

'She's probably just unwell, do you think?' He sounded unconvinced.

Megan shook her head. There was no way that Chloe would have risked everything unless she was dying. Besides, she'd been completely fine yesterday, so what illness could she have come down with so suddenly that it had rendered her unable to even make a phone call? No, there was something wrong, she knew it, but what she didn't know was what she could do about it.

'Do you know where she is staying?' Darren asked.

Megan thought hard, trying to recall their conversations, trying to remember if she had ever mentioned her address. She shook her head.

'Well they'll have something on record here, ask him.' He tipped his head towards Ben, who was walking towards them.

'Ben.' Megan stopped their instructor as he passed their table in the cafeteria.

Ben turned and smiled. 'Yes, Megan?'

'I'm worried about Chloe,' Megan said quickly. Ben's smile faded and he mirrored her frown. 'I don't suppose you would know, or be able to find out where she lives?'

'I don't know, you know,' he said, touching the side of his face thoughtfully. 'Do you think maybe she's just sick?'

'No, she'd have called in.' Megan held her phone up. 'But she's not even picking up. There's no way she'd miss the last two days, I know she wouldn't, what with today being the last exam...'

'I did think it was strange,' Ben agreed. 'Leave it with me, I'll see what I can find out.'

'Thank you so much.' Megan felt suddenly tearful. There was something terribly wrong, she could feel it. Paul's arm appeared around her shoulder and she leaned into him for a moment. 'Maybe she has just broken her phone?'

'Yes.' Paul squeezed her. 'Or she's lost it. I'm sure Ben will get hold of her.'

Megan nodded and pulled herself upright, out of his arm. 'Do you think they will let her get her wings if she's missed a day?'

'I don't know.' Paul sounded doubtful as he shook his head. Megan doubted it too.

The afternoon dragged as they sat through security training, with Megan checking her phone at least ten times an hour. The class seemed incomplete without Chloe in it, nothing felt right. She wondered if Ben had forgotten about his promise to look into things, staying behind as the others left the classroom for a coffee break.

'Give me a second,' Ben said, giving her a nod of acknowledgment as he picked up the phone. 'Hi, it's Ben from training,' he said to whoever was on the other end of the line. Megan waited patiently as he made noises, picking up a pen and writing something down on a piece of paper in front of him. 'Thank you, Diana, appreciate your help,' he said eventually, hanging up the phone and looking at Megan. 'I'm afraid they only have her address in Barnet, not where she is staying here,' he apologised as he handed her the paper he had written on. Megan's heart sank as she read it.

'Did they have a number for her parents?' she asked, knowing the answer.

'I'm afraid not,' Ben replied. 'Just her mobile number.'

'Okay, thank you,' Megan said, turning to see Paul waiting for her at the door.

'Well?' he asked as they walked side by side along the corridor.

'How do I get to Barnet?' she asked, realising what she needed to do.

Chapter Forty-Six

Paul: Guys let us know where you are later and we'll come and find you. Me and Megs just want to make sure Chloe's alright

Maddie: No worries, I hope she's ok xxx

Jen: It's really odd, let us know when you find her xxx

Darren: Shout if you need any help guys

Paul: Will do fella.

Everything always turns out okay in the end used to be her motto, but now she wasn't so sure.

Chloe didn't feel the pain anymore as she pulled with all her strength against the restraints on her wrists. She could feel them cutting through her skin but she had to keep trying... if she gave up *then* what? She had no idea of the time, but it must be the afternoon she decided, as the daylight was still managing to come through the window, although it did seem to be dwindling. She wished that he had left the light on. The thought of being alone, like this, in the dark, didn't bear thinking about.

What did he plan on doing with her? Why had he done this to her? Would he be back once it was dark?... The questions kept coming as she writhed on the floor. Her only hope was to get out of these bindings, but he had tied them so tight, and with both her legs and her arms up behind her, it was impossible to move herself over to anything that she might be able to cut them on. Or was it? If she could get near to something sharp maybe she could do something. Anything.

On her side, Chloe dug her shoulder into the floor and tried at first to pull herself forward, resulting in her losing her balance and ending up face down on the floor. The cold felt strangely nice on her flushed cheeks, but it was harder to breathe. She tried with her knees to push forward, again to no avail. Fighting despair, she rocked left and right until she managed to get back on her side, no closer to anything.

Suddenly the light dimmed. She looked over to the window, thinking that she could see the shadow of someone there on the other side of the dirt-covered glass. She held her breath, listening hard, her heart nearly stopping as she wondered if it was him... Time stood still for a moment as she watched the shadow move a little, lifting its arm.

The smell of cannabis took Chloe by surprise at first, and she inhaled deeply a few times to make sure she was right about it. She had gone through a rebellious stage in her teens, smoking joints with her friends after school. It hadn't lasted long, she hadn't liked the feeling of being out of control, but she always recognized the smell afterwards, especially when Zac took to storing it in his room while their parents were blissfully unaware. It had been a great source of blackmail on her part.

Who was smoking weed behind the garage? she wondered, almost laughing despite her predicament when she realised that it must be Kathryn. She thought back to all the times that Kathryn had come in through the back door, or the time she had come out from behind the garage pretending that she had been weeding. Well, weeding she had been, in a different sense of the word, Chloe thought, amused enough to forget herself for the briefest moment.

She opened her mouth to call out, forgetting the cloth tie. Wordlessly she shouted, the sound muffled, reaching down into her stomach to force it out as loud as she could. Over and over, as loud as she could, watching the shadow, willing it to hear her, to stop smoking and listen to her cries. But she couldn't make herself heard, she must have been too far away from the window for Kathryn to hear her, and she watched as she walked away again, her shadow giving way to what was left of the daylight.

Chloe sobbed. Big, gut-wrenching sobs of despair. What hope did she have? She couldn't move, no one could hear her... all she could do was lie here and wait for him to come back. Come back and do with her whatever he planned to do. She was sure he would be back that night, once the others were inside, under the cover of darkness. It was clear that he would kill her too, what else could he do, after all?

Her poor mum and dad, she cried, would they ever find her body? Would they ever know what had happened to her? Would her mum keep her room as a shrine to her, always hoping that she would be found one day alive? Would the police find her, would they search the garage for her and find her blood on the floor... she could feel it thick and sticky on her hands from the ties on her wrists.

Would he get rid of both of their bodies? Hers and Captain McGhee's?

A new wave of determination came over her, and she grunted as she dug her shoulder into the floor again and inched forward. If she could just get over to the tools then maybe she could get one of these ties off... but at an inch at a time, would she get there before he arrived...?

****

Bea rubbed her eyes as she filled her glass with water.

'Hi,' Kathryn said as she shut the back door behind her and walked through the kitchen.

'Hi,' Bea answered without turning around. She looked at the clock on the wall. It was almost four o'clock, she could have slept longer but she needed to get to the shops before Chloe got home. She was going to cook her a pasta dinner and get some prosecco in for them both. She was so excited for her, remembering how she had felt when she knew that she had passed that last exam and that the wings were going to be hers... there was no feeling like it, and she felt so lucky to be able to live it again through her new friend.

She rinsed the glass and stood it upside down on the draining board before going back upstairs to get dressed, wondering as she did so if she would be allowed to go and watch the ceremony? She would quite like to see it from a spectator's point of view, without the pressure of having everyone watching you.

It was usually just family invited, or it had been when she had got her wings, but perhaps she could sneak in since she was an employee? She made a mental note to ask Chloe later if she would mind her being there...

Chapter Forty-Seven

Sophie: Got a table at TGIs booked for 7:30 to celebrate us all passing that last exam. Booked for 12 as know a few of you can't come, but like this post if you're coming x

Jen: I'm in, haven't had TGIs for years!

Jade. I'm in. Any news on Chloe?

Megan: Just on our way to her parents, don't think we will make it back for then. Enjoy though, and see some of you back in the crew room later xx

Paul: All these weeks and you pick my favourite place the night I can't come. You lot suck. @Chloe you have a lot to answer for!

Paul: Only joking btw but if you are reading this and could let me know you're okay I might make the table!

Paul: Joking again!

Jade: I just checked, she's not been online since yesterday.

Megan: @Chloe we love you and miss you babe xxx

Megan and Paul sat in thoughtful silence as the 17:29 overground train from Crawley pulled into Victoria Station. Neither of them had said much on the journey so far, despite the fact that they had somehow, with their minds a million miles away, passed their final exam just two hours ago. She had been happy of course, but it had felt almost disloyal to celebrate when Chloe wasn't there to join in, when she was potentially not okay. Paul, who was usually the first one to the bar, was concerned too, and had insisted on coming with her. Out of the whole group they were the ones who probably knew Chloe best and knew she would have been there today… if she could have been.

The station was busy, and they weaved through the crowds on the platform. Paul had offered to drive, but with the rush-hour traffic the train would be quicker by far, if less comfortable.

'Victoria Line, northbound,' Megan said loudly over the noise of the announcements, repeating what the satnav on her phone was telling her. She was familiar with the main routes in and around London, but they were heading further north than she had ever been and she needed a map to get her there.

'Right you are,' said Paul, pointing to a sign that would lead them that way.

The smell of McDonald's made them both turn their heads; it was gone six o'clock and neither of them had eaten yet, but neither of them suggested stopping either. Down the escalator the underground train was just pulling in. It looked full, and Megan hesitated before following Paul's lead and stepping up into the packed carriage. She folded herself over, beneath the arms of people holding on to the rails and handles above and around her, only inches away from the doors as they *whooshed* closed. She concentrated on looking outwards as they pulled along, trying to block out the thought of all the bodies behind her. Paul steadied her as a small jolt made her stumble, and she held on to his arm.

The carriage was so full that Megan felt unbelievably hot in her wool coat, the same one that she had been freezing in outside. She was well out of her comfort zone now; she much preferred country life, where there was enough fresh air for everyone, and personal space was in abundance. She counted the four stops down until they arrived at Euston, springing out onto the platform, relieved beyond words to be 'set free'. She took a deep breath to centre herself, pushing it out through her mouth.

'One more train.' Paul patted her on the shoulder and steered her towards the Northern Line. She didn't mind trains, just the ones where you were squashed in like sardines, the ones that had no air, the ones that she was putting herself through because she needed to make sure her friend was okay.

The next train was better, less full, and by the fifth stop they managed to get a seat.

'What if we get there and she's at her mum's, absolutely fine?' Megan asked, wondering for the first time if she was overreacting.

Paul shrugged. 'Well then she is fine and we will be able to stop worrying.'

Megan nodded, sinking back into her seat. Yes, he was right, she thought, taking her phone out of her pocket to call her one last time, just to check. There was no signal.

Outside of High Barnet station they followed the blue dot on Megan's map, along streets of terraced houses until they reached Chloe's. It was strange, Megan thought, seeing where Chloe had grown up without her being here to show her. The houses were all in pairs, semi-detached, some with front gardens, but most with the grass replaced by concrete to hold the cars that couldn't fit on the street. Number 35 was a white rendered building, with a shingle drive, and two topiary trees either side of the dark grey front door. It was smart, modern. A floodlight lit up the dark path as Megan and Paul walked up to the door and pressed the doorbell. Nothing moved inside.

A few minutes passed before Megan pressed the doorbell again, following it up with a hard rap of her knuckles on the glass inlay. Aside from the hallway light she could see now that the house was in darkness, that no one was home. She looked up at Paul.

'We could wait a while and see if anyone comes back?' he suggested.

'Good idea,' Megan agreed, wrapping her arms around herself. It was freezing, and she thought she saw flakes of snow in the air. 'Not too long though, or we'll freeze to death.'

'How about we find a pub and come back in an hour?'

'You know what, that is the best suggestion I have heard all day.' Megan looked on the map. 'And it just so happens that there is one just five minutes' walk from here.'

Chapter Forty-Eight

Jade: Heading to TGIs now, anyone want to share an Uber?

Darren: I will. Any update @Megan?

Megan: Nothing yet, just waiting in pub nearby as no one home, hopefully they will be soonxx

Paul: Meanwhile, the beer is good and the log fire is roaring {image}

Darren: Always a silver lining, looks proper toasty in there!

It was dark, and it was freezing. Chloe had been shivering for so long that her body ached now. Her head still hurt and sharp pains shot along her limbs, screaming in protest at being contorted as they were for as long as they had been...

She pushed forward another centimetre; the tools were probably about a metre and a half away now. She hadn't thought about what she was going to do once she reached them yet, hadn't formulated the next part of her plan. Her only aim right now was to reach them, she would figure out the rest when she got there.

Another centimetre and she cried out, a muffled cry through the cloth as something sharp scraped the side of her knee. Her skin felt even more sensitive in the cold. A change in the darkness made her curl her body forward to look around. There was a shard of light coming from under the big garage door at the front. It must be the intruder light, she realised, the one that came on when you walked up the path in the dark. Someone was coming in, or out, of the house.

She listened, relieved not to hear a car, and the light went off. Was it Bea? Was she home? They were meant to be having drinks tonight, weren't they? She gave in to crying for a moment as she pictured Bea in the house, wondering where she was, oblivious to the fact that she was in *here.* Like *this*. In *danger*.

Something rattled the metal door and Chloe bit down hard on her gag. She wriggled aimlessly, trying even harder to get to the tools. Louder it rattled, making the metallic sound echo around her, through her.

He was back.

Was this it?

Chloe stayed still, petrified in terror.

Time passed and she couldn't hold her breath any longer. She let it out. Nothing happened. The rattling stopped and the light went off. Slowly Chloe unclenched her jaw and loosened her tight muscles. She felt a warmth between her legs and it took her a moment to realise what it was. She had wet herself. She had been so terrified that she had wet herself. The sobs, dry this time as she was empty of tears, came back harder than even before.

****

Bea pulled the front door shut behind her, the outside light coming on as she stepped onto the path. She looked at her watch and sighed loudly. She would have to be quick now, having lost twenty precious minutes looking for the damned garage key. It was so frustrating knowing that her beautiful champagne bucket and glasses were locked away in there and she couldn't use them. Knowing that they would have looked so nice when Chloe arrived back all excited. In frustration she tugged at the door handle as she passed it, on the off chance that it was unlocked, but of course it wasn't, the metal door mocking her with its loud rattle.

Defeated, she set off at pace, walking quickly both because of the time and to keep warm. Chloe would just be happy that she had made an effort for her, she wouldn't care about the glasses she never even knew about, she was sure. The girl would be so excited right at this minute about passing her final exam that she wouldn't care if she gave her a paper cup, Bea thought with a smile.

Chapter Forty-Nine

Darren: Any updates?

Megan: Nothing yet. Defo won't make dinner.

Darren: Ok see you in the crew room

Megan looked at her watch. They had been in the pub for just over thirty minutes and yet neither of them had finished their drinks. They weren't here to enjoy themselves, didn't want to 'get merry,' they were literally both counting down until they could leave again.

'Shall we?' Paul asked.

Megan nodded and stood up, taking her coat from the back of her chair and putting it on as she followed him out. Back at the house minutes later, Megan's heart sank when she saw that it was still in darkness.

'We should have stayed the hour,' she thought aloud.

'Yep,' Paul agreed.

'What are we going to do now?' Megan turned to him. They both knew that they couldn't stand out here all night on the off chance someone turned up, it was too cold for one thing, and they needed to get back.

'We could leave a note?' Paul suggested.

Megan tapped him on the arm. 'Genius. I knew there was a reason I let you come along.'

'I have my uses, apparently.'

Megan dropped her slouch bag on the floor and crouched down to rifle through it, trying to find a pen and paper. As she wondered what she was going to write, a car's headlights shone directly at her, blinding her for a moment.

'Scrap that,' said Paul, offering her his hand to help her up. 'We have company.'

They stood side by side at the front door as the blue Ford Focus crunched along the gravel towards them. The driver eyed them briefly as she turned the car off and opened her door. A young man got out of the passenger side. *She* smiled questioningly at them, *he* scowled.

'Mrs Bashford?' Megan asked, her voice hopeful.

'Yes, that's me,' the lady said, confirming that she was Chloe's mum. 'Shush,' she said, turning to a small spaniel who was still in the car, barking at them through the window.

Megan could see the likeness between Chloe and her mother, and presumed that the man was Zac, the brother, owner of the bike.

'We were looking for Chloe,' Paul stepped in.

'Oh, are you friends of hers?'

'Yes,' said Megan. 'We are training at Osprey with her.'

'Oh.' Her mum looked confused.

'Mrs Bashford...' Megan deliberated what to say next, what would be the best way to say it.

'Please, call me Helen. Is Chloe alright?'

Even in the dark Megan could tell she had turned pale. Zac moved around the front of the car to stand next to his mum. 'What's going on?' he asked, the scowl now replaced by a face of concern.

Megan tried to smile. 'It's just that Chloe didn't turn up for training today, and we don't know her address where she is staying so we came here...' She was aware that she was talking quickly but carried on anyway. 'We just hoped you had heard from her, as her phone isn't ringing and...' She felt Paul put his hand on his shoulder and stopped talking. Chloe's mum had her phone out and was calling someone. Megan was sure that she was calling Chloe.

'Straight to voicemail,' she said, looking up at Zac. 'It's not like Chloe.'

'We didn't think so either,' said Megan. 'If you have her other address we can pop by and check on her?'

'No.' Helen shook her head. 'Jump in the car and we'll all head over there right now.' Zac nodded and walked around the car to sit back in the front. Megan and Paul climbed in behind him, either side of the excited dog who seemed extremely pleased to meet them, his tail wagging furiously.

'Oh, sorry, do either of you mind dogs?' Helen asked over her shoulder.

'Absolutely not,' said Megan, ruffling the long hair on top of his head, finding comfort in the softness of his fur. Paul stroked his back gently and smiled as he shook his head.

'Great.' Helen put the car into reverse and shot backwards on the drive. 'Now let's go find out what is going on with that daughter of mine.'

Chapter Fifty

Megan: Nearly there now, hopefully have an update soon...

A few minutes had passed, and Chloe sucked in as hard as she could through her nose to stop the sobs that were doing nothing to help her. She pushed forward another centimetre, the cold, wet skirt, clinging to the ground now, working against her. She cursed in her head, cursed him, cursed the garage, cursed the uniform... it made her feel stronger, pushing her through the pain centimetre by centimetre. She was sure that her leg was bleeding, and stopped a moment to try to turn onto her other side.

A car drove past on the street. She wondered who was in it. Where were they going? Were they young, going out to have some fun, completely oblivious to her plight as they drove past the house with the garage and the big tree? Outside the world was just carrying on without her, people just going about their day-to-day lives where they thought their tiny problems were so real. Like she had. All along though, other people out there had been suffering in a way that until now had been so unimaginable to her. She read about it, after all, heard about it on the news, watched it on her documentaries... but she realised now that she had never thought of any of the victims as real people, with real feelings... If she ever got out of here, she was sure that she would hear their stories in a whole different way.

Another car. Another push. She was close now, straining her neck to see where she was heading. The workbench loomed over her, tools hanging on the wall. She could see saws, beautiful saws with rusted teeth that were calling to her, calling to her to let them cut her bindings. They were too high though. When she eventually got there, how would she reach them? Could she push herself up the wall between the bench and the boxes? Could she use something to knock them down?

Another centimetre closer. Her heart pounded even harder, adrenalin helping her to ignore the pain. Another centimetre… she was doing it. She was going to make it!

Why had she lain over there, for so long? Why hadn't she started moving, like this, earlier? Maybe she would have been free by now if she hadn't been so pathetic at first?

The regrets came thick and fast.

She had wasted all of this time, and now she was quite sure that he would be back any minute, and what if she wasn't free? She would only have herself to blame. She should have tried harder. Tried earlier. Why had she been so weak? Why hadn't she been…

The light grew brighter, seeping in underneath the metal door. The sound of tyres on concrete were unmistakable. The engine slowed down to a stop and went silent, as one then two car doors opened and then shut softly. The car lights were replaced by the intruder lights as two sets of feet trudged towards the garage and then seemed to go off to the side, towards the house.

Chloe's mind raced, imagining who had come to the house, who had walked in silence together.

One more centimetre.... Another and then another.

She felt the leg of the workbench against her head and pushed herself around so that she could look up at the wall.

Above her, in the dim light, she could see a red-handled saw. She imagined how it would feel in her hand, how it would sound as it cut through her ties. How the rust would flake off the blades.

A murmuring made her stop moving towards the wall. She listened hard to try to hear who it was. They talked in low whispers at the side of the garage, on the path next to the house. She stopped herself from making a noise, held back until she could be sure who it was.

Was it him? Had he come back with someone else to carry her away? Did he have an accomplice to help him with her murder?

The next noise took her a moment to work out. A lock. A key in a lock. A click, before a handle pushed down and a door opened. The door at the side of the garage was being opened and she could hear their voices...

'You said you took all the keys with you anyway...'

She recognized the woman's voice.

'Just shut up, for God's sake shut up!'

And the man's.

'Chloe?'

The fluorescent light clicked on and Chloe blinked in its harshness.

Kathryn.

What was that she had been saying about the key? Was she saved?

'Chloe, where are you?'

Chloe screamed silently from behind the boxes, tucked in between them and the workbench, underneath the saw.

Kathryn's footsteps came closer, until she was there, looking down at her. Here to save her....

'Oh, sister, what have you done now?'

A man stepped up behind her. The landlord. He stood with one hand on his hip, the other half covering his face as he stretched the skin with his palm, pulling it downwards. He shook his head.

Sister?

Chloe stared, wide-eyed, up at Kathryn. Why wasn't she afraid of him? Couldn't she see what he had done to her? *Kathryn, help me*... she screamed in her head. Why wasn't she looking at her though? Why was she looking at him, and why was he shaking his head at her like that?

Chapter Fifty-One

Megan: Guys we aren't going to make it. Something terrible has happened.

The Ford pulled into Addison Road, slowing down from what until now had been a speedy journey across the city. Megan had lost count of the red lights that Helen had jumped through, had stopped looking out of the window. Instead, she had focused on the dog. No one had spoken after the initial introductions, all deep in their own thoughts and worries, and now she peered out, trying to see the house numbers as they slowed to a crawl along Addison Road.

'This is it,' Helen said as they pulled up outside a detached house with garage to its side. Lights were on inside, from every window apart from upstairs, on the right. A car was already on the drive, and so she pulled along the kerb at the front of the low wall that held back the front garden. All four of them got out and walked quickly to the front door. Zac knocked on the glass loudly.

A pretty girl answered. She looked at them one by one, smiling but obviously confused.

'Can I help?' she asked.

'We're looking for my daughter, Chloe,' Helen said, stepping forward.

'Oh, pleased to meet you, I'm Bea, Chloe's housemate.' Bea's smile stretched wider now. 'I was expecting her home a while ago actually, but I think she must have stayed behind with her classmates for a bit. Exciting times for her, hey?'

'No, she didn't come in today,' said Megan. 'We are training with her and just wanted to check she was okay.'

'Oh, that's odd.' Bea's smile faded. 'Maybe she's sick? Come on in, I'll go and check if she's in her room. I'd just presumed she was still out.' She held the door and Megan, Paul and Zac walked in. Helen looked back at the car, where Sam was scratching frantically at the window.

'I'll just get Sam out. I don't know what's wrong with him.' Bea nodded, leaving the door open. 'Chloe?' she called as she walked quickly up the stairs. A moment later she was back, shaking her head. 'No sign of her.'

'Is she there?' Helen called, opening the car door and letting the ball of furry energy escape.

'No,' Zac called back.

The five of them huddled around the doorstep now, Sam sniffing the ground around them.

'So odd,' Bea muttered. 'Her bag is still there, so it doesn't look like she left for training this morning…'

'Can I go and have a look?' Helen asked.

'Please do, I'll show you her room.' Bea led the way.

'Sam!' Zac called as the leadless dog disappeared around the side of the house. 'Mum, Sam's off,' he called before heading around the side behind him, followed by the others.

Sam was behind the garage when they all reached the garden, emerging with his nose firmly on the ground, still sniffing.

'The light is on?' Bea said, her voice confused.

They stopped together outside of the wooden door, where light escaped through the narrow gap around it. Sam appeared at their feet, scratching manically at the wood, the paint flying off, as if trying to dig through it. Instinctively, Megan reached out and tugged the handle, flinging the door open.

'What the…' a man's voice said.

'Get out!' a woman shouted loudly.

Bea appeared behind them and pushed past Megan and into the garage.

'Kathryn?'

'I said *get out*!!' she screamed it now, in case Bea had not understood her the first time.

'Kathryn, what's…'

A muffled, animal-like sound came from behind the two of them. Everyone was in the garage now, all standing behind Bea.

Megan saw it first, the bent legs sticking out from behind the boxes, wriggling as if they were trying to kick, but something was stopping them. She pushed past Bea, knowing exactly who it was, suddenly fearless.

It happened so fast. With each step Megan took, Kathryn took one towards her. Only Kathryn was holding something in her hand, swinging it now, high above her head.

'Watch out!' screamed Bea as the hammer came down towards her. Sam barked loudly, leaping into the air towards the weapon, as the man behind her grabbed her arm, pulling her towards him and wrapping her firmly in both of his.

'No, Katie. No more,' he said firmly as she struggled against him.

Chapter Fifty-Two

Captain McGhee, April 21st 1992

The plane touched down at 0430 from Hong Kong. Captain Anthony Thomas McGhee bid farewell to his colleagues as they reached the carpark and walked along, looking for his BMW. He had a feeling that everything was going to change today, that whatever it was that Nell needed to tell him so badly was going to set the cat amongst the pigeons and send the façade of his normal life into turmoil.

He drove fast, joining the M25, and trying to keep his mind from wandering off to what-ifs until he got there. Wales was a long way to drive, and Fishguard was about as far on the other side of it as you could get. He wasn't complaining though, she had made a similar long journey, getting the ferry over from Ireland just to see him. If he were honest, something about Nell made all of these long journeys, and all the lies, worth it. She was different from the others, had warmed his heart up more than he had known it was capable of warming.

The rain was lashing down, and the wipers on his car couldn't keep up, but still he drove fast, until the sign for the sleepy town was upon him. It was almost midday now and he was feeling tired. He pulled over in a layby and took a last look at the map, memorising the final few turns. It was something he was good at, map reading, a skill honed from years of flying.

The guest house was unremarkable, its whitewash speckled with black from the coastal spray and rain. Nell's small Fiesta was there, and he pulled his car in next to it. He would have liked to have bought her a new, smarter car, she deserved one; maybe he would one day.

And then she was there, standing in front of the door, a smile on her face that made every minute of the five-hour drive worth it. His beautiful Nell, so much younger than him and yet she made him feel the same age as her. He got out of the car and wrapped his arms around her, breathing her in.

'I'm pregnant,' she blurted out into his shoulder, and he felt the worry in her as she said it. He squeezed her tighter, letting her know that it was okay. Somehow, he had known that she was going to tell him this when she had said she would meet him halfway, had known that she wouldn't want him to go all the way in case it wasn't news he wanted to hear. That was her way, selfless and always considering others before herself. Just one of the reasons he loved her.

'Is it okay?'

'Well, I guess I have some things to figure out,' he said. He'd avoided figuring things out until she actually told him, just in case he'd been wrong. Her face fell and he kicked himself, but it was true, he wished it was easier but he had other responsibilities too, and she knew that. 'But of course, it is okay,' he said with a smile. He wrapped her in his arms again. 'Everything will be okay,' he soothed.

That night when he left her the tense feeling in his stomach accompanied him the whole way home. It passed in a blur, until he reached Heathrow exactly twenty-four hours after he had landed there. Jean never questioned him about his rosters, accepted whatever he told her about the length of his flights. For years he had manipulated things to squeeze someone else into his life, and for the past six months he had managed to catch a flight to Dublin most months to see the Irish girl who had stolen his heart on that weekend away for a friend's stag party. He imagined a life with her, and smiled briefly, but there was so much else to consider between now and then, and it wouldn't be easy.

He pulled the car onto the drive, in front of the garage, looking up at the home he had been so proud to buy once. Growing up in care, he'd had nothing. No money, no family, but he had it all now, and he was about to throw it all away. He got out and looked at the metal door. The paint was starting to flake at the edges, it was a job he had planned to do soon but wouldn't get around to now.

Inside the house it was dark and quiet, nobody was up yet, and he walked through to the kitchen, filling the kettle and putting it on, soaking up every second of normality while he could. He looked out into the garden, the last of summer's flowers colouring the borders that Jean tended daily. He would miss sitting on his bench under the window and just daydreaming.

He heard her coming, soft slippers on the stairs as she came down them. He turned to see her, wrapped in her towelling dressing gown, long nightdress poking out at the bottom. She had cut her hair short this summer, struggling with the flushes of menopause, but somehow with the hair had gone the last of her beauty, it seemed to him.

'Morning, love,' she said sleepily. 'Good trip?'

'Tea,' he said without answering her question. She nodded and sat at the table. Although he was quite sure he didn't love her the way he should anymore, he didn't want to hurt her, but putting it off was just as cruel.

'Jean,' he said, putting her tea in front of her and trying to keep his voice calm. 'I have something to tell you...'

****

Anthony rubbed his head with both of his hands and ignored the tears that were running down his face. He looked around the garage, all the things he had accumulated over the years, and memories of their family life; he could only take what would fit in the car for now and he didn't know where to start. He hadn't tried to phone Nell yet, it didn't feel right to call her from the house phone, he would stop at the telephone box when he was on his way.

The sound of the door opening made him wipe his face and pull himself together. Andrew stepped in and pulled the door shut behind him. His face was red and Anthony knew that his son had seen his mother.

'You absolute bastard,' he said through clenched teeth.

He was right, he was, and yet his dislike for his son made him resent it. 'Don't speak to me like that,' he said with as much authority as he could muster.

'I'll speak to you any way I like,' Andrew said, pulling his arm back and swinging his fist at him.

Anthony stepped back and laughed. 'What, you think you can beat me up?' he mocked him. 'You, Mummy's boy,' he sneered. They had been so close when he was little, but now, all he could see was an almost twenty-five-year-old mummy's boy who had no respect for anyone else, had never had a girlfriend and had no intention of ever moving out. He hated to admit that he didn't like his own son.

'How dare you do that to her, and I know it's not the first time,' Andrew stood with his fists clenched by his side. 'She might not want to see it, but I know you've been cheating on her for years. You piece of sh…'

A white mist descended over Anthony and before he could stop himself he had punched him full in the face, knocking him to the floor. He stood over him, waiting for him to open his eyes so that he was sure he could hear him.

'Don't you ever talk to me like that again,' he seethed at the disrespect. 'Ever.'

'DADDY!!' Katie had appeared at the back door and was looking at them both with wild eyes. To him she looked so much like her mother when she was younger, the same fiery, curly hair, the same red, freckled cheeks. She ran past him to comfort her older brother, who sat pathetically on the floor, nursing a bloody nose. Something flashed across her eyes when she turned to look back up at him. It was the look she always got when she was about to lash out, the look she gave when all reasoning was lost and she was going to break something... smash a window, slap her mother, kick a door. They all knew that she had a problem, that her behaviour wasn't *normal,* but Katie was everyone's little girl, she was inherently sweet... despite what the schools might have said when she was excluded time and again.

****

Andrew drove his dad's car back to Heathrow. He had gone to work with him enough times, in the days when they got on, to know where he parked. He locked it and got on the bus to the terminal. From there he took the train home.

In the garden he found his mother sitting on the bench. She was just staring into the distance, the last bit of her spirit that had remained after years with that monster was broken. She had known about the affairs, he had listened to her crying at night when she knew he was with this one or that one, but she hadn't had the strength to leave. She just accepted it, still loved him even. Maybe she had hoped that one day he would stop.

He sat next to her and put his arm around her shoulder, pulling her towards him. 'I'm gonna look after you now, Mum, he can't hurt you anymore,' he said. He wondered whether he should tell her what Katie had done, or would the secret be too much burden for her to carry?

In the garage, later, he emptied the contents of the freezer of the fish that his Dad would bring home from his fishing trips. Had he really caught them though, he wondered, or just bought them on the way back from one of his women? He heaved the body along the floor, the dead weight of him making him sweat. His dad had been a big man, much bigger than him. Finally he managed to get him up and over the edge, stuffing the limbs in, and bending his head forward so that the place where the hammer had hit him on the forehead was hidden from view. She hadn't meant to do it, hadn't meant to kill him. His job as a big brother was to protect his little sister at all costs; that was what Mummy had always told him.

The last thing he saw before he pushed the lid down was the four stripes on his father's shoulder that he had been so proud of. They meant nothing to anyone now.

****

'So he never came home?'

'No, officer.' Andrew shook his head. He looked at his mum; she shook her head too, but said nothing. He had needed to tell her in the end, in case she gave it away and the finger was pointed at them. At the dining table Katie sat quietly doing her jigsaw puzzle; she seemed so detached from everything around her, as if she wasn't even there.

From the day his dad hadn't turned up for his next flight there had been a flurry of phone calls and visits as they, the police and his employers, tried to work out where he was. The only clue had been his car which was still in the car park, and then there was the discrepancy between when the company had said he was due home and when *they* had been expecting him the next day. It seemed he had something to hide but they just couldn't get to the bottom of it.

The whole thing had sent his mother almost mute, and he hated to see what they had done to her, but for now it was best that she was like that. He would make it his mission to make sure the rest of her life was a happy one, once they had stopped looking...

****

Nell looked at the phone. It had been exactly a month and he hadn't called. She rubbed her stomach and took a deep breath. 'Looks like we are doing this alone, little one,' she said, holding back the tears. She should never have let herself believe he would choose her, *them*, but it was okay, she was okay with it now, she had to be.

Chapter Fifty-Three

Chloe smiled back at her friends on the screen. They'd been drinking, all cramming into the picture to wave at her and blow her kisses. She'd had to archive the group chat, she was too out of the loop, and she had nothing to say on there anymore. Maybe she would jump back in one day when this was all over.

'So, I have this little badge here for you,' Megan said, waving the silver wings in front of her face. 'Ben says you can come and do your last exam whenever you are up to it, but don't rush.'

Chloe bit her lip. She so badly wanted to be there with them tonight. For a moment she had believed that she could make it, until the reality of what had happened to her had struck her and the bed in the small hospital room had suddenly become her safe place. There was a knock on the door and she looked up to see Bea there. She beckoned her in.

'I love you, Megs,' she said. 'Say hi to everyone for me. I have to go.'

'We love you!' Megan, Paul and some of the others called as she hung up the call.

Bea walked in, and Chloe could see that her bottom lip was trembling.

'It's okay, I'm okay,' she said, managing a smile to try to comfort her, holding out her arms.

Bea walked over and bent down into her hug. 'I'm so sorry this happened to you,' Bea sobbed.

Chloe shuffled in the bed. Her muscles were sore from being stretched, her skin sore from the multiple cuts on them. Lacerations circled her wrists and ankles; they were covered now by bandages and she hoped and prayed that they wouldn't scar and be permanent reminders.

Bea's wet cheek brushed hers as she stood up and dropped into the chair next to her bed.

'How are you?' Chloe asked.

Bea shrugged. 'Don't worry about me, it's you that has been through it.'

Chloe shook her head and reached out to touch her hand. Yes, she had been terrified, feared for her life, but just because Bea didn't have any physical marks didn't mean that she didn't have the scars.

'What happened after?' Chloe had been in here for twenty-four hours. Her mum had come in the ambulance with her so hadn't known what had happened next either. All she remembered was Megan and Paul cutting off her ties, and her brother picking her up in his arms and carrying her inside while they waited for the police. She hadn't seen Kathryn, or her brother, since.

'Well, Kathryn, my...' Bea took a deep breath, 'My crazy half-sister, was carted off in handcuffs along with my crazy half-brother.'

Chloe pushed herself up on her elbow, holding her hand now and giving it a gentle squeeze. 'And your...' She stopped herself from saying it.

'My dad?' Bea blinked back tears. 'I hear they are thawing him out somewhere now.' She gave a small, dry laugh.

'Oh, Bea,' Chloe said; it was all she could think of. It was the most messed-up thing she had ever come across. 'Are you still at the house?'

'Er, no,' Bea said bluntly, before a small smile emerged. 'I've moved in with Andre for a bit. Not forever, just while I sort myself out, and Mum and Dad have pulled out of the house sale at the last minute, so they aren't going anywhere for now.'

'You have great parents, Bea,' Chloe said, thinking how stressful that would have been to change things so last-minute.

Bea nodded. 'I know. I think I'm going to opt out of the other family, stick with the more stable one.' She raised her eyebrows. 'Can you imagine if Kathryn hadn't killed him? I'd have had to grow up knowing I was related to those two nutters. Oh and her room was like a shrine to her dead dad apparently, I overheard the police say.'

Chloe lay back, mentally running over how things might have panned out for Bea if things had gone differently, and indeed how things might have gone for *her* if her friends hadn't turned up. She still couldn't believe that it was quirky, sweet Kathryn all along though, and it occurred to her that she might never get to ask her now why she had been calling her that weekend, or if she had been looking through her things; maybe she had just wanted permission to touch her puzzle, or to ask if she had wanted dinner? Perhaps she had been looking in her drawer for a lighter to light her joint? That last thought made her smile. Maybe some things, she thought with acceptance, would just have to remain a mystery, and that was alright, because a much bigger one had been solved in the meantime.

'Bea,' she said eventually.

'Yeah?'

'Do you think they'll let me fly with you at first? I think I'll be a bit nervous now, going away on my own.'

'I think that is just the best idea,' Bea replied. 'I'll chat to a manager, see if we can get a buddy roster.' She was smiling now. 'I think we could both do with it... and imagine the stories we'll be able to tell our crew in the bar over a few drinks!'

Chloe laughed at the thought... no one would ever believe them!

The End